THE MUMMY CASE
MYSTERY

THE MUMMY CASE
MYSTERY

DERMOT MORRAH

COACHWHIP PUBLICATIONS

Greenville, Ohio

The Mummy Case Murder, by Dermot Morrah
© 2014 Coachwhip Publications
Dermot Morrah, 1896-1974
No claims made on public domain material.
Simultaneous publication, New York & London, 1933. No
    coyright renewal.
Cover: Sarcophagus © Emmanuelle Bonzami

ISBN 1-61646-250-7
ISBN-13 978-1-61646-250-5

CoachwhipBooks.com

CONTENTS

1
THE DONS

THE HUM OF AFTER-DINNER TALK subsided for a moment as the Provost and Fellows of Beaufort College, Oxford, suspended their several conversations to take an informed and critical interest in the opening of another bottle of port. Denys Sargent, the junior fellow, on whom the celebration of this rite devolved, manipulated his corkscrew, napkins and decanters with the air of a cardinal whose absolute liturgical correctitude is compatible with a certain intellectual scepticism concerning the fundamentals of the faith. Sargent was a master of the art of fine drinking, and treated wine with a seriousness he accorded to few subjects in life; but he contrived, within the bounds of the utmost decorum, to make his every gesture with the corkscrew redolent of a gentle patronage for the college port, and by implication for the Internal Bursar, who was responsible for buying it.

The only guest present looked on with wistful admiration. "You know," he said, "if we in America had had your English faculty for making our wine-drinking a sacrament, the world would never have heard of Volstead."

"I should wait till you've tasted this stuff, Mr. Van Ditten," said Sargent, passing up the full decanter towards the pro-Provost's place; "you may come to the conclusion that it's the sacrament of penance."

Glasses were filled and the suspended conversations broke out again round the massive dessert table of the Fellows' Common Room. At the end nearest the fireplace Van Ditten, seated between

7

Sargent and his own host, Peter Benchley, the Internal Bursar, made himself an audience for them both with that air of childlike receptiveness to the ancient wisdom of Oxford which is the invariable attitude of the visiting American and to whose flattering charm no don has ever failed to succumb. Responding easily to encouragement, Sargent began to talk glibly of historic vintages, while Benchley revealed an encyclopaedic knowledge of the wines of the ancients, the Falernian of Horace, the Opimian of Cicero, and the potion of Pramnian that the fair-haired Hecamede mixed for Nestor.

"And what about your old Pharaohs, Dr. Benchley," asked the guest. "Did they worship the wine-god too?"

"Looks as if your education's been neglected, Mr. Van Ditten," interposed Sargent. "Haven't you read Benchley's book?"

"I wouldn't presoom," the American answered. "I know what's above my intellectual station. But have I made a *faux pas?*"

Sargent smiled sardonically. "You've stepped in where a Chicago gunman would fear to tread, which is between Benchley's battle-axe and the tomahawk of his friend Bonoff, the Bolshevik Bashi-Bazouk."

"I'm mystified," said Van Ditten. "What's it all about, Dr. Benchley? I'm sorry if I've said something I oughtn't."

"You mustn't mind Sargent," replied Benchley. "He's one of our bright young people, and, like most of his progressive generation, he's generally a bit behind the times. He is alluding to a little academic controversy between me and an eminent Russian scholar, which happens to have come to an end. A few—"

"My dear Benchley!" exclaimed Sargent, "you don't mean to say that the bold bad Bonoff has given in at last? We must have another bottle on this!"

"I said the controversy had come to an end," corrected Benchley. "But by all means open another bottle; it'll give me a chance to explain to Mr. Van Ditten. You'd better open some Madeira, since I know your palate isn't educated up to the '04 port."

Sargent reached over to the chest beside his chair, extracted a bottle and busied himself again with the corkscrew. Meanwhile Benchley turned to his guest and began to speak with a gentle seriousness of mien that showed that the subject was very near to his heart.

"You were asking about the Egyptians and the wine-god, Mr. Van Ditten," he began. "It so happens that I published a little essay on the subject some years ago."

"Don't be misled by Benchley's modesty," broke in a fresh voice from across the table. "The little essay runs to two fat volumes, and incidentally it's a world-famous book. It got Benchley appointed as Professor of Egyptology here, besides bringing him honorary doctorates at Cambridge and Heidelberg."

Benchley bowed across the table to the young Reader in Assyriology who spoke. "My colleague Considine is apt to over-estimate me," he remarked to Van Ditten. "You'd hardly believe from the way he speaks that he used to be my pupil. But he's unique among pupils in never having thought it worth while to demolish his tutor's reputation."

Considine blushed as he took a pinch of snuff from the great ramshorn that was slowly circulating. Benchley beamed at him for a moment with obvious affection, then raised his glass and sipped absent-mindedly.

"You were telling me about your book, Dr. Benchley," Van Ditten prompted him.

"Ah yes, my book—my book." Benchley came back to earth with a start. "I'm afraid Madeira will never have another vintage to equal the old prephylloxera days. What was it you wanted to know about my book?"

"Well," said Van Ditten, "weren't you going to tell me about the Egyptian wine-god?"

"The book wasn't exactly about the Egyptian wine-god," the Professor replied. "It was about the Greek god, Dionysos, that I advanced a little tentative theory."

Sargent had been long enough out of the conversation. His self-confident, rather harsh, voice cut across Benchley's diffident murmur with: "What Benchley means to say, Mr. Van Ditten, is that he proved conclusively that Dionysos was originally shipped to Greece from Egypt. Warranted pyramid-bottled, in fact."

"Yes," said Benchley, "that was substantially my theory, though it needs certain reservations, and of course you will understand, Mr. Van Ditten, that the reference to pyramids is a distinct anachronism. The traces of the Dionysos cult in Egypt, that I attempted to demonstrate, related to a period considerably posterior to the Fourth Dynasty, which was, as of course you know, the age of the pyramid builders."

"And how does Bonoff come into this?" asked the American.

"With both feet and a howitzer," said Sargent. "But you mustn't let Benchley talk about him here; Cardinal Beaufort, by whose benefits we are here brought up to godliness and the studies of good learning, made a strict statute forbidding profane language under pain of excommunication. I should hate to see a pious atheist like Benchley excommunicated."

"Our young friend is a little out of touch with Egyptology," rejoined Benchley. "You must forgive him. He is a lawyer, and lives in a world where mutual recrimination is a sacred duty. Feodor Bonoff is a most distinguished scholar, for whose work I have a very high regard."

"Expressed in letters to *The Times*, which I habitually use as texts when discoursing to my pupils on the law of actionable defamation." A second glass of Madeira had left Sargent more determined than ever to go on baiting his senior colleague, but to-night Benchley was no less resolute to maintain his demeanour of sweet reasonableness.

"Yes," he said, "I admit both Bonoff and I have put our views pretty strongly at times. However, as I said, the controversy is over now. But I see you've passed the decanter, Mr. Van Ditten. The pro-Provost has risen, so we're free to go. Shall we move on to the coffee room? Sargent's condemned to be the slave of any toper who wants to go on drinking; but he'll join us when they release him."

As the two men left the common room Humphrey Considine rose also, and the three entered the adjoining coffee room together. Considine walked to the window and looked out.

"Oughtn't we take advantage of the first fine evening this term?" he asked. "I shall take my coffee in the garden. Coming, Benchley?"

"We shall probably be driven in by jazz bands," observed the professor; "but let's give it a trial."

Sitting in deck chairs on the famous lawn of the fellows' garden, the two orientalists and the stranger from the west sipped their coffee and for a few minutes gave themselves up in silence to the enjoyment of that sense of timeless peace which is felt only in an Oxford June. Term was over; but the sound of tuning instruments from the direction of the great quadrangle told of the beginning of that last festivity of the undergraduate's year, a Commemoration ball. A full moon shining through the branches of a copper beech cast dappled shadows on grey walls, which had been venerable when Montrose dined with the Fellows in Hall on the day before he rode north to reconquer Scotland for his King. Beyond the garden the gothic spire of the chapel lifted a dark blade of shadow across the stars, looking down upon the three quadrangles like a watch-tower from which the spirit of the great dead cardinal still kept ward over his college. In the deepening twilight a solitary bat flew in frustrate circles round and round the walled garden, and the hoots of an owl somewhere above the buttery windows were silenced when the multitudinous bells of the churches and colleges began to toll, in ragged harmony, the hour of nine. One by one they chimed and ceased, and as the last echo faded the sombre music of Great Tom began to beat out his hundred and one strokes to call the scholars of Christ Church home.

"I never knew it was possible to travel right back into the Middle Ages like this," said Van Ditten. "Is there a stone in sight that wasn't here before Columbus sailed from Palos?"

"Not a stone," replied Considine, "unless, perhaps, there are one or two in Benchley's new gate over there. But even that's practically hidden from here by that row of laurels."

"And I suppose the place has slept through every tumult that's disturbed the world in all those centuries. It's impossible to believe, sitting here, that there's ever been anything but peace anywhere on earth."

"Ah!" said Benchley, "there, if I may say so, you're rather romanticizing our history. Perhaps you don't know that we should never have been founded if Cardinal Beaufort hadn't had a guilty conscience over the burning of Joan of Arc. The college was the headquarters of a cavalry regiment in the civil war, and forty years later the dons themselves went out with drums and muskets to meet the Prince of Orange. They failed to meet him, and he had them all thrown out when he became King; but not before they'd nearly burnt the college down after celebrating their glorious victory. No, we haven't been so pacific as you think."

"Battles long ago," murmured the American. "Somehow they never seem like real disturbances of the peace. Nothing like an election for mayor in Chicago, for instance."

"Well, if you want the real authentic blood lust," said Considine, smiling, "there's always the great feud of Bonoff versus Benchley. By the way, Benchley, did I really understand you to say that it's all over?"

"Yes, it's all over. I've come to the conclusion that I must modify the position I took up in my 'Prolegomena.' Bonoff has proved his case. I went to see him in the Isle of Wight last week, and we had a most interesting talk. We drafted a joint essay on the whole subject, and it's appearing in the next number of *The Oriental Review*."

"But, my dear Benchley!" Considine was genuinely shocked. "You don't mean to say you've given in to Bonoff on the Dionysos question. Why, it's tantamount to abandoning your whole life's work."

"*Magna est veritas, et praevalet*," the Egyptologist quoted. "When you're my age, my boy, you'll know that that is the common fate of scholars. But I don't think my work is wasted. There's the results of forty years of digging set out in that book; and if the facts don't prove my theory, they'll be useful to somebody else. In fact, Bonoff himself is going to use most of them for a book he's bringing out next year; and my discoveries will live in that."

"Well, if you're convinced, I suppose there's nothing more to be said," remarked Considine. "Certainly, if you and Bonoff join forces, there's no living Egyptologist who'll be able to stand up against you. I wish I'd been present at the signing of the Peace Treaty, though. I suppose it was the first time you'd seen the wild man in the flesh?"

"No, not quite," replied Benchley. "Don't you remember I was asked by the Egypt Association to go and call on him when he first landed in England a year ago? I happened to be travelling to Havre on my holiday the day he landed at Southampton; so I went and looked him up at his hotel. Our little controversy was at its height then, so I'm afraid we didn't exchange more than formal courtesies—not to say chilly ones."

"But you've really made the peace now? Personally as well as academically?"

"Oh, yes, absolutely. Of course, Bonoff's not what you'd call a sociable animal; he has the reputation of a hermit and seems to live up to it. But he received me most hospitably, and we couldn't have parted better friends. In fact it was from Bonoff I got the mummy you're so interested in, Mr. Van Ditten." Benchley turned rather apologetically to his guest, whom he had for the moment forgotten, but who had been listening with an air of rapt interest to the conversation of the two dons.

"Yes, so I had ascertained," said the American. "I may say that I've traced that mummy all the way from Egypt to Russia, from Russia to the Isle of Wight, and from the Isle of Wight to Oxford. The very day I heard that it was the oldest royal mummy in the world, I said to myself, 'That mummy's going into the Luther Y. Van Ditten collection, if it costs a million dollars.'"

"D'you mean you're trying to buy Benchley's famous new toy?" asked Considine.

"I sure am," replied Van Ditten. "That's what brought me all the way from San Francisco to Oxford. But so far, Dr. Benchley won't sell."

"Is that so, Benchley?" asked Considine with some surprise. "I thought you told me you only bought the mummy as a speculation, in order to sell it again."

"Yes, so I did." Benchley was a little embarrassed. "I'm afraid I can't possibly afford to keep it, much as I should like to. Mr. Van Ditten must forgive me if I've been forced to be a little disingenuous with him. The mummy is already sold."

"I knew it!" exclaimed Van Ditten. "That darned Bowery racketeer Lewstein has got in before me!"

"I fear I am not at liberty to divulge the name of the purchaser," said Benchley diffidently. "That was a condition of the sale, and I'm not sure I haven't committed a breach of confidence in telling you as much as I have."

"Of course it's Lewstein," said the American furiously. "Couldn't be anyone else. Didn't he do me out of the glass Landru used for his last drink of rum on the scaffold? And now he's got away with King Pepi I. But I'll be even with the bastard!"

"I fear I am not in a position either to confirm or to contradict your surmise touching Mr. Lewstein." Benchley with his gentlest and most pedantic tones attempted to soothe the ruffled feelings of his guest. "But perhaps you would like me to inform the purchaser, whoever he may be, that you are anxious to acquire the mummy, and he might then communicate with you himself."

Van Ditten felt the implied rebuke in his host's tone. "I'm sorry, Dr. Benchley," he said. "I'm afraid I'm not quite sane where Lewstein's concerned. I've been fighting him in every market in the United States for the last thirty years. But I should hate our little quarrel to disturb the academic calm of Beaufort College. And now—"

A new voice interrupted the conversation. "Ah, so I expected," it said. "When Benchley slinks out of the coffee room directly after dinner, I always know that the pure air of night will shortly be polluted by the fumes of the unclean thing now protruding from his jaw. As indeed the air of day has been continuously polluted since Benchley woke up this morning."

The speaker, who approached across the lawn leaning lightly on Sargent's arm, was the senior fellow of the College, Ernest Monitor, D.M. He had white hair, and his sight was manifestly failing, but the youthful gaiety of his features was curiously accentuated by the mess uniform of the Royal Army Medical Corps, which he insisted on wearing in hall in memory, as he said, of the only useful work he had ever done. He was the last survivor of the old un-reformed fellows, elected "till death or matrimony." He had commanded a casualty clearing station during the War; but since then he had practised the art of medicine only to the extent of being always ready to patch-up one of his innumerable undergraduate friends who wished to persuade a proctor or a board of examiners that he had spent a sober and abstemious evening the night before. To this general solicitude for the welfare of the more excitable junior members of the university, he added a special mission for the preservation of his colleague, Benchley, from premature asphyxiation by tobacco fumes.

On the present occasion, as always, Benchley flushed guiltily behind the enormous meerschaum pipe that he was smoking. "I surrender, Ernest," he said. "I'll just finish this one, and then won't smoke any more to-night."

"You will not smoke any more to-night, nor will you finish that one," said Monitor. "You will hand over that septic object to me here and now. Failing instant obedience I shall call upon Sargent and Considine to confiscate it by force and then hold you down while I perform over you a pleasing little rite for the exorcism of alchemists and other makers of foul odours, which I learnt from an Armenian monk on my last visit to Constantinople."

Benchley meekly handed over his pipe. "I can't stand up to black magic," he said. "When do I get it back?"

"Let me see," replied Monitor. "You're publishing your class list in the School of Oriental Languages and Literature to-morrow, aren't you? You shall have back this pocket instrument of suicide directly I've seen the list and satisfied myself that you've given an adequate class to my little friend Betty Ireland of Somerville. I take it the death-tube is unique?"

"It's my only solace in all the world, you unscrupulous old ruffian," answered Benchley. "You see, Mr. Van Ditten, the academic innocency you admire so much rules out neither blackmail nor robbery under arms."

"Well," said the American, "I suppose the petty larceny of Dr. Benchley's pipe is the most heinous crime that's ever been plotted or committed inside these venerable walls. And now I must say good night. I'm sensible of the great privilege it has been for a poor outer barbarian like me to meet all you learned gentlemen in this most wonderful old college. I hope if any of you are ever in 'Frisco you'll give me an opportunity of trying to repay your hospitality."

With a general murmur of leave-taking the group broke up, Benchley guiding his guest across the lawn to the fellows' private gate, and the old doctor accompanying them. Sargent and Considine remained for a moment watching them disappear behind the row of laurels that concealed the gate from the view of a person looking out of the common room windows or standing on the lawn in front of them; then Sargent spoke in tones of bewilderment.

"I really think poor old Benchley must be breaking up at last," he said. "To think that after all these years he should have made peace with Bonoff!"

"Yes," said Considine, "and you didn't hear the worst of it. He seems to have given in to the old fraud all along the line, and he's going to collaborate in a joint work expounding the Bonoff theory. And that just a month after his letter in *The Times*, saying that the identical theory was the conglomerate product of the imagination of a Münchausen combined with the credulity of the Horse Marines."

"To which, if I remember rightly, Bonoff replied that Benchley's canons of textual criticism were apparently derived wholly from the study of crossword puzzles."

"Yes, they've both got a very similar taste in Billingsgate; in fact it's their very similarity that makes it so impossible to imagine them coming to terms. I never thought the affair could end without murder. Really it's beyond me, Denys. I give up. Come along and let's do our duty by our young barbarians, all at play."

Considine slipped his arm through Sargent's and drew him in through the French windows of the Common Room, whence they issued into the great quadrangle, now occupied by a huge marquee, in which the undergraduates of the college were giving their triennial Commemoration ball.

2
THE UNDERGRADUATES

AS A FAREWELL to university life perhaps no ceremony could be less appropriate than a Commemoration ball. It involves the importation into college precincts of everything that is least characteristic of Oxford—sweet vintages, a London jazz band, hosts of young women not in academical dress. In the undergraduate's memory the last picture of alma mater shows her masquerading as a Bright Young Person of Mayfair, and the dying echo of the voice of the Muses is lost in the blare of saxophones.

But Oxford is all things to all men in all moods, and a Commemoration ball, exotic though it be, remains a gracious thing. Its very incongruity is its greatest charm. Even to conscientiously cynical youth there is romance in the air when one slips out of a quadrangle very effectively converted to a glittering ballroom into a dim cloister that cannot cease to be a sanctuary. It will not be less a sanctuary for the presence at one's side of a creature of shimmering silk and silver, whose divine attributes have recently become apparent to a worshipper lately redeemed from the cult of one of the false goddesses of Eights Week. That, at any rate, was the sentiment of Mark Devereux, commoner of New College, as he guided Miss Daphne Carrothers to a pair of Minty chairs in the darkest corner of the cloisters of Beaufort.

For a moment the magic of moonlight on ancient stone held them both in silence. Devereux was about to go down, and the grey old city was laying its spell upon him with an intensity that revealed for the first time even to himself the profundity of the

17

affection that four years had created. Daphne, leaning lightly on his shoulder, seemed conscious of his emotion.

"I'm afraid you're going to hate leaving all this, Marcus," she murmured.

"Ten days ago I thought I was pining to have done with it," Mark answered. "I thought I was absolutely proof against sentiment. But now I don't think I could bear to leave Oxford if I wasn't sure you were going to marry me before the end of the year."

"You're a mass of sentiment," said Daphne curtly. "You know it, and you've always known it; but I'd rather you sentimentalized over Oxford than over me. I'm out to rationalize matrimony. And one of the first things we've got to be rational about is the date. You can't bury your head in the sand and pretend Uncle Peter doesn't exist."

"But, Daphne dear, what on earth has the old man got against me?" Mark spoke with a peevishness that indicated that an old grievance was being reopened. "Doesn't he give any reason for refusing his consent?"

"Yes, rather," said Daphne. "He produces a different reason every day. This morning, for instance, he said he'd heard you were likely to get ploughed in the Schools, and he wasn't going to have his only relative marrying a congenital imbecile."

"Damn the examiners," exclaimed Mark. "They've no right to let Benchley into the secrets of my private examination papers. I shall sue them for slander—if not publication of indecent matter. And anyhow it seems a pretty poor reason for turning me down. My life isn't going to depend on knowing the difference between a bill of attainder and a gesithcund man. What other objections has the old blighter got?"

"Well, yesterday," said Daphne, "he paid me the compliment of saying that it was my money you were in love with more than me."

"But my dear, you've only got twopence a year, haven't you?"

"About that. That's what makes the compliment such a pretty one. But, of course, I shall come in for his money when he dies, such as it is."

"Still," said Mark, "he surely can't think a problematic succession to his little pile is going to make much difference to me. After all,

I'm not a pauper. White Abbey isn't Blenheim, but it's the biggest estate in the island, and it brings in quite a respectable income."

A puzzled look came over Daphne's face. "D'you know," she remarked thoughtfully, "it may sound extraordinary, but I can't help feeling that his real objection is something to do with your place being in the Isle of Wight. He sees red every time I mention it."

"But the man must be off his rocker," said Mark impatiently. "What the devil's the matter with the island? I don't live in Parkhurst gaol."

"Oh, he trumps up artificial reasons," replied Daphne. "Says the island breeds a criminal type. Result of inbreeding and all that. He's a bit barmy on the subject, because he thinks the same thing ruined one of his old Egyptian dynasties. Still, I'm sure that reason's only invented for the occasion. There's something else underneath it—something that he gets really hit up about."

"I suppose it can't be anything to do with Comrade Bonoff that prejudices him against the island?" suggested Mark. "You know, of course, that the wicked Bolshevik is a neighbour of mine."

"Well, it might even be that," Daphne answered. "Uncle Peter's not quite sane where the arch-enemy's concerned. Blast! That's Humphrey Considine's voice—I'm dancing the next with him. Kiss me quick, Marcus, and I'll see you at supper."

"Look here," said Mark, as he complied with hurried efficiency. "I'm going to have it out with old Benchley.

'Not once or twice in our rough island story
The path of duty was the way to glory.'

The old ruffian shall quail before an islander in his wrath. I'm going to his rooms now. It's only eleven o'clock. He won't be in bed yet."

"Well, good luck," responded Daphne. "Don't be late for supper. Oh, here you are, Humphrey. How clever of you to find me!"

Mark walked away through the farther door of the cloisters into the smallest of the three quadrangles, at one corner of which stood a small isolated building, the Bursary, with the official rooms of

Benchley as Internal Bursar above. Meanwhile Daphne returned
to the dancing marquee on the arm of Humphrey Considine.

The ball proceeded in the accustomed way of Commemoration
balls. The long swinging rhythm of the Eton boat song seemed to
sweep the dancers like a wind that sweeps over a field of ripening
corn. Young limbs, accustomed to being dutifully constrained in
the crabbed shuffle of their generation's measures, relaxed under
the influence of its dreamy sweetness and glided into the grace
of a Victorian waltz. Then negro America resumed its sway, and
reduced the company once more to wriggling pedestrianism with
the syncopated strains of "I'll say ma baby's a cutie," the supreme
musical success of the year. To the dozen undergraduates who had
organized it and now, wearing the red carnations of stewards, pal-
pitated with anxiety for its success, the whole ceremony seemed
the last refinement of sophisticated modernity. To old Dr. Lacy,
the Provost, who had looked in to watch for an hour or so, it brought
back the illusion of time arrested, seeming indistinguishable from
any of the Commemoration balls he had seen since he himself was
a freshman in 1858. That is the sad paradox of Oxford to those
who make their lives there: that whereas the undergraduates, of
whom a thousand go down every year, seem changeless as her
ancient stones, the dons, who go down only to the grave, are but
shadowy types of human mutability.

Daphne Carrothers, steadily dancing her way through a
crowded programme, noticed that Mark had reappeared in the
marquee by half-past eleven, partnering one of the girls of the party
of eight to which they both belonged. But she got no word with
him till, on the stroke of midnight, he emerged alone from the
direction of the cloisters to claim her for supper. Even then she
had only time to murmur "any luck?" and receive the whispered
reply "enemy's attitude hostile. Tell you all about it later" before
they were both caught up into the chattering procession that
flooded into the great library, where supper was being served.
The other three men of Mark's party being all members of Beaufort, they had secured a single round table for themselves and
their partners, and the eight settled down noisily to the important

business of fortifying themselves with lobsters, meringues and champagne for the arduous six hours of dancing that still lay ahead.

Into the cheerful hubbub created by five hundred voices among the echoes of the old library there suddenly broke the tolling of a bell. The sombre and melancholy sound imposed momentarily a puzzled hush, in the midst of which a deep voice began to intone from behind a bookcase at one end of the great room, "In the midst of life we are in death. *Memento, homo, quia pulvis es, et in pulverem reverteris*," and there appeared two young men in evening dress, but with top hats swathed in crape, who advanced down the lane between the bookcases one behind the other, and wheeling between them what looked like a bier. On it lay a bulky coffin-like object, and the two, continuing to chant mixed phrases from the funeral and penitential liturgies of several religions, seemed about to wheel their strange burden through the middle of the supper tables.

But the hush of astonishment lasted but a few seconds. As the mock-tragic procession emerged from the shadow of the bookcases that occupied one end of the library, the shape and bright colours of the object on the bier became visible in the electric light, and were immediately recognized by a score of Beaufort undergraduates. "Well, I'm damned," cried Mark Devereux, springing from his seat, "they've got old Benchley's mummy. This is a bit thick!" Chairs were being thrust back all over the room with similar exclamations, and it looked as if the two practical jokers would be overwhelmed by a rush of indignant undergraduates.

For the ritual of Oxford ragging is delicate and subtle. To any undergraduate who had read Herodotus for Smalls, and knew the ancient Egyptian custom of thus bringing home to feasters the transitoriness of life, this was the obvious thing to do with a mummy. But it was not the obvious time. To produce the mummy at a bump supper, even to intrude it upon the dinner parties of certain dons (but not those of certain other dons—any sound man would know where the dividing line lay) would be wholly canonical. But at a commem ball one does not rag. More especially one does not rag at the commem ball of another college; and it was seen at once that these two were not Beaufort men. Hence it looked as if they were threatened with some very rough handling.

But this rag, it seemed, had been carefully prepared. Scarcely ten seconds had elapsed since the first tolling of the bell had announced their entry, and they had only just reached the half-way point of the long library when half a hundred leapt up to intercept them. At that instant every light from end to end of the two hundred feet of the huge room was extinguished, and the hands, and in many cases heads, of the avengers crashed upon solid oak as the massive central doors, giving upon the great quadrangle, were slammed in their faces. Half a dozen undergraduates, cursing in the darkness, clutched uselessly at one another's hair in a vain groping for the handle, and before they had sorted themselves out the sound of a heavy key turning in the lock outside was distinctly audible to all.

An undergraduate crowd does not easily lose its temper, and the first reaction of the imprisoned dancers was a concerted peal of laughter, in which men and women alike joined. Then a self-confident young voice was uplifted and took command of the situation. It came from Goddard, Steward of the Beaufort Junior Common Room, a rowing blue well accustomed to control an eight in the noise and excitement of a bumping race without the help of a megaphone. "Keep still, everybody," he shouted, "till the lights go on. Manciple, can you get at the main switch?"

"Yes, sir, if one of these young ladies will take her heel out of my mouth," came back a muffled voice from somewhere on the floor, scarcely recognizable as the usually solemn utterance of the chief college servant. There was a rustling in the dark, a heavy tread towards one of the corners of the library, and a sudden outburst of light, which revealed every table deserted and the entire concourse packed into one jostling, disorderly, but exceedingly cheerful football scrum against the locked doors.

"Now then, after them," shouted Goddard. "Never mind the big doors; get out at the ends!" In addition to the main entrance there was a small door at each end of the library, and from these in a few moments, not without much scrambling and rending of garments, a sufficiently formidable pack of hunters debouched into the quad.

Despite the efforts of some of the stewards to marshal the ladies back to their seats, the sporting instincts of both sexes were equally aroused, and the view hallo that went up on catching sight of the quarry vanishing through an archway at the far side of the quadrangle was rendered by nearly as many treble voices as bass.

Across the quadrangle charged the hunt, breaking as it went into the familiar cries of Eights Week. "Beaufort! Beaufo-o-o-ort! Well rowed, Beaufort!" was the predominant call, but its booming was broken by a few Christ Church men with their staccato bark of "House! House! House!" and the still more staccato "One! Two! Three! Four!" of the university cox. They swept through the arch into the second quad and from there, losing ground as they jostled through the narrow gate, into the Fellows' Garden, where the mummy could still be seen in the moonlight as its escort trundled it briskly down the path until it disappeared behind the row of laurels at the far end. Here their pace seemed to slacken, for the pursuers, running diagonally across the grass to cut them off, were close on their heels as they reached the small iron gate leading to the Bursary and the small quad. They were just in time, however, to swing the gate to; it was a self-locking one, and the chase was once more brought to a halt until Humphrey Considine, who was not an athlete and had dropped behind, pushed his way to the front with his key. Before the gate could be reopened the fugitives had stopped at the door of the bursary, lifted the mummy from its improvised bier (which could now be seen to be the college portable fire-engine) and begun to carry it up the stairs to Benchley's rooms.

By the time the crowd of young men and women had squeezed through into the quad, and were massed round the opening of the staircase, the two causes of the disturbance had reappeared at the door. One of them, a tall and impressive figure in the moonlight, raised his hand with a gesture of authority that for a moment arrested the general movement to seize him and his companion. Then, lifting his hat with the trailing streamers of crape flowing fantastically from it in the slight breeze, he addressed the threatening array in the slightly supercilious tones of a practised after-dinner speaker:

"Good evening, ladies and gentlemen," he observed serenely. "I gathered from certain remarks that were wafted to us across the quadrangle, that you desired an interview with my friend and me. Pray forgive is if we were obliged to defer this interesting conversation until we had seen His Majesty the late Pharaoh Pepi I to bed. We are now entirely at your service."

The undergraduate, however infuriated, will never be outdone in ironic formality. The mere disorderly rough and tumble that had been imminent a moment before gave place to diplomatic courtesies. Goddard stepped forward as spokesman.

"Thank you, gentlemen," he said, with no less gravity than the former speaker. "We have indeed looked forward to this meeting. Have you ever enjoyed the view of the River Cherwell, for which this college is so justly famous? You have? But perhaps you would like to admire it again in our company. Allow me to offer you my arm. My friends, Mr. Faraday, Mr. Macarthy, and Lord Stephen Bohun will, I am sure, be delighted to help in escorting you."

Three of the brawniest members of the college promptly stepped forward and, with Goddard, seized each an arm of the two strangers, one of whom murmured, "Gentlemen, you are so pressing," but who offered no further resistance. Before they could be marched off, however, Denys Sargent intervened, carefully entering into the spirit of elaborate ceremoniousness so punctiliously observed by his juniors.

"One moment, Mr. Goddard," he said. "I should hate to come between your—er—guests and the enjoyment of our noted river prospect, which I know you are so competent to display to the best advantage. But as Dean of the College, I feel my office demands that I should make sure of an opportunity of pursuing their further acquaintance. Sir," he continued, turning politely to the taller prisoner, "would you be good enough to acquaint me with your name and college?"

"Certainly, Mr. Dean," was the answer. "My name is Randolph, and this is my colleague, Mr. Nevern. We are both members of Corpus Christi College."

"I am much obliged to you, Mr. Randolph, and will take an early opportunity of communicating further with you, through the President of your college. And now I must not any more delay Mr. Goddard's hospitable intentions. Good night, Mr. Randolph, good night, Mr. Nevern."

"Good night, Mr. Dean," replied Randolph and Nevern together, with unruffled composure, as their captors hustled them off in the direction of the college garden, along the far side of which flowed the Cherwell. The ladies of the party, to their no small disgust, found themselves politely intercepted at the garden gate and shepherded by the dance stewards back into the marquee, where the band was desolately playing a fox-trot to an empty floor. The great quadrangle, however, where the dancing tent was pitched, adjoined the garden, and listening ears were able to detect, in a pause of the music, the sound of two heavy bodies making violent and unwilling impact with running water.

Sargent and Considine were left together at the foot of the Bursary staircase. "Well, that's that, Humphrey," said the former. "Those two deserve all they get."

"*And* they're getting it," replied Considine grimly. "I'm almost sorry the magisterial dignity won't let us join in. The power of delation to the Dean of another college is a poor substitute for the fierce joy of a debagging. *Eheu fugaces!* Remember how we hung old Buggins's check plus-fours from the top of the Martyrs' Memorial?"

"When you hung them, you mean," Sargent retorted with mock indignation. "I, if I remember rightly, was being driven away in an ambulance by Monitor, under the noses of the progs, as a patient requiring instant surgical treatment at the Radcliffe Infirmary."

"And I hope you remember the incident every time our revered colleague jumps your claim to your nightly bag of undergraduate drunks. What about getting back to the dance?"

"Yes, let's," assented Sargent. "But oughtn't we to have a look round first, and see that no damage has been done? You're on more intimate terms with mummies than I. You'd better make an inspection."

"Perhaps it would be as well," Considine replied, leading the way up the stairs. "If we can see that everything's straight without waking Benchley, we shall be doing a good deed. He'll have a fit if he ever knows that sacrilegious hands have been laid on his beloved mummy."

"Oh, he sleeps like a log," said Sargent, turning on the electric light in Benchley's sitting room. "If all that caterwauling in the quad didn't wake him up, we're not likely to disturb him. Anything missing?" he added, and Considine walked over to where the mummy stood against the party wall and examined the painted surface of the coffin.

"Nothing that I can see," said the Assyriologist. "Of course, I'm not an expert. There aren't any mummies on my side of the Euphrates. And I can't tell what the corpse inside may have suffered. But if that's all right, there's no reason why Benchley should ever hear the mummy's been disturbed. Luckily he's going down by the early train in the morning, and by next term all the excitement will have died down."

"Let's hope so," said Sargent, and the two young dons descended the stairs once more and strolled through the small quadrangle and the cloisters back to the marquee. They observed on entering that from the canvas roof at each end hung down a pair of black evening trousers; there was however no other sign of the recent interruption; the ball seemed to have got under way again, and to have gained a fresh sparkle of youthful animation. The *chaperons* in the basket chairs round the margin were decorously dozing; the band, refreshed with a substantial ration of champagne, were revealing the athletic side of music; the stewards, hitherto standing aloof with the anxious demeanour of responsibility, were now themselves dancing lightheartedly, a clear sign that they were satisfied the function was successfully launched. Surely it would now carry itself on by its own momentum to the inevitable group photograph in the chilly dawn, and the breakfast at Henley for the exceptionally indomitable or the praeternaturally obstinate.

But the Beaufort College Commemoration Ball of that year was not destined to follow the course laid down for it by its promoters.

Just as a waltz was nearing its end the scream of the bugle used for announcing a new dance broke across the music, sounding an unfamiliar call. Unfamiliar, that is, to the dancers; but a man in the uniform of the local fire brigade, who had been lounging sleepily by the tent door all the evening, sprang suddenly into alertness.

"That's the fire alarm," he cried, and was out of the tent in an instant, while the cry "Fire, fire!" was taken up by all the dancers near his post and passed from mouth to mouth across the tent. Once more the five hundred dancers surged out into the open, followed this time by the bandsmen, the college servants, and even the *chaperons*. There was no mistaking the direction of the fire. An angry red glow showed above the cloister walls, and the first of the seething crowd to burst into the small quadrangle saw flames streaming from the windows above the Bursary.

Wild confusion followed. The college hose, wielded dexterously by the fireman, was obviously unequal to the situation, and could at best retard the advance of the conflagration pending the arrival of the fire brigade, for which the manciple was frenziedly telephoning. The aged Provost, with the full dress robe of a doctor of divinity hastily flung over his flannel nightshirt, was wringing his hands and wailing, "Save the hall, save the hall" over and over again, while no one listened. Meanwhile, half a dozen undergraduates, led by Devereux and Goddard, rushed up the stairs in a wild effort to rescue Benchley. They found the sitting room still untouched, though the wooden party wall was bulging ominously; but the door in it leading to the bedroom resisted their attack.

"It's locked on the other side," cried Goddard. "Get the poker!" and then "Dr. Benchley! Dr. Benchley, wake up, your rooms are on fire. Fire, fire, fire!"

But no sound but the roaring of the flames came from beyond the locked door, and as Mark Devereux, with furious blows of the poker, beat in the panels, an irresistible wall of flame and smoke swept through the aperture and drove the rescue party back to the entrance. As Mark looked back into the raging conflagration he saw the flames licking round the black and scarlet mummy coffin, whose wooden features seemed to leer at him through the murk with an expression of baleful malignancy.

Stumbling half-blinded down the stairs, the defeated rescuers found that the fire brigade had arrived, and a heavy jet of water directed by skilled hands into the blazing building soon had the flames under control. The stout stone walls of the Bursary stood firm, and by an apparent miracle the ground floor, containing the Bursar's official records, was left intact. But when at last the captain of the fire brigade was able to climb through the window into what had been Benchley's rooms, he found them so completely gutted that it was impossible to say where the sitting room had ended and the bedroom had begun. Only after twenty minutes' digging with shovels and axes in a pile of black and unrecognizable debris did his men come upon a charred and shapeless mass, which Monitor was able to say had once been a human body.

3
THE CORONER

THE MORROW OF A GREAT FESTIVITY has generally an air of desolation; and the quadrangles of Beaufort College on the afternoon following its Commemoration ball would have seemed dismal enough, even without the flag—quarterly of France and England, a bordure gobony argent and azure—drooping at half-mast above the muniment tower. The partly dismantled marquee was a damp mass of canvas, for a drizzling rain had been falling since dawn; and the chairs dotted in couples about the garden and cloisters, which twelve hours earlier had wooed to a romantic intimacy, seemed now to blink in the daylight with an air of guilt surprised.

In the lordly dining hall, where the inquest on Peter Benchley's remains was in progress, the magnificence of the cardinal's architecture was less apparent than its gloom. Bygone Fellows of Beaufort, prelates, statesmen, judges long turned to dust, peered sombrely down from their heavy gilded frames with a brooding remoteness that dwarfed the living and claimed ghostly communion with the huddled relics beneath a sheet in one corner, as something more real than they. Lighted candles stood on the table—while Provost Lacy lived no Fellow dared propose the introduction of electric light into hall or chapel—but their pale gleam seemed only to make more distant and oppressive the time-blackened oak panelling of the walls.

Douglas Weir, the university coroner, was a Magdalen man, and obviously ill at ease in these surroundings. In this privileged court, where the university still maintains its mediaeval right to

29

be exempt from all secular jurisdiction—the last relic of benefit of clergy—custom prescribed that he should form his jury from the Provost and Fellows of the college in which he sat; and consequently he felt like an importunate and blundering stranger who has thrust himself into the midst of a mourning family party. He always had this feeling; but mercifully the occasions on which he had to exercise his almost sinecure office were very rare; for dons as a class do not die violent deaths.

The present case was clearly a straightforward one, and he was anxious to spare everybody's feelings, and not least his own. To Daphne Carrothers, who gave evidence as Benchley's only surviving relative, he was paternally considerate.

"Now, my dear young lady," he began, "you will understand, of course, that we have to go through certain formalities in order to be sure that it really is your poor uncle who is dead. But I am not going to harrow your feelings by asking you to examine his body, because I am afraid you would not be able to recognize it. I think it will be enough if you tell the jury whether you have seen any of these objects before. This one, for instance."

Daphne took something small and smoke-grimed from the coroner's hand. "Yes," she said in a low voice, "this is my Uncle Peter's wrist watch, and it looks as if this thing attached to it is the remains of the expanding metal bracelet he wore it on."

"Are you quite sure about it?" asked Weir.

"Yes, certain," replied Daphne. "I can just make out his coat of arms engraved on the back—a shield with a sort of slanting line, all cut into notches."

"Party per bend indented," said the coroner. "That is the object," he explained to the jury, "that Mr. Goddard has just told us he found attached to the wrist of the deceased. Now will you look at this, Miss Carrothers?"

"This is obviously the remains of a bunch of keys on a ring," said Daphne. "I suppose you want me to say they are my uncle's keys. But I can't be sure. They look all right, but there seems to be one missing. A big gilt one."

"How lately had you seen that key?"

"I noticed it only yesterday afternoon. I had lunch with my uncle, and he took out his keys to get a bottle of sherry out of his cupboard. His gold key was on the ring then."

"Very curious, very curious," muttered the coroner. "Still it can't be of any importance; he must have—ah, what's this?" and he put on his horn-rimmed glasses to read a note that had been passed up to him by a member of the jury. "Ah, I see Dr. Monitor thinks he can explain the discrepancy. We will hear him in a minute. It's unusual for a member of the jury to give evidence, but not, I think, without precedent. Then, apart from the absence of the gold key, Miss Carrothers, you think that bunch resembles your uncle's?"

"I can't be sure," said Daphne; "but they're certainly very like his."

"Well, taken with the wrist watch, I think we may take that as sufficient evidence of identity. What was Dr. Benchley's demeanour at luncheon?"

"Oh, very much as usual. Heavy guardian, and all that."

"What exactly do you mean by 'all that'?"

"We sparred a bit, you know. We always did. He found out what I was going to do, and told me not to. But that was Uncle Peter's way."

"Did he seem to have anything on his mind?"

"Only work, I think. He turned me out without any coffee, because he said he had a thousand and one things to attend to before dinner time. He was going abroad for his holidays today, you see. And he said there was an American millionaire coming to see him about his mummy."

"But so far as you could see, he was in his usual spirits?"

"Judging from the way he put it across me, I should say he was at the top of his form."

"Thank you, Miss Carrothers, that will do. I am sorry you seem inclined to treat your uncle's distressing end with something like flippancy. Dr. Monitor."

Daphne, who had been really fond of her uncle, and whose slightly off-hand manner in the witness box had been merely the result of a resolute determination not to give way to tears, flushed angrily at the rebuke and seemed about to reply. She thought better of it, however, and walked back in silence to her seat beside

Mark Devereux. Monitor took her place, and prepared to address the coroner's court with the same gentle discursiveness with which he would treat any social assembly, from a meeting of the Royal Society to a group of rowdy undergraduates in the smoking room of the O.U.D.S.

"It's quite simple, you know, about this key," he began. "Last night—hullo, what's this? A bible? Oh, you want me to swear. Certainly, my dear fellow, certainly. There's a rather nice Maltese oath I picked up last year, all about Dathan and Abiram—however, I expect you prefer your own." And he proceeded to swear in the customary form of words.

"Now you wanted to know about the key," he resumed, fixing in his eye the rimless glass that depended from a broad black silk ribbon round his neck. "Really nothing could be simpler. It was a key like this, of course." He drew from his own pocket a gilded key of curious shape, about four inches long, and held it up. "That's the one, I suppose, Daffy?" he asked conversationally, and Daphne from her seat nodded assent. "Good girl, good girl. Well, you know, Douglas," he went on, turning to the coroner again, "there's no need to waste time on the key. It belongs to the little gate leading from the Fellows' Garden into Grammar Lane. We all have them—all the fellows, that is. I always thought it was so unfair the undergraduates weren't allowed to have them too—I constantly had to lend mine to young friends who wanted to come into college after hours. But my colleagues—oh, well, yes, I suppose since you say so, all this isn't strictly relevant.

"Now, where was I? Had I told you about the American? No? Well, an American came to dinner with poor Peter last night—a most interesting man, reminded me strongly of a Rumanian carpenter I used to know. Perfectly charming, and so was this American. Such a pity he was a millionaire. However, I can see you think that isn't relevant either. But it is, in a way. You see, this American was staying at the Crozier, just where Grammar Lane runs into Holywell. It's the worst beer in Oxford there, but I suppose any drink tastes good after living in America. Now this American had been to see Peter in the afternoon, and Peter had lent him his key,

THE MUMMY CASE MYSTERY

so that he could get into college for dinner that way, instead of going all the way round by the main gate. It's perfectly simple, you see, and I can't think why you've spent so much time on it."

"Thank you, Dr. Monitor," said the coroner. "Could you tell us, very briefly, just how you knew the key had been lent?"

"Certainly, certainly. That's quite simple too. Peter and I walked over after dinner to the private gate to let the American out, and then poor Peter remembered that he hadn't got his key. But the American had, and gave it back to him then and there. Nothing could be simpler."

"Then Dr. Benchley did have the key in his possession after all. Did he put it back on his ring?"

"Now let me think, Douglas, let me think. No, he didn't; I'm sure he didn't. He just dropped it loose into the side pocket of his dinner jacket."

"Thank you, that is what we wanted to know. I think you might stand down, Dr. Monitor. The court is much obliged to you. It is clear that these keys found on the body tally with the description of the bunch Dr. Benchley might have been expected to be carrying. No doubt the loose key will turn up later. Mr. Devereux."

Mark was in a bad temper with the coroner, owing to his unsympathetic treatment of Daphne, and was resolved to be uncommunicative. He gave formal evidence of having seen Dr. Benchley alive about eleven o'clock, and of leaving him then apparently about to go to bed. He went on to describe his unsuccessful effort at rescue. He had heard, he said, no sound of life from beyond the locked door in the bedroom, and, judging from the force of the flames that drove him and Goddard back when the door gave way, he felt sure that the Professor must have been dead before they ever came on the scene.

Mark was the last witness, and the coroner was obviously impatient to have done. He made no attempt to thaw Mark's frozen reserve, but turned immediately to the jury.

"Gentlemen," he said, "I will not detain you with more than a few sentences. The evidence, I am sure you will agree, is perfectly clear. Miss Carrothers's identification of the watch and keys,

together with the fact that the body was found in Dr. Benchley's
rooms, will no doubt satisfy you that it is that of Dr. Benchley himself. The medical evidence of Dr. Inchcape" (who had preceded
Daphne) "was to the effect that the remains were so affected by
fire that he could not say with certainty what was the cause of death.
But Mr. Devereux has told us that the deceased was alive at eleven
o'clock, only two hours before his body was discovered, so we may
reasonably conclude that death must have been caused by the fire
itself. The facts seem best described as 'accidental death'; and that,
I presume, will be your verdict?"

There was a subdued murmuring round the table at which the
jury were seated, and then Dr. Lacy, who was acting as foreman,
rose shakily in his place. "I am sorry to delay you," he said in his thin
and rather mincing tones. "But one of my younger colleagues has some
points that he thinks we ought to discuss in private. So, with your per-
mission, the jury would like to withdraw to another place for a short
time, after which we will acquaint you with our conclusion."

The coroner was annoyed, and showed it. "I can't think what
there is to discuss," he said grudgingly. "Still, you're of course
entitled to do as you like. I hope you won't be long."

The Provost rose, bowed to the coroner, and led the way out of
hall and across to the door of the Fellows' Common Room. Here
he halted, for the common room is the sanctuary of the fellows,
and the Provost may not enter save by invitation.

"Will you do us the honour, Mr. Provost," said Townsend Lake,
the pro-provost for the year, "of joining us in the common room?"

"It is always a pleasure to accept the hospitality of the fellows,"
answered the Provost, and, honour having been satisfied, followed
Lake into the room. While the others, however, removed their
gowns, he retained his, in token that in this room he was a stranger.

"Dear, dear me," he lamented in a quavering voice. "Those ashes
all that's left of poor Benchley. Such a promising young man. This
is the most painful thing that has happened in the forty years I've
been Provost of Beaufort. But we mustn't let our feelings get the
better of us; we must remember we're a coroner's jury, and not

just Peter Benchley's friends. Let me see, Sargent, it was you, wasn't it, who asked for this adjournment?"

"Yes, Mr. Provost," answered the junior fellow. "There was a point in the evidence that I feel sure must have struck everybody as remarkable. When I say a point in the evidence, perhaps I should say a point that was not in the evidence."

"It all seemed only too plain and complete to me," muttered Lake, and there was a general murmur of agreement.

"Then if I am the only member of the jury who noticed it," Sargent continued, obviously pleased with his own acumen, "I had better put it more explicitly. Did no one think it extraordinary that the witnesses found only one body?"

"Only one body!" exclaimed Gurney, the Chaplain. "But how many would you have expected them to find? Surely, poor Benchley was alone in his rooms?"

"I should have expected them to find two bodies," replied Sargent calmly. "If Benchley was in his rooms at all, which does not seem to me to be proved, he was certainly not alone."

"Then who was with him?" asked three fellows at once.

"Hasn't everybody forgotten King Pepi I?" retorted Sargent, manifestly enjoying the sensation he caused.

"The mummy!" The startled exclamation came in half a dozen voices simultaneously. Then there was a puzzled silence, as ten minds tried to rearrange their ideas. At last the Provost recollected his responsibilities as foreman.

"This is certainly an important point that you have raised, Sargent," he said. "Let us be quite clear what is your contention. Are you suggesting that our friend Benchley is still alive—a conclusion that would render us all devoutly thankful—and that the remains that we have all examined and assumed to be his are in reality only those of the Egyptian mummy that he had recently introduced into his rooms?"

"Unless someone can explain how the mummy left Benchley's rooms after half-past twelve, when Considine and I saw it there, that seems to me the only possible conclusion."

"I'm sorry, Mr. Provost," broke in Considine, "but this theory, much as I should like to believe it, is altogether out of the question."

"Indeed, Considine?" said the Provost. "I suppose you mean that it fails to account for the disappearance of Benchley, which, on Sargent's hypothesis, is a very strange circumstance. But not necessarily impossible, surely, Considine, not necessarily impossible?"

"No, Mr. Provost, I'm afraid the difficulty is much greater than that. We have all seen the bones of—well, I fear I must say Benchley. I think you'll all agree that the skeleton showed no marks of injury— in particular, that the skull was intact. Isn't that so, Monitor?"

"Yes, yes, yes. Magnificent head he had, poor fellow. Certainly it could never have been injured in his life. I've got a picture of him in my room taken when we were in the Dolomites together, that shows—"

"Yes, but that's not quite the point, Monitor," interrupted Considine. "You've just seen the skull in the hall. Was it intact *then?*"

"Oh, absolutely, absolutely."

"Then that disposes of the mummy theory straight away. Pharaoh Pepi's skull was cleft in two from crown to chin by the battle-axe of the high priest of Erech, at the battle in Sinai where he was killed. I've got a cuneiform tablet in my rooms that gives a full account of the fight. If you'll excuse me a moment, Mr. Provost, I'll go and fetch it."

"This is an extraordinary complication, my dear Considine," said the Provost. "But can we take it into account? It has not been put in evidence before us, you know."

"If you'll allow me to speak as a lawyer, Mr. Provost," remarked Sargent, "I think Considine is quite in order. A coroner's jury isn't quite in the position of a common jury. We don't swear to decide according to the evidence, and it is perfectly permissible for us to use any special knowledge we may possess."

"That's so, Provost," came in a new voice from near the door. Sir Theodore Mainwaring, Regius Professor of Constitutional History, scented a pet subject of his own. "Sargent's point is quite sound; the distinction has an important historical significance. The coroner's jury represents the old Anglo-Saxon idea of the voice of common fame, and—"

"Really, Mainwaring, that doctrine is surely rather *démodé* nowadays." Gurney was an antiquary before he was a parson, and long before he was a juror. "You would do better to look for the origins of the coroner's jury in Richard Coeur de Lion's duchy of Aquitaine—"

"Or possibly even in Athens," suggested Saunderson, the Mods Tutor. "There are certain aspects of the phratries—"

"Gentlemen, gentlemen." The Provost despairingly tried to call his wayward pack off the false scent. "We are trying to investigate the circumstances surrounding the death of our dear friend Benchley."

"Of King Pepi I," said two or three fellows together. Sargent glanced round quickly. Apparently Gurney and a scientist, named Gaunt, had been converted to his view.

"Well, let us not pre-judge the issue. Shall I say that we are trying to decide whose these relics are? You say, Considine, that you have a tablet showing that the—does one say the 'original'?—of Benchley's mummy had his skull cut in two. I won't ask you to produce the tablet, for I fear you are the only one of us who could read it. But do you think it is possible that the account it gives may be mistaken? After all, it's a long time ago."

"I can see no possible reason to doubt it," said the orientalist. "It's the official dispatch sent home from the battlefield to Assyria, and written the very day of the battle."

"Still, you know," put in Monitor, "some easterns have very odd notions of truth. There was a dragoman I came across in Baghdad, who rather shook my faith in all documents from that part of the world. He told me that—"

"I hardly think, my dear Monitor," interrupted the Provost, "that we can go into general questions relating to the veracity of orientals. Considine assures us, on authority whose weight, it seems to me, he is best qualified to judge, that these remains do not tally with what is known of the mummy in Benchley's rooms. That is a point on whose importance we must all make up our minds. But it occurs to me that the mummy must surely have been examined at some date more recent than that of Considine's cuneiform tablet."

"Curiously enough, Mr. Provost," said Considine, "I believe it was never examined; or at any rate no result of the examination was ever made public. Of course, I'm not an Egyptologist, but I did know a little about this particular mummy through Benchley himself. It appears that its late owner, Professor Bonoff, absolutely refused to disclose anything about it: said a full description would appear in due course in his next book. So far as I know, nobody has ever opened the coffin except Bonoff, and perhaps Benchley; if I didn't know that Benchley had spent practically his last penny on it, in the hope of a profitable resale, I should have said it was quite probable there was no mummy inside at all. That often happens, you know, owing to the depredations of tomb robbers. I asked Benchley about it yesterday morning, when the mummy arrived from the Isle of Wight; but he was disposed to be mysterious too. He said he wasn't going to open the coffin till next term, since he was just going on his holiday. But he must have looked inside when he went to see Bonoff and bought it."

"It seems to me, Mr. Provost," said Edward Newton, the External Bursar, "that we shall have to ask the coroner to adjourn the inquest for the evidence of Professor Bonoff."

There was a chorus of protest. Half the men present had arranged to leave Oxford within the next few days, and nobody knew how long it would take to produce the Russian. Besides, he was a stranger, and this was essentially a college affair.

"Come, come, Newton," said the Provost. "That surely is unnecessary. Somebody must have handled the mummy, and could no doubt tell from the weight if there was anything in the case or not."

Considine shook his head. "I doubt it," he said. "I saw it arrive yesterday. It was taken up to Benchley's room by the two Carter-Paterson's men who brought it; it was inside a big packing case, so I doubt if they could tell us anything definite even if we could trace them. And Benchley unpacked the case himself. The only people I can think of who might be able to help us are those two Corpus undergraduates who played that trick at the ball last night. They ought to know; they carried the mummy up and down the Bursary stairs. Sargent has their names."

"Alas," said Sargent, as all eyes were turned upon him. "I'm afraid there's another snag. I reported those two to Corpus early this morning; and here is a note, handed to me just before the inquest, in which the Dean of Corpus presents his compliments to the Dean of Beaufort and begs to inform him that no such names as Randolph and Nevern appear on the books of his college. He's a bit peevish about the suggestion, I think."

"False names!" exclaimed Newton. "That's very unlike the usual undergraduate. Still, we can't help it, and it seems to bring us back to the necessity of getting Bonoff's evidence."

"It brings us back to the necessity for a little common sense," said Lake impatiently. "Mr. Provost, I appeal to you. We can't possibly assent to Newton's suggestion; it'll make us the laughing-stock of Oxford—calling in a foreigner none of us has ever seen to help us decide a perfectly plain case. All this talk about the mummy is a mere red herring. What are the facts? Considine has told us that the body may never have been in the mummy case at all, and that if it was, it must have borne marks that are not on the body we are inquiring about. Surely, that disposes of the mummy finally. We are left with an unrecognizable body, found locked in Benchley's rooms. Benchley was last seen in those rooms, and is now missing. The inference is obvious. I don't know what the law is, but I suggest we take a vote on the question of identity, and then regard that part of the discussion as closed. I move that we decide that the body is that of Peter Benchley, Doctor of Letters, Professor of Egyptology in the University and Fellow and Internal Bursar of Beaufort College."

"I second the pro-Provost's motion," said Considine quietly.

"All this seems to me rather unusual," quavered the Provost, "and I don't like taking a division in the college on a personal matter touching one of our own Fellows. Still, we can't go on debating all night. Will those in favour of identifying the body as our friend Benchley's raise the right hand? Thank you. And now those against?

Anybody except Gurney, Gaunt and Sargent wishing to vote against the motion? No? Then the motion is carried. Now we have decided that this is Benchley's body; we still have to make up our minds how the poor fellow came to his death. Does anybody suggest any other cause than accident?"

"I can't quite understand how the accident happened," mused Mainwaring. "This is the warmest June we've had for years, so Benchley can hardly have wanted to light a fire. Where did the original ignition come from?"

"Oh, that's simple enough, I'm afraid," said Gurney. "Benchley *would* smoke in bed—that horrible great meerschaum of his. I've often warned him of the danger."

"Yes, but he didn't smoke in bed last night." Monitor's voice had taken on a new incisiveness. "He would never smoke any pipe but that one, and that's lying on my mantelpiece at this moment."

"On your mantelpiece!" exclaimed Gurney.

"Yes," corroborated Considine. "Monitor took Benchley's pipe away from him last night. It certainly is odd. How *did* the place catch fire?"

"And how was it that Benchley didn't even succeed in getting to his bedroom door to unlock it?" asked Mainwaring. "It must have been an astonishingly rapid conflagration."

"But what other explanation is there?" asked Lake.

"Have we any evidence that Benchley was not already dead before the fire started?"

"Then how did he die?"

"It seems to me at least conceivable that we may have to deal with suicide—or even murder."

"Oh, nonsense, Mainwaring," expostulated Lake. "You've been reading too many books by Galahad Baines." There was a suppressed titter round the room, for Sargent had recently unearthed the secret of the *nom de guerre* under which Mainwaring added to his income by writing detective stories of the more flamboyant type. "Suicides don't burn themselves to death, and murderers don't leave their victims in rooms with the door locked on the inside."

"How do we know it was locked on the inside?" persisted Main-waring. "Those two undergraduates who tried to rescue Benchley could see that the key wasn't on their side of the door; but they couldn't possibly know that it was on the other. The murderer might have taken it away with him."

"My dear Mainwaring," said Lake, "your imagination is running away with you. There is not a particle of evidence that a murderer ever existed. Our only difficulty is to account for the starting of the fire; and after all, unexplained fires occur every day. Again, Mr. Provost, I appeal to you to close the discussion and bring in a verdict of accidental death."

"I won't press my point," said Mainwaring. "Though I still think there's more in it than Lake will admit."

"Does anybody wish to take exception to a verdict of accidental death?" asked the Provost.

"I suppose you won't accept an amendment, Mr. Provost?" inquired Sargent, "so as to read 'Killed in action by an act of Pharaoh's enemies'?"

"I'm afraid that's the point we've already decided to dismiss, Sargent."

"Very well, then, Mr. Provost; I join Mainwaring in reluctant acquiescence."

"Ah, then we are all agreed. I suppose we ought to put our verdict in Latin." The company smiled at the Provost's well-known conservative ways. "We are a university jury, and ought to set an example by sticking to the official language of the university—now, alas, so sadly neglected even in Congregation. Yes, we will say, 'mortuus per accidens'."

And so, when at last the verdict was delivered to a coroner purple with impatient indignation, he declared the inquest closed with an acid expression of surprise that it should take the united scholarship of the Provost and Fellows of Beaufort an hour and a half to translate "accidental death" into dog Latin.

4

THE SCOUT

"Well, Humphrey, what do you think of that performance?" asked
Sargent, as the two junior fellows sat over a belated tea in Considine's rooms.

"Legal solemnities certainly don't show the fellows of the college to the best advantage," was the reply. "It would have shaken
my faith in government by discussion, if I'd ever had any."

"But what do you make of the result?"

"Frankly, Denys, I really don't know what to say. On the face of
it, it seems wildly impossible that the thing should be anything
but an accident; but I confess I'm not satisfied about how that fire
started. Are you?"

"I'm dissatisfied with the whole business from beginning to
end," said Sargent decisively. "I'm not convinced that was
Benchley's body. I'm not convinced the fire was accidental. I'm sure
there was more than met the eye in that monkeying with the
mummy last night. I think we shamelessly scamped the question
of what was really in the mummy coffin, which is probably the crux
of the whole case. And I should like to know what became of
Benchley's key of the garden gate."

"I think we've got to make up our minds that it really was
Benchley's body," said Considine. "It cannot possibly be Pharaoh
Pepi's."

"Have you got that tablet, Humphrey?" asked Sargent. "I should
like to know exactly what it does say."

"Yes, I can show it to you, if you like." Considine went over to a glass-fronted cupboard, and extracted one of a number of small objects of baked clay, closely filled with incised writing in small wedge-shaped characters. "Here it is. It's just a straightforward military dispatch. Here, you see, is where the relevant bit begins. 'In the wilderness of the Sinai I laid low Pharaoh and all his host, I the High Priest. King Pepi, King of the Egyptians, with my right hand I slew him, I slew him. With my axe I smote him, I clave him from the crown even unto the chin, so that his brains gushed forth, so that the right ear of Pharaoh fell a cubit's span from the left, so that men took up the head of Pharaoh in two pieces. I the High Priest destroyed him with my own hand. So perish all the enemies of the great god."

"Pretty vigorous work for a clergyman," remarked Sargent. "It certainly doesn't leave much room for ambiguity. I suppose you'll swear it's authentic?"

"I dug it up myself in unbroken ground," answered Considine. "It couldn't conceivably have been forged."

"All right then," said Sargent, "I give up the mummy hypothesis for the time being. But I still don't accept accidental death as proved. There's another point just occurred to me. You remember those keys that the coroner examined Miss Carrothers about?"

"Yes. They didn't strike me as amounting to much."

"No, they didn't. But where were they found?"

"On the body. Goddard gave evidence of that."

"Yes, that's what strikes me as the significant point. Everybody seems to have assumed that Benchley went to bed, and was burnt to death in his sleep. But he wouldn't have taken his keys to bed with him, whatever he might have done with his wrist watch. On the other hand, if he'd been still up and dressed, I can't see how he could have been so taken by surprise that he failed to get to his bedroom door and unlock it."

"But then what do you conclude from that?"

"That Benchley was dead before the fire started."

"But that means suicide."

"You forget the difficulty you yourself raised about how to account for the starting of the fire. It seems to me far more like murder."

"Oh, really, Denys, you're getting as bad as Mainwaring. Who could want to murder Benchley, of all people?"

"That's what I'm going to try and find out. You don't agree with me about the murder, and I won't argue with you now. But you don't agree with the coroner either, do you? So will you join me in trying to get to the bottom of it?"

Considine reflected a moment. "I think you're on a wild goose chase," he said at last. "But, as I said, there is a point that I'm uncomfortable about—I mean the origin of the fire—and I should like to clear that up. So, as long as you don't ask me to commit myself to your theory, I'll do what I can to help."

"My dear Humphrey, I haven't got a theory. I'm as much in the dark as you are. So we start fair."

"How *do* we start, by the way?" asked Considine.

"That's a point, certainly. I believe Sherlock generally started by having a look at the scene of the crime. Suppose we go over and have a search in the ruins."

"What do you expect to find?"

"I haven't the faintest idea. But if we go with open minds there's always the chance that something may turn up. If you want a definite objective for the search, we might begin by looking for the key."

"Which key?" asked Considine.

"Oh, yes, I'd forgotten that. Of course there are the two keys to look for—the key of the garden gate and the key of Benchley's bedroom door. Either of them might turn out to be important. We'll look out for them both. Shall we go across?"

"All right, come along." Considine replaced his cuneiform tablet lovingly in the cupboard, and the two went out into the quadrangle and walked across towards the Bursary.

As they went Considine, whose features indicated growing bewilderment, suddenly reverted to the earlier topic of their discussion. "Denys," he said, "I'm not going back on what I've just put to you; your theory about the mummy is absolutely incredible. But for all that, the mummy has me utterly at sea."

"Why, Humphrey, I thought your chunk of brick settled the matter to your satisfaction."

"So it does, so far as it goes. It proves that the body in Benchley's rooms was not the mummy, and therefore must have been Benchley himself. But we're left completely in the dark as to what became of the mummy."

"Isn't the obvious solution that the coffin was empty?"

"It would be the obvious solution, but for the fact that Benchley bought that mummy as a definite investment, in the belief that it was unique and he could make a big profit on it. I know the price he paid ran into thousands, and he told that American guest of his last night that he had already resold the thing. But if it was just an empty coffin it wouldn't have anything like the value; the whole point of it was that it was the oldest royal mummy in existence. Empty mummy cases are as common as dirt; I've seen one myself going back to the Third Dynasty, whereas King Pepi belonged to the Sixth."

"You don't think old Bonoff could have sold him a pup? Judging from some of Benchley's public references to him he might be a cross between Professor Moriarty and Al Capone."

"You're not paying much of a compliment to Professor Moriarty or Al Capone if you think he'd try and sell an empty coffin as a complete mummy to the greatest living authority on the subject. No, Denys, you've got to accept the fact that that coffin came into college yesterday morning with a mummy inside it."

"And to reconcile it with the fact that there's no mummy now?"

"Exactly. It seems to me what we've got to look for is a mummy without a coffin."

"Common object of the countryside. Well, I'll leave that side of it to you, Humphrey. Round up as many of them as you can find, and we'll have a look at 'em together. Hullo, Newton, are you after me?"

The External Bursar had thrown open the Bursary window, and was waving to them to come in. "It's Considine I want really," he said, "but if you don't mind coming in, too, I won't keep you more than a moment."

Inside the Bursary there was no sign of the havoc wrought in the rooms above by last night's conflagration. The massive stone vaulting, dating from the Founder's time, had easily withstood the strain, while the upper story, added by less conscientious Victorian builders, had collapsed like a house of cards. In contrast with the mediaevalism of the greater part of the college, this room would have struck a stranger with something of a shock, for it was filled with card indexes, filing cabinets, and the rest of the paraphernalia of an up-to-date office. The large-scale maps of the college estates, on the walls, however, some of them executed with the elaborate penmanship of the seventeenth century, were more in keeping with the architecture that framed the whole.

"I've been going over Benchley's belongings," said Newton, as Sargent and Considine came in, "and I've found this. I think I ought to hand it over to you at once." He gave Considine a folded document on blue paper.

"Ah, yes," said Considine, "his will. Yes, he told me he was making me his executor. But I'm afraid I can't make head or tail of this jargon. Here, Denys, you'll have to translate; Assyrian's my language, not solicitor's English."

"It's a dialect specially devised to confine the knowledge of the law to educated men," said Sargent, taking the will. "However, let us try and interpret for the benefit of the vulgar. Let me see. Your takings, Humphrey, amount to twenty-five pounds. His pipe to Monitor, with £500 to provide it with a home. Then his books and antiquarian objects relating to the study of Egyptology are bequeathed to the College. That's interesting. It means we get the mummy, or should have if it hadn't been burnt."

"We may still get the mummy," said Considine. "That is if the sale Benchley spoke of hadn't been completed. The only thing we know has been burnt is the coffin. The mummy may yet turn up."

Newton lifted his eyebrows in surprise, but said nothing. Sargent made a grimace. "Gruesome sort of exhibit," he remarked. "Still, it'll hardly be noticed among the portraits of former Fellows in Hall. Then there's a list of small legacies to the scouts. Fifteen pounds for the Manciple, twenty for Bloggs, etcetera, etcetera. And the residuary legatee is 'my niece, Miss Daphne Carrothers'. And that's the lot. Oh no, it isn't, though," he added, turning over a page. "Here's a codicil. Well, that is odd."

"What does it say?" asked Considine and Newton together.

"It makes Miss Daphne Carrothers a ward in Chancery. That's to protect her from your evil designs, Humphrey, my lad. I suppose it's good in law, by the way. It's generally a parent who plays that sort of trick on his offspring, not a mere uncle. But this is the odd bit. 'And I express the hope that the court will not, in the exercise of its discretion, assent to the marriage of the said Daphne Carrothers to Mark Devereux, of White Abbey, near Bembridge, Isle of Wight, Esquire, while the said Daphne Carrothers remains below the age of twenty-one years.' What do you make of that?"

"That's the undergraduate who gave evidence," said Newton. "He seemed an inoffensive young man, and obviously wrapped up in the girl. What's the objection to him? Lack of cash?"

"No, it can't be that," answered Considine. "I believe he's pretty comfortably endowed; he's the local squire in those parts. Father killed in the War, and the son's going down this term to take over the management of the property."

"Oh, you know him then?" said Sargent.

"I met him once in Monitor's rooms with a mixed crowd of effervescent juveniles of both sexes. But for the fact that any undergraduate you find there is pretty sure to be wanted by the progs, I should have said he was a most eligible young man. Certainly I liked him myself."

"He was the last man who saw Benchley alive," said Sargent reflectively. "I wonder what he was doing up in the old man's rooms in the middle of the ball last night. We ought to look into that, Humphrey."

"Probably something to do with Daphne, don't you think?" replied the orientalist. "He must have known Benchley's objection to him as a nephew-in-law. He was probably making a last effort to bring him round before going down."

"Still, it wants looking into," said Sargent. "Well, we mustn't take up Newton's time, or the college will be in the bankruptcy court. I suppose you don't mind our having a look round the ruins, Newton? You presumably act as Internal Bursar as well as External, *vacante sede?*"

"Go up, by all means," replied the Bursar. "In fact I imagine that Considine as executor is the proper man to take possession. But I'm afraid you'll find damn little left."

There was indeed little enough to be recognized when they emerged into the open air at the head of the staircase. The roof had fallen in, and broken tiles and debris of building materials were strewn thickly over the underlying strata of ashes, which represented all that was left of Benchley's furniture and belongings. Here and there among the rubbish, pools of dirty water, left by the hose of the fire brigade or the morning's downpour, made the mess seem even more dismal and forbidding.

"Looks like a big job, Denys," said Considine. "We shall have to get help if we're to work through all this in less than a week."

"So I was thinking," Sargent agreed. "There's Bloggs coming across the quad. He was Benchley's scout, wasn't he? Bloggs!" he called, going over to the empty window opening. "Bloggs! Come up here a moment."

"Very good, sir; just coming, sir," replied Bloggs, and a moment later his wheezy panting was heard as he slowly ascended the rickety stairs.

Bloggs, an ancient man even as college servants go, had the appearance of an ecclesiastical dignitary who, having had the misfortune to be unfrocked after reaching a considerable position, had since run badly to seed. He always seemed to be rendered speechless with gratitude at the honour of being addressed by one of the Fellows, but if spoken to harshly was liable to burst into tears. On the other hand, he regarded undergraduates as his natural prey, and fleeced them unmercifully in all the innumerable ways elaborated by countless generations of predatory scouts.

"Bloggs," said Sargent. "I want some boys. Do you think you could find some?"

"Well, sir, Henry is the boy on this staircase. I could send him to you, sir. But is it nothing I could do for you myself, sir?"

"Oh, we shall want your help too, Bloggs. But at present I want boys, lots of boys, not just Henry. Mr. Considine and I are going to dig through all this rubbish and see if there's anything of Dr. Benchley's that we can save. So I want you to go and round up all the boys you can find in the college and bring them here. You'd better find the gardener too, and borrow all the shovels and spades you can."

"Yes, sir, thank you very much, sir," said Bloggs with deep humility. "I shall have to speak to the other bed makers, sir. Each boy is under the orders of the bed maker of his staircase, sir. Have I your authority, sir, to say that the boys are required for your personal service?"

"Yes, of course, Bloggs," answered Sargent impatiently. "Get along quickly and collect them. And you may as well get a garden sieve and a wheelbarrow while you're about it."

"Yes, sir, thank you very much, sir," replied Bloggs, and departed.

"Come along, Humphrey," said Sargent. "Let's make a start. *Littera scripta manet.* The college legacy seems to have suffered less than the rest," and he pointed to where, along one wall, a mass of solid and largely unburnt material was still recognizable as books. "We'll begin by clearing those away; that'll give us some space to work in."

They set to work, and had succeeded in stacking a large part of the books on the stairs by the time that Bloggs reappeared, followed by a procession of half a dozen youths in green baize aprons, armed with shovels and spades. One of them pushed a wheelbarrow in which lay a gardener's sieve.

With this reinforcement the excavation proceeded apace. Considine's professional instincts, trained in more than one expedition to the ruins of Babylon, were quickly aroused, and he took command of the proceedings with systematic thoroughness. First, he commandeered two waste paper baskets from the Bursary downstairs. Bloggs, with the sieve, was posted in the doorway, Considine standing beside him, and Sargent with a notebook sitting on the top stair. One boy was occupied in collecting the tiles and other obvious parts of the fabric of the building from the heaps of debris. Three more worked steadily forward on parallel lines across the room, shovelling everything indiscriminately into Bloggs's sieve. The finer ash was sifted through into one of the waste paper baskets, which boy number five was detailed to carry backwards and forwards to the wheelbarrow waiting outside. Such objects as remained in the sieve were carefully examined by Considine, and, if in any way recognizable, catalogued by Sargent in his notebook, together with particulars of the positions in which they were found. Thus one page of the notebook was headed, "Trench No. 1; along south wall," the next, "Trench No. 2; parallel to Trench No. 1, five feet further north," and so on. After the work had been going on for about an hour, a typical extract from the page dealing with No. 2 trench read, "Five feet from east; Leg of chair, glass ink-pot (broken), tobacco-jar. Eight feet: fragments of table, book, title illegible, piece of china plate, paper knife, apparently silver." All these objects, after being classified, were deposited in the second waste paper basket and carried down by the sixth boy to a dump in one corner of the quadrangle. The ashes in the wheelbarrow were from time to time emptied on another heap alongside.

Considine was thoroughly enjoying himself; the problem, as one of pure archaeological technique, had begun to grip him, and he had long forgotten the very existence of Benchley. If suddenly challenged, he would almost certainly have advanced some theory dividing the remains into the various stages of culture to which the different strata bore witness. Sargent, though the more eager for the investigation at the outset, had no professional interest in the method, and quickly became bored. "Do you know what time it is, Humphrey?" he asked, as the boy working trench No. 1 poured his last shovelful into the sieve. "It's a quarter past seven, and dinner's at the half-hour. We ought to go and dress."

"Oh, damn dinner," replied Considine impatiently. "I don't want any. We ought to keep on with this while the light lasts. Can't you forget your belly for a bit?"

"I owe it too much reverence," replied Sargent firmly. "Still, I'll meet you half-way and cut hall. Bloggs, will you go over to the cook and ask him to send along some sandwiches for Mr. Considine and me, and a bottle of claret? We'll have a scratch meal in the Bursary. Then you and the boys can knock off till eight o'clock and get something to eat yourselves."

"Certainly, sir, thank you very much, sir," said Bloggs, and he and the boys disappeared. Sargent rose from his cramped position at the stairhead and stretched himself. "I wouldn't be an archaeologist for much," he said; "thank heaven there's no navvy work in the law." He strolled down one of the "trenches" into the middle of the room.

"Fat lot of navvy work you've done," retorted Considine. But Sargent was not listening.

"Have you any idea what this is, Humphrey?" he asked, stooping down to pick up a small object from the debris.

"Catalogue it, man, before you start playing with it," exclaimed Humphrey. "This isn't crude rule of thumb, like shelling *subpoenas*. This is exact science. You'll never make an archaeologist. Here, let me stick it down." He picked up Sargent's notebook, and began to write with punctilious detail, "one foot north of trench No. 3, twelve feet from east wall." "Now what is it you've found, Denys?"

"That's what I was asking you," replied Sargent. "Have a look at it."

Considine took from him the small piece of blackened metal, and looked at it for some moments in silence. "Doesn't seem anything to make a song and dance about," he said; "but I admit I don't quite know what it is. Anyhow, we'd better make a note of it." And he proceeded to complete his entry with the words: "hollow metallic hemisphere, radius about one inch, small ring attached to the middle point of convex side, screw socket middle of other side."

"No, it isn't much result for over an hour's digging," assented Sargent. "But it's the only thing we've found that wasn't perfectly obvious. I wish I could think what it is. I feel sure I've seen something like it somewhere."

"It's rather like the top of a bicycle bell," said Considine thoughtfully. "But then what's this ring thing for? Besides, Benchley didn't ride a bicycle."

"I've got it," exclaimed Sargent. "You know those cheap tin alarm clocks. It's the bell part of one of those. They often have a ring at the top to pick 'em up by in the morning, when you want to sling the damn thing out of the window. That's what it is."

"Yes, I suppose you're right." Considine was clearly not enthusiastic. "It doesn't seem to get us anywhere. Hardly worth disturbing the symmetry of my excavations for such a trifle. It can't have anything to do with Benchley's death, or even with the missing mummy."

"Don't be too cocksure, Humphrey. It's odd, anyhow; and anything odd is worth noticing when you haven't got a clue."

"I don't see that it's even odd," objected Considine. "Cheap alarm clocks are as common as dirt."

"Not in Benchley's rooms," retorted Sargent. "Did you ever know him come down to breakfast before ten o'clock? But here's Bloggs; he'll be able to tell us. Bloggs, did Dr. Benchley possess an alarm clock?"

Bloggs, who had just appeared in the doorway, seemed deeply hurt by the suggestion. "Oh no, sir," he said. "Certainly not, sir; he couldn't have had any use for one, sir. I called him myself at half-past eight every morning, sir, and again at nine o'clock in case he had gone to sleep again, sir."

"Yes, but wasn't he going to catch an early train this morning?" put in Considine. "I expect he set the clock to wake him up for that."

"I beg your pardon, sir." Bloggs was still more pained. "Dr. Benchley had asked me to call him at seven o'clock this morning, sir."

"Well, he seems to have had a second string to his bow," said Considine.

"I don't think that's likely, sir, if you will allow me to say so, sir. Dr. Benchley was good enough to have absolute confidence in me, sir." Bloggs's voice was beginning to sound tearful, and Sargent hastened to reassure him.

"I'm sure he had, Bloggs," he said. "So have we all. Perhaps there's some other explanation of this bell. After all, we haven't found the rest of the clock. We'd better have a look for it now."

"Thank you very much, sir," said Bloggs. "But what I came up to say, sir, is that dinner is served, sir, in the Bursary."

"Oh Bloggs, Bloggs," said Considine reproachfully, "we said we'd have sandwiches, and now I suppose you've given us a six-course meal. I should like to take you out to Nineveh and teach you the elements of the simple life."

"Yes, sir, thank you very much, sir," said Bloggs, and stood aside to let the two dons pass down the stairs into the Bursary, where one of the tables had been laid with a white cloth and a considerable array of the famous college plate.

Once faced with the admirable meal that only a college kitchen can produce on the spur of the moment, Considine forgot his impatience to continue the excavations and seemed to enjoy his food and wine as much as Sargent. By tacit consent they avoided the dominant topic while they ate, and it was with minds as well as bodies refreshed that they eventually returned to their labours on the floor above.

Once more the shovels, the sieve, and the notebook were brought into play, and the party worked on methodically until the late darkness of June suspended their operations. By that time less than half of the floor space of Benchley's rooms had been cleared, and most of the objects retrieved and catalogued were commonplace enough. But trench No. 4, which ran along the line of what had been the wooden partition wall between the bedroom and the sitting room, yielded two finds of some interest.

The first was the lock of the communicating door. Sargent, as the excavations approached the spot where the door had been, left his place on the stairs, and was standing over the boy with the shovel at the moment the mass of metal came into sight. He pounced on it at once, thrust the boy aside, and began to grope with his hands among the wreckage round about where it had lain. After a few minutes he stood up triumphantly, holding over his head a key. He tried to fit it into the lock, but it was too badly bent by the heat to enter the keyhole. Still, it was obviously a key of the ordinary domestic pattern, and Considine agreed with him that there was no reasonable doubt it was the key of the bedroom door.

"But what does that tell us?" he asked sceptically. "We knew all the time that the door was locked, and therefore that there must have been a key."

"It's evidence," replied Sargent. "Negative evidence, I admit, but still evidence. If we'd found the key in the lock, it would prove that the door had been locked on the inside, and therefore that Benchley was alone when he died. For I don't think we need seriously consider the possibility of a murderer's having locked the door on the inside and then got away by the window; he'd certainly have broken his neck, unless he was a monkey."

"But the fact that we didn't find the key in the lock doesn't prove the door was not locked on the inside," said Considine.

"No, of course it doesn't," said Sargent. "That's why I said it was negative evidence. Benchley might have locked the door and taken the key out, though I can't at the moment suggest any reason why he should. Or it may just have fallen out of the lock when Goddard and Devereux were banging on the door. You notice the lock was a little way further into the bedroom than the key. As the door was battered down, it presumably fell inwards towards the bedroom; and therefore if the key had already fallen out of the lock the result would be as we have it. On the other hand, suppose Benchley was murdered. The murderer then set light to the bedclothes, went out, locked the door on the outside, and shoved the key back under the door. That would fit the facts, too; the key would still be found on the sitting-room side of the lock, unless he shoved it a hell of a long way with a stick or something."

"Then really we've discovered nothing at all."

"Oh, I don't know about that. Personally, I think the first idea, of the key falling out of the lock, is much the less likely of the two. It isn't easy, I should say, to shake a key out from the other side of the door at the best of times; and when it's pretty nearly red hot it must be a lot more difficult. Metal expands with heat, you know."

"Yes, but if the key expanded so would the lock," objected Considine.

"The metal of the lock would expand," said Sargent. "But that means the hole would get smaller, doesn't it? I'm not very sure;

I'm not a physicist. We shall have to ask Lake—unless we burn down your bedroom door by way of experiment. But anyhow, I think the idea of the key having been pushed back under the door is a shade the likelier of the two. I can't press it, because, as I said, it's just conceivable that Benchley himself may have taken the key out after locking himself in. But at least you'll admit that the facts so far don't destroy the murder theory, as finding the key in the lock would have done?"

"Yes, I'll admit that," answered Considine, "for what it's worth. Of course, Benchley might have taken out the key if he was going to commit suicide and wanted to put people off the track."

"Well, we won't rule out suicide yet," assented Sargent, and returned to work.

The second discovery in trench No. 4 was more unexpected. Inextricably tangled in the remains of the wire mattress of Benchley's bed, which had stood against the wooden partition, was found an almost formless mass of metal, in which, however, a few cogwheels survived in a sufficiently intact state to identify it as the missing alarm clock. Sargent obviously attached great importance to this find.

"What did I tell you, Humphrey?" he said, exultantly. "Benchley did have an alarm clock after all; or at any rate an alarm clock got into Benchley's rooms last night. If it had been there before, Bloggs would have known of its existence. What do you make of that?"

"Simply that Benchley didn't put all his faith in Bloggs's punctuality after all, and got the machine to put under his bed and wake him up in time for his train."

"Having previously removed the bell part and left it in his sitting room?" asked Sargent quietly. "No, Humphrey, my lad, there's more in this than meets the eye. I'm going to bed to think it over."

5
THE EGYPTOLOGIST

SARGENT WAS THE FIRST TO ARRIVE next morning in the common room, where those fellows who were resident in college habitually breakfasted together. With a copy of *The Times* propped against the coffeepot he settled down to combine the consumption of fried eggs with the study of the career of his late colleague.

"PETER MANNINGTON BENCHLEY," the obituary notice began, "whose lamented death in a fire at Oxford is the subject of a report on another page, was by the common consent of scholars throughout the world the supreme authority on the mortuary customs of the ancient Egyptians. In the wider sphere of general Egyptology he had done more to advance the boundaries of knowledge than any researcher since Young and Champollion deciphered the inscription on the Rosetta Stone.

"Born on July 19th, 1864, the only son of the late Wilfred Benchley, he was educated at Harrow and Pembroke College, Oxford. His early training did not suggest an archaeological career, for he took a first class in Mathematical Moderations in 1884 and a second class in the Final Honour School of Natural Science two years later. He continued his scientific studies for another year at the University of Bonn. It was the comparatively accidental circumstance of his appointment as research chemist to the Anglo-Egyptian Cotton Company that turned his thoughts in the direction of Egyptology. The eminent Italian orientalist, Orlando de' Conti, who was at that time studying the development of the art of mummification, invited the assistance of the young scientist in elucidating some of the chemical questions involved. Benchley plunged into the work with enthusiasm, and eventually collaborated with de' Conti in his famous work *La Necrologia Egiziana*. This proved the turning point in his life; in 1890 he resigned his industrial appointment to become Keeper of the Mummies in the Ghizeh Museum, and henceforth devoted himself wholly to Egyptological research.

"It was while engaged in collecting materials for his work on the festivities of the Pharaohs, *The Fleshpots of Egypt*, published in 1905, that Benchley became attracted by the problem of the relation between Egypt and the earliest Hellenic culture. He advanced the remarkable theory that the Greek wine god, Dionysos, could be identified with a spirit of vegetation worshipped in Lower Egypt at the time of the Twelfth Dynasty. This contention led him into wider fields of speculation, and when his thesis was at last set forth in full in his *magnum opus*, *Dionysos at Memphis* (1910), it was found to cover the whole field of the ancient religions of the near and middle east. The work was immediately hailed by scholars as a contribution to learning of the first importance, and when the Khedival Chair of Egyptology was founded at Oxford in the following year, the election of Benchley as its first occupant was a foregone conclusion.

"At Oxford, where his professorship carried with it a fellowship of Beaufort College, Benchley devoted himself once more to that study of mummies and funerary customs generally which had been his first interest, and on which his fame with scholars, as distinct from the general public, is most likely to rest. But shortly after the War he was drawn into a prolonged controversy by the attacks of the Russian Egyptologist, Feodor Bonoff, on the thesis of *Dionysos at Memphis*. Benchley, whose slashing style of argument in public debate was in strange contrast with his shy and modest manner in private intercourse, engaged his antagonist at all points, and the result was a warfare of print that raged for twelve years in learned periodicals and even in the pages of this less technical journal. Since there is certainly no living Egyptologist competent to judge between the adversaries, the question of the validity of their respective contentions must be left for posterity to settle.

"For many years Benchley visited Egypt annually, generally accompanied by Oxford pupils, for excavation work in various parts of the country. Both in these expeditions and in his lectures and private tuition at Oxford he showed himself a teacher of rare insight, and won the personal affection of all who came under his instruction. It is safe to say that all the best work that has been done by the younger generation of English Egyptologists is based on Benchley's teaching.

"As Fellow of Beaufort, Benchley entered fully into the life of the college, which he served for the last ten years of his life as Internal Bursar. In this capacity his early mathematical training stood him in good stead, and he proved a most able and devoted steward of the college interests. He served the office of pro-Provost in 1927-28.

"Benchley never married, and his only surviving relation is a niece, Miss Daphne Carrothers, daughter of the late Sir Matthew Carrothers of the Indian Civil Service and of the late Lady Carrothers, who was Benchley's only sister.

"Benchley was a Doctor of Letters at Oxford, an honorary Doctor of Laws of Cambridge and Heidelberg, and a Fellow of the British Academy. He was President of the Egyptian Research Society in 1920, and of the Fédération Internationale d'Archeologie in 1929."

"Professor Feodor Bonoff writes as follows:

"'To the Editor of *The Times*,
"'Sir,
"'The untimely death of Professor Benchley is a loss from which the science of Egyptology can never recover in our time. To his monumental work, *Dionysos at Memphis*, we are indebted for practically every fact of importance to the study of Egyptian religion that has been discovered in this century. It is true that the fundamental thesis of that work is untenable, as I have demonstrated in previous letters published in your columns. The book none the less remains, as a repository of facts, unsurpassed and unsurpassable.

"'It is not generally known to the learned world that Professor Benchley himself had recently abandoned the controversial positions taken up in his book. I had the honour of entertaining him not long ago at my home in the Isle of Wight, and he then, with the generosity of the great scholar he was, freely admitted that the arguments, mainly based on his own discoveries, which I had been able to advance against him were conclusive. Not only this, but he placed at my disposal the whole of the unpublished material that he had collected on the subject. This material will be incorporated in my forthcoming

volumes, to be entitled *Religi Pharaonis*, which I
hope to publish early next year. My modest treatise,
therefore, will gain a distinction it little deserves,
as the memorial of the life's work of that illustrious
scholar, Peter Mannington Benchley.

"'I am, Sir, your obedient Servant,
"'Feodor Bonoff.'"

"What do you think of that, Humphrey?" asked Sargent, push-
ing the paper over to Considine, who had just entered the common
room and walked over to the sideboard to help himself to porridge.

"What is it?" said Considine, with the spoon poised in the air.
"Oh, Benchley's obituary? I wrote it myself a year ago. I'm afraid
it doesn't do him justice; but you can't really put a man like that
on paper."

"Oh, I don't mean the obituary," said Sargent. "I guessed that
was you straight away. No, look at the letter underneath."

"Bonoff, is it? He's pretty quick in the uptake. What's he got to
say?" Considine read the letter in silence. "Smarmy sort of document,"
he said when he had finished. "Looks as if he's mainly concerned
to get a free advertisement for his own book, and saw a golden opportunity to trade on poor Benchley's reputation—steal it in fact."

"Yes, that was my impression," agreed Sargent. "Still, it's true,
isn't it, that Benchley had given in?"

"Yes; he told me so himself the very night he died," Considine
answered. "But there was no need to go trumpeting it over his dead
body. It's just like Bonoff, though."

"How did he get on to it so quickly, do you think?"

"Oh, it was in the evening papers last night. I expect the re-
porters were on Bonoff's doorstep; he was the obvious man to go
to. Fleet Street's a nest of ghouls."

"What about Assyriologists who write up their friends' obitu-
aries while they're still hale and hearty?" asked Sargent.

"*Touché*," said Considine. "Good morning, Lake," he went on,
as the pro-Provost entered the common room. "Have you seen this
effusion of Bonoff's?"

Lake took the paper and read. "It's like a crocodile going into mourning," he said.

The door opened again, to admit Gurney and Newton, followed a moment later by Gaunt. Each in turn read the obituary and the letter, and a general discussion ensued, in which the prevailing opinion seemed decidedly unfavourable to Bonoff. Sargent and Considine took an early opportunity to slip away.

"Well, Denys," the latter began, as they paced the lawn of the fellows' garden, "have you solved the mystery of the dissected alarm clock?"

"I've got an idea that may account for it," replied Sargent. "But I don't think I'll tell you what it is at present. We oughtn't really to be formulating theories till we've got some more facts to base them on; and if I put ideas into your head that may turn out to be moonshine, it may quite easily have the effect of leading you to overlook some bright inspiration of your own. Don't you agree?"

"That seems sound, up to a point," said Considine. "But on those lines, how exactly do we collaborate?"

"We collaborate in collecting the facts, and try to keep our interpretations of them out of it—help each other to keep an open mind, in a word. Now, about this alarm clock, for instance. We ought to be able to find out some more facts about that."

"What sort of facts do you mean?"

"There seem to be three obvious things it would be useful to know." Sargent ticked them off one by one on his fingers. "First, who put it there? Secondly, when? Thirdly, where exactly was it put? Fourthly, of course, why?—but that's a borderline case between fact and interpretation. If we can find the answers to the first three it'll probably answer itself."

"Number three seems an easy one, at any rate," said Considine. "Surely the clock must have been put where we found it."

"Yes, but where precisely was that?" asked Sargent. "Remember your trench No. 4, where the clock was, followed the line of the partition between the two rooms. Also it was all tangled up in the remains of the bed, and that's where the firemen were digging when they found the body. Therefore we can't be sure whether the

clock was really put under the bed, or whether it was in the sitting
room, close up against the partition, and got tangled up with the
bed during the digging."

"But the whole length of the partition was taken up by bookcases," Considine objected.

"Except about three feet in the middle," said Sargent.

"You mean where the mummy stood?"

"Exactly."

"But—but—" Considine grew suddenly excited. "Are you suggesting that the clock was inside the coffin and was used for starting the fire? That would mean that those two undergraduates who
ran off with the mummy put it there, locked poor Benchley in, and
left him to burn to death. How ghastly!"

"Now my dear Humphrey, we agreed to keep our theories to
ourselves," Sargent reminded him. "I'm not going to discuss this
one, except just to mention that you seem to have forgotten about
the key."

"Yes, that is a difficulty," said Considine thoughtfully. "Of
course they might have shoved it exactly under the door itself,
where Benchley wouldn't see it, so as to give the impression of
suicide."

"But wasn't the whole show more designed to give the impression of accident?" asked Sargent. "Anyhow, I repeat, we agreed to
suspend theories and look for facts. The next fact to tackle is when
the clock was put there."

"We haven't much to go on for that," said Considine. "The only
thing I can think of is that Bloggs didn't know of its existence, so it
couldn't have been in Benchley's rooms long. There's not much that
prying old scoundrel wouldn't have ferreted out."

"Oh, I think we can be a bit more definite than that," Sargent
suggested. "Think of the way those alarm things work. You have a
little hand like a seconds hand, and you set it to the time you want
the machine to go off. Say you set it to ten o'clock. Then it'll start
to buzz the next time ten o'clock comes round. That means you
can't set it for more than twelve hours ahead. Now the fire broke

out round about one o'clock in the morning. Doesn't it follow that, if the clock was used to start it, it must have been wound up not earlier than one o'clock the previous afternoon?"

"*If* the clock started the fire," said Considine. "It's pure theory that it had anything to do with it."

"Yes, you get me there," Sargent admitted. "Still we must allow a little theory, just enough to guide us in deciding what to inquire into. Let's put it this way: the clock can't be of any significance unless it was put there after one. If we find evidence that it was there earlier, we dismiss it from the case. Agreed?"

"Agreed."

"Very well, then. Let's try the remaining question about the clock. Who put it there? If it was planted before Wednesday afternoon the planter doesn't matter. So we need only inquire at the moment who could have put it there at one o'clock or later on Wednesday. Now who went to Benchley's rooms between one in the afternoon and one in the morning?"

"That's impossible to check," said Considine. "Anybody could go in when Benchley was out."

"I'm not sure that it's so impossible as all that," said Sargent. "He was in all the afternoon, I'm pretty sure. Didn't Miss Carrothers say at the inquest that he was going to work from lunch time till dinner?"

"Yes, I believe she did. I'd forgotten about her. She was there to lunch, so that brings her within the time limit. But I take it you don't suspect her of murder."

"We're dealing with facts, not suspicions," said Sargent reprovingly. "Let's make a note of the presence of Miss Daphne Carrothers. Now, who else went up to Benchley's rooms?"

"Let me think," said Considine. "There was Van Ditten, coming in the afternoon to try and buy the mummy, and again later for dinner. Benchley brought him into the hall, so I suppose they had a rendezvous in his rooms. Then that undergraduate, Devereux, went up to see him during the ball—at eleven o'clock, I think he said. After that, the two blighters who ran the mummy rag. And finally you and I, to see that everything was straight—as it was. That was about half-past twelve, and doesn't leave much time for a later visitor. Can you think of any others?"

"Only Bloggs," said Sargent. "He must have gone up to put out Benchley's evening clothes. Oh, and of course Monitor. I'd forgotten him. Of course, he took Benchley up to bed after they'd seen Van Ditten off."

"My dear Denys, I draw the line at hustling poor old Monitor to the gallows. It would only remind him of some endless story about how he once went gay with the public hangman of Nijni Novgorod."

"Never mind, we'll put him down for the sake of completeness," said the punctilious Sargent. "The list seems to run: Miss Carrothers, Van Ditten, Bloggs, Monitor, Devereux, two unknown undergraduates, ourselves. Those are the people we've got to find out about. But I suggest we start with the ones we know least about already."

"Those would be Devereux and Van Ditten, I suppose," said Considine. "And perhaps Daphne Carrothers."

"Yes, I think those are the three," agreed Sargent. "How shall we get at them?"

"Well, as executor of the will, I thought I ought to see Daphne at once. So I've already asked her to come to tea this afternoon. And as Devereux is mentioned in it, I can make that an excuse for seeing him, too. I'll send a note round to New College asking him to call on me. Shall we have them separately or together?"

"We ought to see Devereux alone, don't you think?" said Sargent. "He was definitely on bad terms with Benchley. If Miss Carrothers comes into it at all, which I should say was very unlikely, it could only be in connexion with him. So suppose you ask him to come about half an hour before her; then we can tackle him separately and afterwards the two of them together?"

"Right," said Considine. "I'll ask him to call at half-past three. You can be there as legal adviser to the executor—without fee, by the way. Now I must be getting along. I've got to see Benchley's bank manager. Can you be trusted to carry on with the excavations on your own account?"

"A good deal better than you can be trusted loose in a bank," retorted Sargent, and walked with him towards the porter's lodge. Seeing the porter standing at the gate, he stopped on a sudden impulse and spoke to him.

"Good morning, Collins," he said. "I'm afraid poor Dr. Benchley's death will be a blow to you. He was a good friend to you and Mrs. Collins, wasn't he?"

"He was a good friend to all the college staff, sir," replied Collins. "I've served under seven Bursars in my time, sir, and none of them did as much for the servants as Dr. Benchley did. We're all very much distressed about it, sir."

"I suppose you don't remember, do you, whether Dr. Benchley had any visitors the day he died?"

"Why, I should think so, sir. I've got a pretty good memory. Let me see now. There was that mummy was brought in by two men from a Carter-Paterson's van."

"What time would that be?"

"I should say about half-past ten, sir. Then Miss Carrothers came to lunch; she was Dr. Benchley's niece. But of course, Mr. Considine knows her. And an American gentleman came to see Dr. Benchley about three o'clock in the afternoon."

"And that was all?"

"That was all, I'm pretty certain, sir. Dr. Benchley let the American gentleman out himself by the fellows' gate about a quarter-past four, and after that he sported his oak till nearly dinner time."

"Can you remember if either Miss Carrothers or the American was carrying a parcel?"

"That's rather an odd question, sir. But I think I can answer it. Miss Carrothers was carrying about half a dozen parcels, of all shapes and sizes. Looked as if she'd been out shopping. The American gentleman had a little square case in his hand—sort of thing to carry papers about in."

"Thank you very much, Collins. I'm sorry to mystify you, but Mr. Considine and I have to clear up Dr. Benchley's personal affairs, and all this has to do with it. Well, Humphrey, I'll see you at lunch time. Don't forget that note to young Devereux."

"I haven't forgotten," said Considine. "I'll call in at New College myself on my way to the bank," and he departed in the direction of Holywell.

The manager of the New Bank, in the Broad, made no difficulty about explaining to the executor the state of Benchley's financial affairs, although, pending probate of the will, he was of course unable to make any payment to the heiress.

"I'm afraid, Mr. Considine," he said, "your unfortunate colleague's death could not possibly have come at a more disastrous time, speaking from a pecuniary standpoint. He had only within the last few days drawn a cheque that practically wiped out his entire capital."

"That would be to Professor Bonoff, of course," said Considine.

"Ah, you knew of the transaction. Then you will also be aware that the money was the purchase price of a certain mummy?"

"Yes, I knew that. I don't know exactly how much he paid."

"The cheque was for the sum of 10,000 guineas. It struck me as a most exorbitant price for a single mummy, but of course I'm not a scholar and don't know what value collectors set on these things. And Dr. Benchley assured me that he knew of a purchaser, an American I believe, who would quite certainly give him at least double the price for the mummy. And so we allowed a large overdraft on the security of certain shares we hold for Dr. Benchley. I am sorry to say that the sale of these shares will barely suffice to cover the overdraft."

"Then Miss Carrothers will get nothing?"

"Oh, it's not quite so bad as that. Dr. Benchley's life was insured for £5,000, and so far as I know there are no debts to set against that. So Miss Carrothers will be left with a small income from that source. There is also the fire insurance money."

"Won't that cover the mummy?" asked Considine.

"I'm afraid not. The policy allows for a maximum payment of £1,000—which, of course, you should be able to obtain. I strongly urged Dr. Benchley to insure the mummy for the short period it was to be in his possession, but he was most unaccountably obstinate about it. He said it was a unique object, which no insurance company could replace. A very inconclusive argument it seemed to me, where £10,000 was involved; but you know what the Professor was like when he chose to dig his heels in."

"I do indeed," said Considine. "It's a bit hard on Miss Carrothers, but it might be worse. I suppose you don't know who was to be the buyer of the mummy. I understood from poor Benchley that it was already sold."

"I'm afraid I don't," said the manager. "All that Dr. Benchley said was that it was an American millionaire collector. Certainly no money came into the account in connexion with the sale, and I fear it's hopeless to expect it now."

"Benchley didn't mention the name of one Lewstein?"

"Milton P. Lewstein of New York? No, he didn't mention him, but he's quite a likely man, especially as he happens to be in London now."

"Indeed? Perhaps I ought to get into touch with him. I suppose you don't know his address?"

"I should think that Worldograph Limited, in Wardour Street, would always find him. It's his chief film company on this side."

Considine shuddered at the barbarous hybrid. "Very well," he assented, "I'll write care of—what you said. I think that's all I need ask you for the present, Mr. Nicholson. Thank you very much for your help. Good morning."

"Good morning, Mr. Considine. Please let me know if there's anything more I can do."

Considine took his leave, and, after a short and colourless interview with Benchley's solicitors, who could tell him nothing new, paid a visit to the Crozier Hotel. Here he met with a check.

"Mr. Van Ditten, sir?" said the clerk in the reception desk. "I'm afraid Mr. Van Ditten isn't here. He left yesterday."

"Could you give me his address?"

"I understand he has gone back to San Francisco, sir. He was summoned home unexpectedly, and left in a great hurry to catch the *Berengaria* from Liverpool."

"Ah, I'm sorry to have missed him," said Considine, and walked thoughtfully home by Grammar Lane and the fellows' gate. He went straight to the Bursary, where he found Sargent supervising the last stages of the clearing of Benchley's rooms.

"Well, Denys," he said, "have you dug up any more clues?"

"Nothing of any importance," was the reply. "One more scrap of negative evidence; Benchley's key of the garden gate definitely isn't here."

But Considine thought he detected a new eagerness in his colleague's manner. "Come off it, Denys," he said; "I can see you've got something more exciting than that up your sleeve."

"If I have," said Sargent, "it's for your privy ear alone. Come over to my rooms." He led the way down into the quadrangle, and, once out of earshot of Bloggs and the boys, broached his news.

"I've got something that's going to surprise you quite a lot, Humphrey," he said. "You remember your intelligent suggestion that what we had to look for was a mummy without a coffin?"

"Yes," said Considine eagerly. "Go on. You don't mean to say you've found it?"

"No," replied Sargent. "The search for a mummy without a coffin has so far failed. What we've found is a coffin without a mummy."

6
THE WOMEN STUDENTS

"WHEN I SAY 'FOUND,'" Sargent went on, after Considine had indicated suitable astonishment at his bombshell, "I don't mean to claim personal credit for the latest addition to Egyptological knowledge. The actual discoverers were two young women."

"Do I know them?" asked Considine.

"I don't think so; they're undergraduates. They're coming to see you at two o'clock."

"Oh, Denys, what have you let me in for? You know how I hate boot-faced zeal for learning, wrapped up in a mackintosh."

"I doubt if these are likely to be of that sort," Sargent reassured him, "though I haven't seen them in the flesh. They come from that nunnery up the South Parks Road—Cherwell Edge, it's called, isn't it?—where I think they cultivate a rather frivolous attitude to the seven liberal arts. It's the place where the young sirens one meets in Monitor's rooms generally come from."

"If you haven't seen them," Considine asked, "how do you know they've found the mummy?"

"My dear Humphrey, they haven't found the mummy. That's the whole point. But they've found the coffin, and were intelligent enough to take the glad news to the Ashmolean Museum. Ashmole told them to ring up you, which they did, and as you were out I told them to call at two o'clock."

"Where did they find the mummy?" asked Considine.

"I don't know," Sargent replied. "They wouldn't say. They're going to take you to it. It's my opinion they don't want to miss the chance of vamping you, my lad."

"Well, you'll have to go instead," Considine grumbled. "Strange women terrify me. You're the expert on the breed; the college gates are simply blocked with female bicycles when you're lecturing."

"That's only because I once exercised my legal right to confine my audience to men. Actually it was because I couldn't get the big lecture room, but they all thought it was because I wanted to tell a risqué story, and they've flocked to my feet ever since in the hope of hearing another one. Such is the path to academic fame. However, I'll come and hold your hand this afternoon if you like."

"I suppose that'll have to do," Considine grumbled. "But you'll have to do all the talking."

"If they're the kind I expect," said Sargent, "we'll be lucky to get a word in edgeways between us. Tell me how you got on this morning."

Considine gave him a short summary of the results of his interviews with the banker and the solicitor, ending with his visit to the Crozier and the discovery of Van Ditten's sudden departure. "Don't you think we ought to report that to the police?" he concluded.

"Good heavens, no," exclaimed Sargent. "What on earth for?"

"Well, he was on our list of suspects, and this hurried flight surely makes him twice as suspicious."

"But my dear Humphrey," Sargent protested, "as far as the police are concerned there's been no crime to suspect him of."

"What about the theft of the mummy?"

"We don't know that the mummy was stolen, and if it was there's not a scrap of evidence against Van Ditten."

"Still, telling the police doesn't necessarily mean laying a charge; and if we don't tell them it seems to me that anybody we do suspect can always get away. We haven't the resources to track them down."

"Now look here, Humphrey; once and for all, let's make up our minds that we don't want any heavy-footed copper charging about among our clues. The university is a privileged corporation, with its own criminal jurisdiction and its own machinery for the maintenance of law and order. I want to show that we're quite equal to the task of dealing with our own crimes and criminals; and this is a golden opportunity, because the civil power doesn't know that any crime's been committed."

"Still, it's a pity to risk letting a murderer escape on a point of academic punctilio."

"Ah, then you admit that it was murder." Sargent was on him like a knife.

"No, of course I don't. I—er—oh, well, I suppose you must have it your own way. You shall keep your amateur status. Let's go and get some lunch."

Two o'clock found them back in Considine's rooms, awaiting their visitors, who arrived with unexpected punctuality, dispensing with the usual escort of the porter. Miss Patricia Foley and Miss Aileen O'Connor bore no resemblance to Considine's grim description of the female undergraduate he so much dreaded. Both were excellent examples of that modern type of female beauty which has so diplomatically reconciled the conflict of art and nature; and they were arrayed, not in mackintoshes, but in flimsy and frivolous garments of the kind dear to the artists who design the covers of summer numbers. Their manner showed that easy and confident self-possession which, contrary to the general belief, is the special product of a convent training.

"Good afternoon, Mr. Considine," said the taller of the two, "you asked us to come and tell you about the mummy, I think. I'm Miss Foley, who spoke to a friend of yours on the telephone, and this is Miss O'Connor."

"Let me introduce Mr. Sargent," mumbled Considine unhappily.

"How do you do?" said Miss Foley. "I don't know if we ought to have come in gowns. We searched the statutes, but we couldn't find what was the correct costume for taking unknown dons on the river."

"We could only find a Latin regulation, apparently meaning that a commoner's gown must reach to the heels," said Miss O'Connor, "which seemed out of touch with modern fashion, and unjust to Miss Foley's new stockings."

"Did I understand you to say you proposed to take us on the river?" asked Sargent.

"Oh yes, that's where the mummy is, you know," replied Miss
Foley. "We've brought a canoe; Miss O'Connor's going to punt it,
so you'd better bring umbrellas."

"We seem to have our movements very effectively planned out
for us without regard to our grey hairs," said Sargent, smiling. "You
didn't, I suppose, look up the statute '*de reverentia juniorum erga
seniores*'?"

"Sorry," answered Miss O'Connor cheerfully, "I'm afraid we're
both illiterate. But you'll get your own back next month, Mr.
Sargent. I'm up for *viva* before you in the Law School."

"And that's the only security for your life," added Miss Foley.
"She simply daren't spill you into the river with the whole of her
young career hanging on whether she can scrape a fourth."

"That's all very well for Sargent," said Considine, as they meekly
accompanied their effervescent captors out into the quad; "but it
seems a bleak prospect for me. I suppose neither of you is reading
the school of Oriental Languages and Literature?"

"That's an idea, Aileen," said Miss Foley. "I should think we
might be rather well qualified by our discovery. Why shouldn't you
write a D. Phil. thesis on 'Evidences of Egyptian Colonization on
the Upper Cherwell'?"

With similar interchange of irreverent badinage the two undergraduates led Sargent and Considine across the college to the landing stage, where a Canadian canoe of ominous instability was
moored. Sargent cast an ironical glance at the large notice-board
facing the water—"Private landing stage for members of Beaufort
College only"—then submissively inserted himself into the narrow
space in the bows indicated by Miss Foley. She herself took a position in the middle, squeezed into intimate proximity with the still
bashful Considine, while Miss O'Connor, springing lightly into the
stern, seized a punt-pole and pushed off.

There are few forms of conveyance that seem to the inexperi-
enced passenger more precarious than a Canadian canoe when
it is punted instead of paddled, and Sargent and Considine made
the first stage of the journey in a silence of acute apprehension.
Miss O'Connor, however, proved an accomplished mistress of her

graceful art, and the overladen craft made smooth and swift progress upstream. As the Cherwell slid, faintly musical, past the bows, all three passengers gradually surrendered to the drowsy charm of the summer afternoon. The river was almost deserted, for the mass of the undergraduate population had already gone down, and the time had not yet come for the invasion of its silences by the townspeople or the uncouth hordes that descend upon Oxford annually for the summer schools. Even the honeymoons of the clergy, which are generally so conspicuous here in the summer time, contributed nothing to the river scene this afternoon. Only here and there a punt moored beneath a willow, with a pair of white flannel-clad legs at full length upon the cushions, while their owner's face was concealed by a large book slipping sideways from an unconscious hand, told of the imminence of *viva voce* examinations, and suggested the happy compromise between the two rival theories of preparation—last-minute cramming and complete rest before ordeal.

The canoe had passed along the shore of the Parks and come to the great bend where the river broadens out between the open meadows in front of Lady Margaret Hall, before the irrepressible Miss Foley once more took up her ingenuous prattle.

"It's not very far from here," she said, "that we found it."

"Found what?" asked Considine absentmindedly. He had been watching the flight of a kingfisher ahead, and was in a world far remote from their curious quest.

"I believe you've been asleep, Mr. Considine," his companion reproved him. "You've forgotten all about the mummy in the bulrushes; and here am I, full of the pride of Pharaoh's daughter, and I don't get any appreciation at all."

"Wasn't it a baby she found?" murmured Sargent in sleepy correction.

"Well, yes, I believe it was," Miss Foley admitted. "But a mummy's so much less compromising, don't you think, at any rate to a young maiden *in statu pupillari?* Princesses can get away with these things, where the poor downtrodden undergraduate would be gated for life. Wasn't it somewhere about here, Aileen?"

"It's just five yards past that sunken stump," was the reply, and a moment later, with a graceful thrust of her pole, Miss O'Connor had swung the canoe lightly round and was heading it apparently for the right-hand bank. "Heads," she cried, as they glided under an overhanging bush, and then they were crunching through the undergrowth into what proved to be a tiny concealed backwater, not more than four feet wide, but long enough to allow them to push their way through the reeds to a distance of some thirty yards from the main stream. "This is our private backwater," she explained, as an overhanging bough swept Miss Foley sideways into the arms of Considine, "and you're both sworn to secrecy. All change here!"

Considine, restoring Miss Foley to an upright position with a shy haste that concealed an unexpected pleasure in the sudden contact, felt a bump as the canoe slid alongside a stationary punt and came to a standstill. Simultaneous excitement seized all four passengers, who rose as one man and one woman and scrambled into the punt. Sargent missed his footing and plunged ankle-deep in Cherwell mud, while Considine went sprawling into the bottom of the derelict vessel; Miss O'Connor and Miss Foley, with superior agility and better watermanship, transferred themselves without mishap.

The punt had been roughly covered over with light boughs broken from the willows and hawthorns that overhung the backwater, with sufficient effect to hide it from the casual glance of any person walking through the riverside meadows and not actually looking for it. At the stern end however (or the bow to a Cambridge man, for in no matter of scholarship does the gulf between the two seats of learning yawn so wide as in the question of the proper position of the navigator of a punt), the branches had been cleared away, and disclosed the foot of an unmistakable mummy coffin. Without a word, moved by a unanimous impulse, four pairs of hands set to work to push the remaining greenstuff overboard and in a very few minutes the coffin lay uncovered from end to end. It was open and empty, while beside it the lid, painted with the effigy of the dead Pharaoh, gazed up to the green canopy above with that air of bland and solemn mystery that seems to preserve all the secrets of old Egypt from the thieves, the scholars, or the idly inquisitive who in fifty generations have come to violate her tombs.

For a moment the four young representatives of the twentieth century looked down in silence, held by the austere dignity of this sombre relic of old mortality lying in the lap of green and sunny England. A stately cadence of Sir Thomas Browne drifted across Considine's memory, and he murmured beneath his breath: "Man is a noble animal, splendid in ashes and pompous in the grave, solemnizing nativities and deaths with equal lustre, nor omitting ceremonies of bravery in the infamy of his nature." Then the fresh and prattling voice of Miss Foley dispelled the romantic illusion.

"Well, Mr. Sargent," she asked, "is the dear departed a Beaufort man?"

"Considine's the expert on mummies," replied Sargent. "What do you make of it, Humphrey?"

"I can't make head or tail of it," said Considine, who had gone down on his hands and knees in the bottom of the punt and was closely examining the coffin and lid. "For the umpteenth time, I'm not an expert on mummies; but you and I looked at Benchley's mummy together on Wednesday night, and I could swear this was the same case. But Benchley's rooms were burnt only about an hour after we saw the mummy there; and I don't see how it could possibly have been taken out in that time. The quads were crawling with people sitting out from the ball, not to mention that it would have been quite impossible to get it past Collins at the porter's lodge. No, it certainly couldn't have been got out of college that night."

"In fact, we can prove that it must still be there, burnt to ashes?" said Sargent with a sardonic smile. "Meanwhile, here it is. What are we going to do about it?"

"I suppose I ought to take possession as an executor," replied Considine doubtfully. "And we certainly ought to have a look round for the mummy itself."

"Still harping on that," said Sargent. "I don't think there's any chance of finding the mummy round here. If it was ever in the coffin, the thieves would hardly have taken the trouble to hide the two in different parts of the same field. Besides, why steal the thing at all if they're going to leave both behind? No, I think we can take it for granted that the mummy's well away by now. Always supposing there ever was a mummy, of course."

"Then we'd better take the punt and the coffin back to college," said Considine. "Remember we've got this undergraduate coming at half-past three."

"Yes, we shall have to get back," Sargent agreed. "But I don't like the idea of parading this mummy case publicly through the college. I can't see what it means yet, but it's obviously an important clue, and if we give away that we've got it we may be putting someone on his guard."

The two girls had been listening in some bewilderment to this conversation, but Aileen O'Connor seized eagerly on the promising word "clue." "We seem to have got in with a pack of sleuths, Patricia," she exclaimed. "Isn't there a part for two modest young Watsons, Mr. Sargent? We know the methods."

"I don't think there's anything—" Sargent was beginning, but Considine interrupted him. "I think it's very kind of Miss O'Connor to suggest helping us, Denys," he said firmly. "As Benchley's executor I can't leave the coffin out here in the open. Yesterday's rain hasn't improved it as it is, and besides, the thieves might come back. On the other hand, we haven't time to deal with it now. Do you think you could help us to get it under cover, Miss O'Connor— somewhere where we could arrange to come and fetch it after dark and get it into college without being seen?"

"How about it, Patricia?" said Aileen. "We could hide the mummy in our boathouse, couldn't we? We're the only two still up, so nobody would be likely to go there before tonight."

"It all sounds very nefarious to me," Patricia replied. "I think if we come in you ought to tell us all about the ghastly crime, Mr. Considine. Otherwise, how are we to know whether you're Sherlock or Moriarty?"

"I'm sorry." Sargent spoke hastily, for he detected signs that Considine was about to become communicative. "I'm afraid we've

got to be rather mysterious for the present. That, as you will remember, my dear Watson, is the authentic sign of the master. But,
as Considine says, we should be very grateful for your help, and
perhaps we'll tell you what we can when we can."

"I suppose that'll have to do," Patricia grumbled. "But you'll
have to let us join in the hunt afterwards. Otherwise we shall blackmail you. Now I suggest that Aileen and I drop you at Beaufort and
then go back to Cherwell Edge and pick up a supply of rugs and
things. Then we'll come up here again, cover up the mummy and
punt it down to our own boathouse. It'll look odd, of course, but
there aren't many people about to-day, and if anyone does notice
a bulky object covered with rugs in a punt, I doubt if his first
thought would be to cry out, 'there goes Pharaoh!'"

"That sounds quite simple and straightforward," said Considine. "It's very good of you to undertake it. Where is your boathouse, by the way?"

"It's that little green erection by the entrance to New College
backwater. I'll bring you the key after we've put the mummy to
bed. We're both coming in to Beaufort this afternoon, to tea with
Dr. Monitor."

"Right," said Sargent. "Thank you very much. Then that's all
there is to arrange, isn't it?"

"We've still got to arrange what reward we get for our services,"
said Patricia firmly. "We won't ask to be let into the grisly secret
at once, but you simply must let us do some of the sleuthing. For
instance, couldn't we shadow the Vice-Chancellor, disguised as the
Bedell of Arts?"

"I'd much rather shadow the Bedell of Arts, disguised as the Vice-
Chancellor," Aileen amended. "I'm sure bedells lead secret lives. But,
seriously, Mr. Sargent, you will let us go on helping, won't you?"

"I promise that if anything turns up that you could help with
I'll ask you," said Sargent. "Meanwhile, please go on keeping the
mummy dark. By the way, have you told anybody else about it?"

"No," said Patricia. "Luckily there was nobody to tell, because
everybody else at Cherwell Edge has gone down. We told the man
at the Ashmolean, of course—Baker, I think his name was."

"Baxter, do you mean?" asked Considine. "A little man with a glass eye? I can square him."

"Then that's all right," said Sargent. "Now before we go, hadn't we better try and identify the punt? They have some sort of registration mark put on by the Thames Conservancy, don't they?"

He knelt down in the punt and ran his eye rapidly along the side, looking for the little enamelled tablet bearing the registration number. The others followed his example. Suddenly Considine sprang up with a cry of surprise, holding up a shining brass object in his hand. "Look at this, Denys," he exclaimed excitedly.

"Good heavens," cried Sargent with no less excitement, "it's the key of the fellows' gate. What's the number of it?"

Considine examined the haft of the key. "Thirty-seven," he read out.

"That was Benchley's own number," said Sargent with a puzzled frown. "I looked it up in the Bursary books this morning. This is the last place I expected to find it."

The two girls were also on their feet again. "Your red herring seems more exciting than the original fox," said Aileen O'Connor. "But I've identified the punt, if it's still of any interest to you. It's one I've been out in dozens of times. I don't know anything about Thames Conservancy marks, but I couldn't mistake this little Chinese image stuck in the bows."

"Well, whose punt is it?" asked Sargent and Considine together.

"It's Dr. Monitor's," she replied.

7
THE CHANCELLOR

IT WAS TEN MINUTES after the half-hour before Sargent and Considine were back in college, and they found Mark Devereux already waiting for them. Considine, with his eye on the clock, plunged straight into business.

"Good afternoon, Mr. Devereux," he began. "We have met, I think, in Dr. Monitor's rooms, but I don't think you know my colleague Mr. Sargent. I have asked you to call in connexion with Dr. Benchley's will, of which I am executor. Mr. Sargent is looking after the legal side of the matter."

"How do I come in, sir?" asked Mark. "I, surely, can't be mentioned in Dr. Benchley's will. I only met him twice, and I'm afraid he didn't approve of me."

"You are mentioned, Mr. Devereux," Considine replied, "though not, I am afraid, in a very complimentary way. I believe there was some question of a possible engagement between you and Dr. Benchley's niece, Miss Carrothers."

"We *are* engaged," said Mark with vigorous decision. "We're going to be married in the autumn"

"That, I am afraid," said Considine uncomfortably, "is the point at which the will affects you. I asked you to come here because I thought I ought to tell you at once that Dr. Benchley constituted Miss Carrothers a ward in Chancery."

"What exactly does that mean?" asked Mark.

"It means," said Sargent, "that among other things the ward, while under age, cannot marry without the consent of the court."

79

"Oh, if that's all," said Mark with relief, "there can't be much to worry about. The court of Chancery can't have anything against me. It isn't as if it were the progs."

"I'm afraid that isn't all," said Considine. "Benchley left an express request in his will that the court should not consent to the marriage of Miss Carrothers with Mr. Mark Devereux of Bembridge."

"The dirty dog!" Mark broke out vehemently, and then quickly recollected himself. "I'm sorry, Mr. Considine," he went on. "I didn't mean to speak like that of a dead man. But it does seem unfair, doesn't it? After all, I can offer Daphne a good home, and I think I can claim a sound enough reputation. Is it legal to try and stop her marrying me like that?"

"He couldn't lawfully prevent your marriage," Sargent explained. "That is left in the absolute discretion of the court, which acts on certain well-defined principles; I could give you an account of them sometime, if you liked. But the point you're up against is that the court will certainly attach very great weight to the known wishes of the testator from whom it derives its guardianship."

"Even if those wishes are obviously unreasonable?" asked Mark indignantly.

"I think they will assume he had reasonable grounds for his objection," said Sargent, "in default of clear evidence to the contrary. I thought you might perhaps be able to think of some such evidence. Suppose you tell us what had passed between you and Dr. Benchley, and then we might consider whether there is anything we can put before the court to induce them to depart from the codicil. For instance, if we could prove what were the grounds of the objection, it might be possible to remove them."

"But that's the whole trouble," Mark exploded. "He simply hadn't any grounds at all; he knew nothing about me."

"Well," said Sargent patiently, "let's take it in order. How long have you known Miss Carrothers?"

"Let me see," said Mark reflectively. "It was just after Eights Week; I think it'll be a month to-morrow. I met her at a Monitor mix-up. You know Dr. Monitor's evening parties for undergraduates, sir? Rather cherry shows, though sometimes rowdy."

"In my official capacity as Dean I have sometimes become aware of them," said Sargent with a sardonic smile. "But Miss Carrothers isn't an undergraduate, surely?"

"No," said Considine, "she lives with an ancient female cousin in north Oxford, and used to spend most of her time looking after her uncle. But she goes about a good deal with friends in the women's colleges."

"I see," said Sargent. "And when did you become engaged, Mr. Devereux?"

"Oh, the same night," Mark replied. "I drove Daphne home from the party—by rather a circuitous route, I'm afraid. I didn't get back to my digs till three in the morning, and I had hard words with the Warden next day—gated for the rest of the term and so on. However, it was in a good cause."

"And did you ask Dr. Benchley's consent to the engagement?"

"Rather. I did the thing in the best mid-Victorian style. Went straight to him, with my ears still burning with the Warden's rude language."

"And what did Dr. Benchley say? I suppose he took exception to the shortness of your acquaintance with Miss Carrothers?"

"Curiously enough, he didn't. I was naturally a bit shy about that, but he took it like a bird. Said he liked young men to be impulsive, and if he'd followed his own impulses more lightheartedly fifty years ago he'd probably have led a happier life. In fact, at the beginning of our interview he was simply all over me with effusiveness. It almost seemed as if he was delighted to get rid of the responsibility for Daphne. And then he suddenly dried right up, and said that on second thoughts he must take time to consider the matter. And next day he wrote me a very chilly letter to say there was nothing doing. Daphne was too young, he said."

"Do you think it was anything you said that made his manner change?"

"That's what I've been puzzling over. I simply couldn't imagine what caused it at the time, but something Daphne said at the ball on Wednesday night gave me an idea. Only it seems to be so silly as not to be worth mentioning."

"Never mind; let's hear it."

"Well, according to Daphne, her uncle seemed to be developing a monomania against people who lived in the Isle of Wight. I have a little place near Bembridge, you know. And, thinking back to my talk with Dr. Benchley, it does seem to be true that he started to freeze up just about the point when I told him where I lived."

"That's odd, certainly," said Sargent. "Did he say anything against the place then?"

"No, nothing that I can remember. What is there to say, after all? He'd never even been there, I remember he told me."

"Yes, that's so," put in Considine. "When he went to see Bonoff there last week, I remember his mentioning to me that it would be the first time he had set foot in the Isle of Wight."

"That's another point I'd thought of," said Mark. "In fact, I put it to Daphne myself. I believe Dr. Benchley had some sort of feud with Professor Bonoff, who lives not far from me in the island. Do you think it's possible his obsession against the place could have anything to do with the fact that Bonoff lived there? It seems far fetched, but really it seems impossible to think of a more sensible reason."

"I should think it's just conceivable," replied Sargent. "Benchley had some rather eccentric ideas. But if that was the case, I fear it won't altogether account for his objection to you as a husband for Miss Carrothers. You see, when he visited Bonoff last week, they had a complete reconciliation, and presumably his dislike of islanders, if it was based on Bonoff, then came to an end. But the codicil making Miss Carrothers a ward of court, and containing the request that she shall not be allowed to marry you, is dated the day *after* his return."

"Yes, that seems to demolish the Bonoff excuse," Mark admitted with a wry grin. "I suppose I must blame my criminal cast of countenance after all."

"It does seem as if the explanation breaks down," said Considine. "But till we can see an alternative, ought we not to keep it in sight? Did Dr. Benchley mention Bonoff to you, Mr. Devereux?"

"Oh, he just asked if I knew him. That's when I told him I lived at Bembridge, of course."

"And do you know Bonoff?"

"I know him by sight, as I told Dr. Benchley. I doubt if anybody knows him any better. He's the mystery man of the village. Lives all by himself in a house alleged to be full of mummies, and only emerges into the daylight about once a week. I don't think I've seen him more than half a dozen times in the last three vacations, since he came to live in the island. But since then—"

He was interrupted by a tap on the door and the entry of Considine's scout with the announcement: "Miss Carrothers."

Daphne, dressed in black and now much more subdued in manner than when she had stood up in the publicity of the coroner's inquest, greeted Sargent demurely on introduction, kissed her hand to Mark, and subsided on the sofa beside Considine.

"Well, Humphrey," she said. "All this looks very grim. Is it a meeting to determine my future? I gather you are now my revered and terrifying guardian."

"I wish I were, Daphne," said Considine, "much as I should shrink from the responsibility. No, your guardian is the Lord High Chancellor of England."

"Oh, but how nice," exclaimed Daphne. "That's the old gentleman who got an honorary degree at the Encaenia on Wednesday, isn't it? He looked charming. Where do I go? Do I live with him in the House of Lords? That will be fun."

"The guardianship, I fear, is not quite so intimate as that," said Sargent, "though I am sure no one will be more disappointed than the Lord Chancellor. The actual custody of your person is committed to a lesser watch-dog."

"Ah well," said Daphne resignedly, "I suppose to keep me and the King's conscience in one establishment might be a bit of a handful. Tell me the worst. Is it Humphrey?"

"Alas, no," said Considine. "The honour goes to a certain Mrs. Antony Shelmerdine, whom I don't think I've had the pleasure of meeting."

"Not Aunt Matilda," cried Daphne in unfeigned dismay. "She's a hundred and twenty, lives in Wigan and dribbles. Swathed from head to foot in bombazine and thinks the female ankle obscene. Mark dear, we shall have to get married at once."

"I only wish we could," said Mark gloomily. "But the wretched old man's forbidden it till you're twenty-one."

"Who's a wretched old man?" Daphne, however restive under the control of her uncle when alive, was quick to resent disrespect to him now he was dead.

"In effect it's the Lord Chancellor," said Sargent hastily. "There's a direction in the will, which we think the court will act on, that no consent shall be given to your marriage with Mr. Devereux. Considine has explained the position to him, and he'll tell you all about it. I don't suppose you want to go into it again now."

"But I don't understand," Daphne complained. "What court are you talking about?"

"The court of Chancery," said Sargent. "You're what is known as a ward of court."

"Oh, Iolanthe stuff," said Daphne. "Yes, I think I get the position now. But what happens if we just get married without bothering the Lord Chancellor?"

"Then Devereux goes to prison for contempt of court," Sargent pointed out.

"I call it putting a premium on immorality," said Daphne indignantly. "I shall simply have to come and live with you unmarried, Marcus."

"My dear Daphne!" exclaimed Mark in horror, the inbred conventionalism of the landed proprietor quickly submerging the undergraduate's superficial scorn of the traditional moralities.

"No, I mean it, Mark," said Daphne. "Quite seriously. I know you're an atheist, and so's Humphrey. I expect Mr. Sargent's one, too. Why should anyone be shocked if we act on our convictions? Don't be a hypocrite."

"You won't shock me, Miss Carrothers," said Sargent, looking very shocked indeed. "But I'm afraid you might shock the Lord Chancellor, who's paid to take a conventional view of his wards' behaviour. And the penalties for taking a ward out of the custody of the person appointed by the court are apt to be even more severe than those for marrying her without the court's consent."

Daphne looked dashed. "The brutes," she said. "They seem to think of everything. If they were nice-minded men, such a thing as a ward of chancery living in sin would never have occurred to them. Can't we get round it anyhow?"

"That's what we were discussing when you came in," said Considine. "Sargent thinks if we could get at the reason for your uncle's objection to Devereux, and then either remove it or prove it unreasonable to the satisfaction of the court, we might get the ban lifted."

"So we were asking Devereux to tell us all he remembers of his dealings with your uncle," Sargent added. "He'd just given an account of the interview when he went to ask for Benchley's consent to your engagement."

"Well, you'd better go on, Mark," said Daphne. "Or perhaps I had. You see, Mr. Sargent, Mark didn't see Uncle Peter again till Wednesday night, just before the fire. For the last month all the negotiations have been done through me." And she proceeded to describe her various rebuffs when attempting to conciliate Peter Benchley's hostility to her lover, repeating the substance of what she had told Mark himself in the cloisters of Beaufort during the Commemoration ball.

"H'm," said Sargent, when she had finished. "I'm afraid it doesn't get us much forrader. He seems just to have trumped up one makeshift excuse after another, and to have kept his real objection hidden all the time."

"But isn't that just what you want," protested Daphne, "when you're trying to prove that his objection was unreasonable?"

"Er—yes," said Sargent, rather disconcerted, for in his anxiety to discover something bearing on Benchley's death, he had quite forgotten the ostensible purpose of his enquiries. "Yes. That would be all very well, if we could prove it by his public actions, or by the testimony of some independent witnesses. You see, you're so obviously an interested party that I don't think your evidence would count for very much. But what happened that last night, Devereux? I rather got the impression you could have said more than you told the coroner."

"Yes, I could," said Mark. "He was so damned rude to Daphne that I made up my mind I wouldn't tell him a thing more than he chose to force out of me. But I wasn't trying to defeat the ends of justice. Nothing happened that could possibly have any connexion with Dr. Benchley's death."

"But what did happen?" asked Considine, handing round the tea that had been silently produced by the scout.

"Well," said Mark, "I went up about eleven o'clock, as I said at the inquest. I knocked at Dr. Benchley's door, but I got no answer, so I walked in to see if he was out. But he was in the sitting room all right; only he seemed terribly embarrassed to see me. He'd got his mummy case open on the floor, and was kneeling down beside it, doing something or other to the mummy inside. Directly he saw me he shoved the cover on in a great hurry."

"Did you see the mummy?" exclaimed Considine with irrepressible excitement.

"Of course I saw the mummy. You can't hide a great thing like that. It was as close to me as you are now."

"Yes, yes," said Sargent impatiently. "But Mr. Considine means the mummy itself, not the coffin. Did you actually see the body inside?"

"Yes, I saw that too," said Mark stolidly. "I don't mean I saw the creature's face. It was all wrapped up in tight brown bandages—looked like very mouldy canvas. It was the mummy all right—I've seen them in the British Museum. Is that very important? It looked like the usual kind of thing to me."

The two dons exchanged significant glances, and it was Sargent who replied guardedly. "Mr. Considine's an orientalist himself," he said, "and he's got a theory of his own about that mummy. It doesn't affect your concerns and your fiancée's. Let's hear the rest of your story."

"There really isn't much to tell," said Mark. "We had a pretty stormy interview, I'm afraid. I was a bit worked up, because of what Daphne had told me of her uncle's goings-on against islanders, and I put it to him hot and strong. It was bad tactics of course, for it only got his back up. He gave me all the old arguments that Daphne's told you about, and in the end he more or less chucked me out. But I got a very odd impression all the time I was there that he was in a desperate hurry to get rid of me—as if he couldn't concentrate his attention on me at all. He seemed to be expecting something to happen, and to be fearfully worried lest I should be still there when it did."

Sargent and Considine could no longer conceal that their interest in the story was more direct than the mere question of the will could cause. "Have you any idea what he could have been expecting?" asked Sargent.

"I had no idea then," Mark answered, "and of course I didn't think much about it at the time, beyond feeling that his distraction wasn't very polite to me. After all, you do expect a man's whole attention when he's kicking you downstairs. But naturally I've thought quite a lot about it since."

"And what was the result?"

"Well, if I was a superstitious sort of bloke, I'd have said he had a presentiment that he was going to be dead in a couple of hours. His manner really was uncanny. In fact, that's what I should probably have thought as it was, if it hadn't been for another curious thing I saw the same night."

"What was that?" asked both dons together.

"There may be a simpler explanation, but it struck me as very queer, and I should have told the coroner about it if he hadn't got my goat as he did. I didn't have a partner for the last dance before supper, the one beginning at twenty to twelve, so I just wandered round the college by myself, thinking over what the old man had said to me, and wondering what chance there was of bringing him to reason about me and Daphne. There was absolutely nobody about, except a few couples sitting out in the cloisters; everybody else seemed to be dancing. But just as the bugle went for supper I was passing under the arch leading from the second quad to the big one, and I saw a man slink out of the staircase at that corner and slip away in a tearing hurry towards the other side of the quad."

"Do you mean towards the fellows' garden?" asked Sargent.

"I'm afraid I don't know this college very well," said Mark apologetically. He rose, walked to the window and pointed. "That's the way he went," he said.

Sargent nodded. "Yes," he said, "that's the garden. Go on. Why do you think this man had anything to do with Dr. Benchley? That isn't the way to the Bursary."

"I know it isn't. What surprised me was who the man was. It was pretty dark, of course, and he kept his hat low, but he passed under a lamp, and I feel absolutely sure I recognized him."

"And who was it?" The question came like the crack of a gun.

"It was the most unlikely man to see at an Oxford commem ball that you could possibly have imagined," said Mark with quiet emphasis. "It was my mysterious neighbour, Professor Bonoff."

"Well, I'm damned!" exclaimed Sargent. "Sorry, Miss Carrothers, but this is a bit of a shock. Where did you say he came out of, Devereux?"

"That's another surprise," said Mark. "I saw him shut the door at the foot of the stairs, and it happened to be that of the only set of rooms in Beaufort that I'm at all familiar with. They were Dr. Monitor's."

8
THE SENIOR FELLOW

"MY DEAR DENYS," SAID CONSIDINE, "this is what comes of amateur dabbling in detective work. It's all very well to go trailing after an imaginary murderer. But when your clues start leading you to Monitor, of all impossible people in the world, I give up. Give me a nice, fat, heavy-footed, unimaginative copper."

The two were waiting in the common room for the arrival of Monitor, the only other fellow who had put his name down for dinner on Friday evening. The new discoveries of the afternoon, connecting their colleague's name first with the empty mummy case and then with the mysterious visit of Professor Bonoff, had left them in a fog of bewilderment, and they had been engaged in a futile argument over these disconcerting facts ever since Mark Devereux and Daphne Carrothers had taken their departure. A flying visit from Patricia Foley, who had slipped in, on her way to Monitor's rooms, to report the safe transport of the coffin to the boathouse and to deliver the key, had not interrupted the discussion for more than a few moments.

Sargent's mood was subdued and even depressed. He was very conscious of the check, and showed no pugnacity when his friend took him to task. "I know, Humphrey," he said. "It does look as if I'm making an ass of myself. I can't really imagine Monitor coming any nearer to a murder than the man in the moon. But it's the routine thing to do to suspect everyone, however unlikely, and I'm going through the form of it, just the same. Put it down to my damned obstinacy if you like."

89

"But when you come up against an impossibility," Considine objected, "isn't it a waste of time to go on? Oughtn't we to give up that line and try a quite different one?"

"Yes," Sargent agreed, "if there is a different line. In this case there isn't."

"There's the very simple line of turning the whole thing over to the professionals," Considine pointed out.

"Simple, yes, but surely quite ineffective. How should we ever convince the police there's been a murder at all? Collins is an ex-sergeant of police, and I should think an exceptionally intelligent specimen of the breed. Suppose you go and try and persuade him that Benchley was murdered?"

"We needn't say anything about murder. We could just put them on to the stolen mummy, and that might lead them to the solution of the murder, if there was one."

"The stolen mummy's coffin was found in Monitor's punt. The police always follow the obvious clue first, and they'd simply make the poor old man's life a burden to him for nothing. We can follow that line just as well ourselves, and do it a bit more tactfully."

"Yes, but what's the good of doing it? We know it's a dead end."

"Oh, I'm not disputing that," said Sargent. "But it's surprising what a lot you can find by exploring blind alleys. You ought to try chess problems, Humphrey. But then, of course, you play chess for the county, and I know that the highbrow player would rather die in a ditch than be caught solving a problem. But you probably know enough about them to understand what I mean. If you see a clumsy move like a check or a capture that looks like leading to mate, you know quite well it can't be the real key. But you look into it all the same, because in finding why it won't work you're quite likely to hit on the move that will. That's the sort of idea I've got about these Monitor clues. There must be a flaw in them somewhere, quite apart from 'evidence of character.' Let's act as if we suspect him until the flaw comes out, and we may stumble on the proper solution. Of course you can drop out if you like, but I'm going on."

"Oh, I shan't desert you," said Considine. "I'm getting quite an enthusiasm for wild geese myself. Now here comes Monitor. I'm going to let you do your own cross-examining."

"Am I late?" asked the old doctor as he entered the common room. "I'm so sorry. Yes, Richard [to the common room butler], we'll have the soup in at once, please. I've had a lot of young people in my rooms, and they never go, you know, they never go. Not unless you turn them out, and I hate doing that. So charming of them to come at all, isn't it, to see an ancient relic like me? But you two boys are young yourselves, you wouldn't appreciate it as I do. Ah, here's dinner. *Munda, quaesumus, Domine, has creaturas tuas in sustinentiam servorum tuorum, per Jesum Christum Dominum nostrum.* Let's have a look at the menu. Canard Rôti sounds encouraging, don't you think? What a mercy that letter was delivered on Good Friday!"

"What letter was that, Monitor?" asked Considine, obviously mystified.

"You children don't study the college archives as you should," answered the senior fellow. "But then, of course, you're all heathens nowadays, so our most priceless privileges mean nothing to you. Shall we drink wine together?" They filled their glasses, bowed to one another in silence, and drank according to the simple old ritual. "Let me see, I was talking about Pope Clement, wasn't I?"

"No, wasn't it about a letter that was delivered on Good Friday?" said Sargent.

"Yes, yes, of course," replied Monitor, "but then you see it was to Pope Clement the letter was sent. Pope Clement VII. And he got it on Good Friday. And that's why we got the bull."

"Sorry, Monitor," said Sargent, "I'm out of my depth. What letter? What bull? I'm not well up in cattle breeding."

"Dear me, dear me. How I do tell stories backwards. You ought to stop me. But then, you see, I've known the bull by heart for fifty years, and I always seem to take it for granted the junior fellows know it too. I've never seen the letter—I believe it was burnt in the sack of Rome. No, that won't do—that was in 1527, four years before it was written. Anyhow, I'm sure it was destroyed sometime. It was written by all the fellows of Beaufort jointly to prove that Henry VIII was lawfully married to Katharine of Aragon and so couldn't divorce her. It reached the Pope on Good Friday, and he was so delighted with its theological learning that he dispensed the fellows of Beaufort from the observance of Friday abstinence for ever after. They all turned Protestant directly Henry VIII died, but we've still got the bull in the muniment tower, and that's why I can eat roast duck with you to-night. Dear Pope Clement. I'm sure he'd be glad to know what a lot of pleasure he's given a rather greedy old leech."

"But does the dispensation hold good even when the college has become Protestant?" asked Considine.

"Well, you know, that's rather a nice point. I've often wondered about it. I've asked several of the pundits. Father Gregory Dunstable, of the Dominicans here, says the college has ceased to exist in canon law, and so all its privileges have lapsed. There's a horrid cold-bloodedness about the legal mind—you'll have to guard against it, Sargent—it gets even the clergy. Anyhow, no decent Beaufort man could take a view like that, could he? I must ask Father Gregory to dinner sometime on a Friday when there's duck on the menu, and perhaps he'll see the question's more subtle than he thought. Anyhow, I put the same point to a most delightful Uniat monk in Cettinje, and he quite saw the other side. And I act on his opinion, because not to do so savours of disrespect to the memory of Pope Clement, don't you think?"

"A most cogent piece of legal argument," said Sargent with a smile. "You ought to have been called to the bar, Monitor."

"I did think of it, once upon a time," said the old man. "But I chose medicine because it gives more scope for bluff. Your clients are always liable to find you out, but my patients only discover my mistakes when they're safely dead and buried. And now, of course, I don't need any legal knowledge any more. When I'm run in for murder I shall brief you, my dear Sargent, and be sure of getting off."

Sargent bowed gravely. "I'll be honoured to accept the brief at the Old Bailey," he said, "but I shall want an enormous fee before

I appear for you before St. Peter in the matter of your Friday duck—
with his vested interest in the fish trade, too."

"Yes, that's a point," assented Monitor. "Still, you know, even
a fisherman wouldn't want me to be unsociable and not join in a
common meal. How nice it is, the small parties we get at dinner in
vacation, so that everyone can take part in one conversation. I think
three is the ideal number. I remember a little dinner for three in a
hermitage by the Nile—oh, it must be twenty years ago now. Just
the Coptic Patriarch and his chaplain and myself. They're said to
be the only two men in the world who still speak Coptic—though I
believe our poor old friend Benchley could have taken them on in
it if he'd tried. It's the genuine original language of the Pharaohs,
you know, but it's only used for church services nowadays, and
there are just these two dear old fellows who understand it. Grubby,
of course, but perfect mines of out-of-the-way knowledge."

"Do you think any of the learning of the old Egyptians has been
handed down by the Copts?" asked Considine.

"Oh, dear me, yes—all sorts of things they know. Things you'd
never expect. Science for instance; even my line of business. They
showed me a most valuable treatise on medicine—full of prescriptions I could never have thought of for myself. How would you cure
Leucoma of the eyes, for instance? You don't know. Neither did I.
But they could tell me. You take the brain of a tortoise, grind it up
and mix it with honey. Then you recite over the mixture an incan-
tation about a shouting in the darkness of the southern sky and an
uproar in the northern, and you smear it over the patient's eyes
and he's cured straight away. I expect he is, too. There are men in
Harley Street who'll make you out prescriptions with just as much
sense behind them all day long, at five guineas a time. All bluff,
you know. We just guess, like the old Egyptian medicine men. And
why should we be able to guess any better than they?"

"Did you ever talk to Benchley about that side of Egyptology?"
Sargent asked him.

"Oh, often, often. Poor old Peter. He could have prescribed for
Pharaoh himself in the correct manner of the age. He was a scientist himself when he was young, you know, like so many of the big

Egyptologists of the old school. Both Champollion and Young were brought up on stinks. Benchley stuck to his chemistry all through. That's what made him such an authority on mummies. He was always experimenting on them and knew the whole process from alpha to omega. And that's what put an idea into my head when you were talking about that mummy at the inquest yesterday. From what I knew of old Peter's habits, it seemed to me quite likely he'd taken the mummy out of the coffin himself to try some of his drugs on it."

"But if he did, where did he put it?" exclaimed Considine. "It only arrived on Wednesday morning and an undergraduate saw it—"

"I don't think Benchley could have taken it out of college without its being noticed," Sargent interrupted hastily, kicking Considine under the table.

"I wonder," said Monitor pensively. "There are lots of things people don't notice that happen right under their noses. Has either of you considered what became of Peter Benchley's luggage?"

"His luggage?" echoed the two junior fellows together.

"Yes, his luggage. He was going on his holiday yesterday, you know, and he always sent his luggage in advance. A most dangerous habit that I outgrew myself donkey's years ago. When you're as old a traveller as I, you'll know that you should never let yourself be separated from your portmanteau. I made the mistake once, and it led to my being presented to the Dowager Empress of China in khaki shorts with a scarlet patch on the seat. I didn't mind, but it nearly led to a diplomatic crisis, and the British Minister fairly hauled me over the coals about it. The worst of it was I had to appear before him in the same garments. Still, that's beside the point. What I was saying, when you led me into that digression, was that old Peter always sent his luggage in advance, and if you inquire what became of it on Wednesday you're quite likely to come on the track of the mummy. Newton tells me it's bequeathed to the college, so we ought to find out about it. Is either of you having any more port? No? Then shall we all go on to the coffee room? What are you two going to do with yourselves this evening?"

Sargent at last saw his chance. "We'd rather thought of going out on the river for a bit," he said. "I wonder if you'd mind lending us your punt? Or even coming out in it with us yourself?"

"Now isn't that a pity?" Monitor lamented. "D'you know, I haven't got the punt at present. I lent it to someone for commem week. Now who was it? Let me see. Oh, I remember, it was little Daffy Carrothers, Benchley's niece. She's engaged to that nice undergraduate from New College, Devereux he's called, and I think they've got the punt round in New College backwater. Yes, that's where it is, I remember their telling me. I don't suppose they're using it tonight, so you could go round and take it if you like."

"Oh, thanks very much, but it was only a passing whim," said Sargent. "On second thoughts, it's hardly worth the walk; it'll probably get pretty chilly in an hour or so. I think we'll stay here after all."

"Then, in that case, suppose you come over to my rooms with your coffee," suggested Monitor. "This place is too vast for a small party; I always feel overawed by it."

Accepting the invitation with alacrity, for it offered further opportunity of unobtrusive collection of evidence, the two junior fellows, coffee cups in hand, accompanied the doctor across the fellows' garden to his rooms adjoining the archway between the first and second quadrangles. The sitting room was typical of its owner, who had occupied it continuously since 1882. The panelling was believed to have been designed for the college by Grinling Gibbons, and the furniture was wholly by Chippendale; but on these austere foundations Monitor had imposed a superstructure of the debris of half a century's travels in every corner of the earth. There were assegais from Zululand and a whale's ear-drum from the Arctic, a human scalp presented by a Choctaw chief and a dried head acquired from the head-hunters of Borneo, the skin of a Siamese temple cat and the stuffed head of a kangaroo, the alleged egg of a dinosaurus and the sentence of death, signed by Lenin, which had been passed on Monitor himself during a visit to Russia shortly after the War. The bookshelves testified to an astonishing multiplicity of interests and a total disregard of the boundaries between the various domains of knowledge. A German treatise on the chemistry of the blood stood next to the *Arabian Nights* in the original Arabic, and there followed in succession *Bishop Hoadly's Sermons*, *Baedeker's Guide to Somaliland*, Dante's *Vita Nuova*, Bower on

Actionable Defamation, the *Septuagint*, and *The Times Book of Crossword Puzzles*. On the shelf below, which alone showed signs of considered arrangement, the seven volumes of *The Constitutional, Political, and Juridical History of the Court of Star Chamber*, by Sir Theodore Mainwaring, were carefully interspersed with *The Bowl of Blood*, and five works of equally lurid title, by Galahad Baines. But the most remarkable feature of the room was the heterogeneous collection of images, representing almost every known religion, that stood on every available shelf and table. Gurney was wont to declare that whether you were an ancient Greek, a Hottentot, an Aztec, a Buddhist, or a Fiji Islander, a Nestorian, a Monophysite or an Anabaptist, a Spiritualist, a Theosophist or a sergeant in the Salvation Army, an Australian bushman or a Parisian Satanist, a worshipper of dragons, crocodiles, unicorns or cats, you could always find something to say your prayers to in Monitor's room. Monitor's habitual reply was that he had in his time received visits from members of all these denominations, and he liked to give them all the opportunity of keeping touch with heaven. Did not the college chaplain pride himself on the comprehensiveness of the Church of England? And might not a poor Papist endeavour to live up to that example?

He went now to a cupboard in a corner of the room, from which he extracted three grotesquely ornamented brass cups and a curious leather bottle.

"I want you to taste this liqueur," he said. "It's sent to me by a friend in Thibet, who assures me that it helps to exalt the mind towards the eternal verities. The cups were given me by a shepherd in Siberia for curing one of his rams of the results of a spell put upon it by a local wizard. It's an odd drink. I think they must make it of fermented goat's milk, but I shouldn't be surprised if there were more enterprising ingredients." He poured a little of an aromatic colourless liquid into each cup. "Some of the recipes of those parts would make Macbeth's witches turn green with envy."

Considine and Sargent sipped gingerly, while Monitor watched them with childlike amusement. "I think I'd rather not inquire into its precise origin," said Considine, "but it's not an unattractive flavour."

"Good," said their host. "But Sargent's the connoisseur. What do you make of it?"

"It has the great merit of not resembling any vintage in the college cellar," said Sargent guardedly.

Monitor laughed heartily. "Splendid," he chuckled. "I didn't think you could get out of it like that. How sad to think I shall never again hear you and old Peter sparring over the wine. That's his pipe up there on the mantelpiece, you know. I suppose I'm getting sentimental in my dotage, but I can't bear to throw it away."

"Did you know he left it to you in his will?" asked Considine.

"Did he now? Did he? Dear old Peter. How exactly like him, to remember all the times he and I and that pipe had shared together. He nearly blew me off the top of the Matterhorn with its fumes once. Well, I certainly can't part with it after that. Do you know, on Wednesday night I don't think I realized the old fellow was gone till I got back to my rooms and felt in my trouser pocket, and there was Peter's pipe. Dear me, I mustn't get maudlin. But it's a dreadful thing, losing Peter Benchley like that. Dreadful."

"You must have been the last of us to see Benchley alive," remarked Sargent. "Did you think he was quite himself that night?"

"Oh yes, why shouldn't he have been, poor fellow? He couldn't have foreseen what was going to happen. Perhaps it was better like that, too. Wasn't it Caesar whom they asked just before the Ides of March what was the best death to die, and he answered 'that which is least expected'? Not a Christian sentiment, of course, but then Peter was a conscientious pagan, and I expect they'll make allowances for him on the day of judgment. Invincible ignorance, you know. It's a plea that must go against the grain for a professor, mustn't it?—but Peter wasn't conceited. And he was *anima naturaliter Christiana* all right."

"Well, I'm glad you think he died happy," said Sargent. "I remember Considine and I were rather worried about him that night. It seemed so unlike him to have given in to Bonoff like that. By the way, did he talk to you about Bonoff after we'd left you?"

"Oh no, I only stayed with him two or three minutes. Besides, I always kept out of that subject. I don't like controversy, you know, so Peter always took care to let me off hearing about the Bonoff feud."

"I must have made a mistake then," said Sargent, with a well-simulated air of surprise. "Somebody told me that you actually knew Bonoff, that you'd met him when you were in Russia ten years ago."

"Now I wonder where that idea can have come from. I never set eyes on Bonoff in my life. I tell you who I did meet, though— another Russian Egyptologist called Gregorovitch. At least, he started life as an Egyptologist, but then he turned missionary. He had an entirely original brand of salvation of his own, a sort of compound of Christian Science and physical jerks. He tried to flood my soul with uncreated light by teaching me to sit down on the floor without bending my knees. You wouldn't believe what bruises it gave me. But Bonoff—no, I never came across him."

"Oh well, the man who told me must have mixed you up with someone else," said Sargent carelessly. "At any rate, it looks as if Bonoff wasn't really on Benchley's mind so much as we thought. I suppose you were in bed when the fire broke out?"

"Now, my dear Sargent, don't make me out more of a Methuselah than I am. I'm only seventy-seven, you know, and I haven't missed a Beaufort commem ball since I was eighteen. I went straight from Peter's rooms to the dancing tent, and from the time I arrived I don't believe I had a single blank on my programme till the fourth extra, which would have been about lunch time, if the ball hadn't been cut short. No, I expect you were too excited to notice me, but I was helping the fireman with the hose. I only wish I could have done something more effective."

"I'm afraid there was nothing for any of us to do," said Sargent. "I still can't make out how that fire started, and how it got such a hold so quickly, but I suppose we shall never know now. Well, Monitor, we shall have to be getting along; we've both got work to do. Good night, and many thanks for the elixir. I hope it'll help you to make progress towards the eternal verities."

"I hope you're satisfied," said Considine, as they walked across the quadrangle. "Personally, I think your cross-examination was indecent; but then I haven't the legal mind. And that's the man you're prepared to suspect of murder."

"My dear Humphrey," said Sargent, "I've never suspected him for a moment. You know we arranged just to go through the motions of suspicion in the hope of getting some new evidence."

"And you haven't got a scrap."

"On the contrary, we've got at least two new facts that may be important."

"And what are they?"

"Well, what struck you?"

"I suppose his lending the punt to Devereux is one, so far as it goes; and then that he wasn't in his rooms when Bonoff was there."

"*If* Bonoff was there. I'd forgotten that one. But there's a third point that you've left out."

"I can't think of another," said Considine after a moment's consideration.

"Didn't you listen to what Monitor told us about Benchley's pipe?"

"What about the pipe? Surely there was nothing we didn't know already. We were both there when he took it from Benchley, and we heard at the inquest that he'd still got it."

"Oh, well," said Sargent, "perhaps it's an insignificant point after all, and I won't try and bias your mind by insisting on it now. You heard what Monitor said, and if it didn't seem worth noting to you, perhaps I'm exaggerating it. I must keep clear of theories. Only I can't resist the impression that the pipe may turn out to be the key to the whole mystery, though I don't quite see its bearing just yet. Now I should think it's dark enough for us to go and collect that mummy coffin. We can bring it up to the college landing stage. The garden's locked up, so there won't be any undergraduates to see us, and Monitor's the only fellow in college. If he goes out anywhere, it'll be in the fellows' garden, so the coast's as clear as it ever will be."

Leaving the college by the fellows' garden and the gate in Grammar Lane, they took their way along the South Parks Road, once a pleasant rural walk, but now transformed into a highway of science and empire, where the great Zimbabwe bird of Rhodes House perpetually grimaces in the odour of sulphuric acid from the grim row of laboratories opposite. Passing Cherwell Edge, the home of their companions of the afternoon, they followed the footpath towards Mesopotamia and presently diverged from it to where a small green shed, large enough to contain two punts, stood by the waterside. There was a door at the landward end, and another giving directly upon the river, which was invisible from the path. Sargent, taking the key from his pocket, bent to the padlock on the door at the nearer end.

"Hullo," he said, "somebody's been here before us. This lock's been forced."

He flung the door open as he spoke, and Considine, looking through the opening, saw the dark gleam of water in moonlight beyond. The further door stood wide, and the boathouse was empty.

9
THE EXAMINERS

"HAVE YOU SEEN THIS?" exclaimed Considine next morning, bursting into Sargent's rooms with a newspaper in his hand.

"Hullo, Humphrey," replied Sargent, "so you're up at last."

"What do you mean by 'up'," retorted Considine indignantly. "I'm not only up, but I've had breakfast, and I haven't seen you in the common room yet."

"Alas, Humphrey, I hate to dash your young enthusiasm on the one morning of the year when you've been up with the lark. But I happen to have had breakfast an hour ago. And I'd been for a walk before that."

"My dear Denys, don't say you're turning hearty. Where have you been at that hour?"

"I went round to New College field. You know they've got a little backwater off the Cher that runs along one side of it, and the under-graduates keep their punts and canoes there. I thought I'd just have a look at them."

"And what did you see?"

"I saw what I expected. There were only two punts left there; I gather they're closing down for the long vac. to-day. But one of those two was Monitor's; I recognized it at once by that little brass image we noticed on it yesterday. Then I had a little talk with the boy who looks after the boats up there. He's the son of the New College waterman, and quite an intelligent youth."

"What had he got to say?"

"Not as much as I hoped. He confirmed that the punt had been borrowed by Devereux and brought round to New College field last Sunday evening. But he wasn't there either when it was taken out on Wednesday or when it was brought back. In fact, he thought Devereux must have returned it to Monitor on Wednesday night, and was surprised to see it there this morning."

"Then we can't discover anything about its movements at the crucial time?"

"Nothing very positive, I'm afraid. But he told me definitely that the punt was there when he went off duty on Wednesday night, and not there at the same time last night. Now, he knocks off at nine o'clock, and we were at the boathouse, which is less than a hundred yards from the field, at about eleven last night. That fixes the time when the women's boathouse was raided within about two hours."

"Not necessarily. They may have hung about before taking the punt back. Or they may have made a journey in it to deliver the mummy."

"I don't think so," said Sargent. "I work it out like this. As the thieves, whoever they were, took the mummy—or rather the case—and left the punt, the inference is that they got it away by land. But it's a cumbrous thing to dispose of, and they'd have had to get some sort of car or van down to the water to meet it. Therefore, they must have brought it ashore close to a road. Now where could they go? They couldn't go downstream, because they'd have had to pass the Rollers, and the men on duty there would be bound to spot the mummy and ask questions. If they went upstream, the only possible landing place for several miles is just outside our fellows' gate, in Grammar Lane, and the lane's too narrow to let an adequate vehicle down to the water. The only other way for them would be to follow up the backwater, which would bring them to the landing stage in Manor Place, a perfectly suitable spot for their purpose. But to get there they'd have to pass New College field, and being in a punt stolen from there they must obviously wait till the boat boy had gone home. So I think it's safe to say the boathouse was broken into after nine and before eleven last night."

"Sounds all right," Considine assented. "Does it help us much?"

"Not enormously, I'm afraid," said his colleague. "But any scrap of information may be useful before we've finished. The time-table of Wednesday night may be more important."

"Why's that?"

"Well, we know once more that the punt was taken out from New College field not earlier than nine o'clock. Our commem ball started at half-past nine, so that anyone who took the punt could scarcely have been here for the beginning of the ball, unless he punted it in full evening dress, which is rather a conspicuous thing to do for an intending murderer. The times there may turn out important if we have to consider alibis. But all this is rather remote at present. What was exciting you in the paper?"

"This," said Considine, pointing to a paragraph at the foot of a page. It was headed "Russian Savant for U.S.A. Dr. Bonoff's Appointment," and ran as follows:

"The President and Trustees of Yale University have appointed Dr. Feodor Bonoff as Peabody Visiting Professor of Egyptology for the forthcoming academic year. Professor Bonoff will sail for the United States almost immediately, and will take up his duties at the beginning of next semester (term).

"Although of Russian origin, Professor Bonoff has for the past twelve months resided in England. He was born in 1869, and before the revolution was one of the most distinguished scholars associated with the University of Moscow. His political views, however, rendered him unacceptable to the Soviet régime, and he had consequently lived mainly in retirement since the Bolsheviks came into power. In June last year his alleged public expression of bourgeois opinions brought the official persecution to a head, and he was obliged to leave his native country. The greater part of his property having been confiscated, a number of English admirers of his work subscribed to present him with the small house in the Isle of Wight, where he now lives.

"Professor Bonoff is best known to the public in
this country for the vigorous attacks that he has
made during the past ten years on the Egyptological
theories associated with the name of the late Professor Benchley, the well-known Oxford expert,
whose tragic death by fire we announced only yesterday. He also created a considerable sensation a
few years back by his discovery of the mummy of
King Pepi I, the oldest royal mummy in existence."

"H'm," said Sargent. "That's both the combatants in the great
feud removed within a week. It's an interesting coincidence. It can't
very well be anything more."

"I wouldn't be absolutely certain," said Considine. "These ap-
pointments aren't as a rule allowed to get into the press directly
they're made. We can be pretty sure that Benchley knew about it
before he died. The Yale people would have been sure to consult
him. In fact I happen to know that he was sounded himself about
taking the job."

"I see. Yes. It seems to become relevant as a point that might
have influenced Benchley's mind. It's probably also the reason why
Bonoff parted with the mummy; I expect mummies get held up on
Ellis Island; they probably count as wops. Yes, we ought to make a
note of it. Is that something more you've got?"

"Yes, it's another check, I'm afraid," said Considine, holding
out a letter. "This is what I get in reply to a telegram I sent yesterday to Lewstein."

Sargent took the letter and read:

> "Worldograph Filmophones, Inc.,
> "500 Wardour Street, W.1,
> "June 24th, 1932.
> "Dear Sir,
> "In reply to your telegram of even date, I beg to say
> that I have not had the pleasure of any dealings

with your friend the late Prof. Benchley. I am a one
hundred per cent up-to-the-minute republican, and
set no stock by the bodies of kings, particularly those
who lived in backward countries and have been dead
for thousands of years. You will find a more likely
buyer for your curios in Mr. Luther Y. Van Ditten,
of New York, who is, I believe, in England, at
present.

"I might, however, be willing to make you an
offer for the film rights of some of your old-world
ceremonies, particularly those featuring co-eds.
            "Sincerely yours,
            "Milton P. Lewstein."

"That seems a dead end all right," said Sargent, handing back
the letter. "Which reminds me that I've had another slight setback
this morning. I thought of following up Monitor's suggestion about
Benchley's luggage. But there's nothing doing. I spoke to Bloggs,
who says it's quite true Benchley always used to send it in advance,
but this time for some reason he wouldn't do it. It was all packed
and ready, and got destroyed in the fire. You remember we've got
a lot of entries under your trench No. 7 of unrecognizable fragments of leather. That must have been his trunks."

"Hence the mummy didn't get out of college that way," said
Considine. "Hence also, surely, it was stolen with the coffin, but
for some unknown reason taken out of it by the thieves. We really
ought to get down to a serious investigation of what did happen to
that mummy."

"Yes, we ought," Sargent agreed. "In fact, I think it's time we
overhauled our ideas on the whole problem. Practically we haven't
answered a single question with any certainty yet. When you came
in I was just finishing a list of the points we want light on, and I
suggest we go over it in detail together. It's rather formidable." He
walked over to his writing table and produced the following document.

"THE BURSARY FIRE

Principal Questions still requiring answer.

1. Whose is the body? Possible answers: *a* Benchley, *b* the mummy, *c* some third person unknown.
2. If the answer to 1 is *a*, where is the mummy? If *b*, where is Benchley? If *c*, where are both Benchley and the mummy?
3. Supposing the body to be Benchley's was death due to accident, suicide or murder?
4. Was the fire started by accident or design?
5. On the supposition of murder, what is the evidence connecting the following persons, who may have had access to Benchley's rooms at relevant times, with the crime?
   a. Bloggs
   b. Miss Carrothers
   c. Van Ditten
   d. Monitor
   e. Devereux
   f. Randolph and Nevern (so-called)
   g. Bonoff
   h. Some unknown person or persons.
6. How, when and by whom was the coffin stolen from Benchley's rooms?
7. By whom was it stolen from Miss Foley's boathouse?

Secondary questions whose answers
may have a bearing on the above.

8. What lies behind Benchley's surrender to Bonoff?
9. Why did Benchley object to Devereux as a husband for his niece?
10. What is the significance of the alarm clock?
11. How did Benchley's key get into the punt?
12. How did Bonoff get into college?
13. Why did Bonoff visit Monitor's rooms?

14. Why was the mummy not insured?
15. Why did Benchley not send his luggage in advance?
16. Who was the buyer of the mummy?"

"It certainly seems a stiff examination paper," said Considine, having read the list through. "A few of them are fairly easy though. Number 12, for instance. Surely Bonoff must have come in on a ball ticket. The college was closed that night to anybody else."

"It isn't as simple as all that," replied Sargent. "I've been talking to Collins about it. He was on duty at the gate till well after midnight, and he has the most marvellous memory for faces of any man I know. Even among Oxford porters it's extraordinary. You remember the description of Bonoff that Devereux gave us—'Small, flaming red hair, scar on the left cheek and always wears smoked glasses.' Pretty distinctive, I think. But I repeated it to Collins, and he's absolutely certain no one answering the description passed through the big gate that night."

"Then he must have got in by the fellows' gate," said Considine. "He couldn't have come by the river, because I know there was a scout on duty by the undergraduates' landing stage to stop gate-crashers."

"Yes," Sargent agreed, "if he came at all I think it's pretty certain that he came by the fellows' gate. Which means that he either had the stolen key or was let in by one of the fellows."

"Meaning Benchley," exclaimed Considine. "Or Monitor," he added as an afterthought.

"Well, if you don't mind," said Sargent, "I think we'll postpone that point. My idea in drawing up this catechism was that we should go through it in order and try and take stock of what we know and what we've still got to find out. Will you do that with me?"

"Isn't it rather giving up your ruling about keeping our theories to ourselves?"

"To some extent it is. But only apparently, I think. All I really want to do is to set in order the evidence we've got together so far, and just remind ourselves what materials we've got for an answer to each question. I'm afraid we shall find we can settle scarcely any of them at present."

"None, I should think," said Considine. "But go ahead."

"Very well. Question one: whose body? What's the evidence that it's Benchley's?"

"*Prima facie* probability in the first place," said Considine. "The fact that it was found in Benchley's rooms, where Benchley was known to be just before. The fact that it was wearing his watch. The fact that Benchley is missing. And the fact that his bedroom door was locked, presumably on the inside. What's the evidence against?"

"I won't try to put it in full," answered Sargent, "because it'll come out under some of the other questions. Shortly, it's the existence of evidence that the fire wasn't accidental, coupled with the lack of motive for the suicide or murder of Benchley. To which must be added the difficulty of accounting for the mummy. Which brings us to the second part of the question. Is there any evidence that the body is the mummy? Simply that the mummy was known to be in Benchley's rooms before the fire, and hadn't his ability to walk away. That you counter with your Sumerian brick. I take it you're still convinced the mummy must have had its head smashed open?"

"Absolutely."

"All right. That seems to complete the evidence on that point. Now for the third. Have we any reason to suppose that the body belonged to a third party?"

"None whatever, so far as I can see."

"None that I can see either. Still, it's a logical possibility, and we oughtn't to rule it out. It's conceivable that evidence might turn up. Now I've summarized most of the evidence on question one, Humphrey. Just to show there's no ill-feeling, suppose you tackle number two."

"If the body is Benchley's, where is the mummy?" said Considine reflectively. "Well, let me see. There seem to be two main possibilities, don't there?"

"Either that it never was in Benchley's possession, or that it was removed before the fire?" suggested Sargent.

"Yes. The first seems to be practically ruled out. We know Benchley paid Bonoff for it, and we know that he was far too great an expert for anyone to try to deceive, least of all Bonoff, who had the knowledge to appreciate him. We know the mummy was delivered on Wednesday morning and not taken out of college during the day. We ourselves saw the coffin in his rooms that night."

"That was after the hanky-panky by Randolph and Nevern," Sargent reminded him.

"So it was," Considine admitted. "But young Devereux saw the coffin open and the mummy inside, and that was before the rag. If the mummy was never in Benchley's rooms, we shall have to assume he was lying."

"True," assented Sargent. "But we mustn't take anyone's veracity as dogma. Remember Devereux's on our list of suspects."

"All right, I'll be as pedantic as you like. Anyhow, we're not forming a conclusion, are we? That's the evidence for what it's worth, bearing on the theory that there never was a mummy. Anything to add?"

"No. Now what about the possibility that it was taken away?"

"Since we're going on the assumption that the body found was Benchley's, the evidence that the mummy was in his rooms in the morning is also evidence that it was taken away before the fire. In addition, we've got the definite fact that the coffin was stolen."

"That's the strongest point, of course," said Sargent. "Only it raises the further difficulty of why anyone who had taken the trouble to steal the mummy should abandon the coffin as they did. Still, we mustn't anticipate questions six and seven. What about the second part of number two?"

"If the body was the mummy, where is Benchley?" said Considine. "I'm so convinced it couldn't be the mummy that I haven't given the question a thought. You'd better deal with that one yourself."

"All right," replied his colleague. "Of course, we haven't anything to speak of in the way of evidence. But we ought just to note down the ways Benchley might possibly have disappeared."

"How do you mean?"

"Alive or dead? And if alive, voluntarily or involuntarily? It's only for the sake of theoretical completeness I include the notion that he disappeared dead. It's almost incredible that anyone who had murdered him should have disposed of the body in any other way than by leaving it to be burnt. But it's worth putting in, because there's just one way in which it could possibly have been done."

"How was that?" asked Considine with some surprise. "The whole college was buzzing with people all night."

"Nevertheless a bulky object was in some way abstracted under their eyes. And it happens to have been an object specially devised for the safe transport of a corpse."

"The coffin!" exclaimed Considine. "I never thought of that. By Jove, yes. That's an idea. It would account for the theft *and* for the abandonment."

"Don't be in such a hurry to eat your own words, Humphrey. It would not account for the finding in the ashes of the body you claim to have proved is not the mummy. And it wouldn't explain why they should burden themselves with the body at all, with the fire ready to hand."

"The fire might have been unconnected with the crime."

"Even that lands us with the theory that the murderers brought another corpse in with them."

"Isn't it possible that one of them was killed in the struggle, that they took Benchley's body away in the coffin and started the fire so as to get their dead accomplice taken for Benchley?"

"Why not leave the real Benchley and take away the accomplice?"

"He might have been injured in some way that couldn't be disguised even by fire," suggested Considine. "Like King Pepi I."

"My dear Humphrey, what a wonderful plot for a shocker you can turn out at a moment's notice. We ought to get Mainwaring to write it up. A hand-to-hand fight with broadswords between Benchley and an unknown number of professional assassins. All conducted in dead silence, so as not to disturb the flappers in the dancing tent. And this is what comes of my innocent attempt to take into account every possibility, even the wild off-chance that Benchley was taken away dead."

"Sorry, Denys," said Considine, flushing slightly. "It really comes of your being too clever. I don't myself think we need consider the theory that Benchley disappeared at all. But let's get back to the main line. You were going to tabulate the evidence for or against the theory that Benchley disappeared alive."

"It's not quite that," said Sargent. "If the body wasn't Benchley's and he wasn't taken away dead, he *must* have disappeared alive. The only question is whether he disappeared voluntarily or otherwise."

"And the evidence?" inquired Considine.

"Practically none," replied Sargent. "We've really got to keep two blank spaces, so to speak, ready for any evidence that may turn up. But there's one fragment that may have a bearing. That key we found in the punt. Of course, it might have been taken off Benchley's body by his murderers. But on our present hypothesis that he wasn't murdered, it would be consistent with his having left the college in the company of the thieves who stole the coffin."

"In that case he might have been taken away inside it after all."

"Could he breathe inside?"

"You'd have had to make some arrangements for ventilation; a mummy coffin is a pretty tight fit. You didn't examine it for breathing holes, did you?"

"No, I'm afraid I didn't. Pity we didn't reckon on its being stolen again."

"Nor did I," said Considine regretfully.

"But let's think this out before we go on," said Sargent. "If there were breathing holes, Benchley must have been in the plot. He couldn't have been kidnapped; the kidnappers wouldn't have had time to rig up the breathing apparatus."

"If you think Benchley would deliberately cut holes in a unique Sixth Dynasty mummy coffin," protested Considine indignantly, "you've got a very different estimate of him from mine. It would be like vivisecting his own child."

"Then the inference is that, if he went out of college alive, willingly or not, it wasn't inside the coffin."

"Unless Bonoff made the holes before he sent it off," suggested Considine. "Oh, but you're leading me into more wild impossibilities, Denys. Benchley never did leave college. Do let's get back to something practical."

"We're trying to exhaust all the alternatives," Sargent reminded him.

"You can't have more than two alternatives," said Considine wearily. "I'm beginning to think there's a good deal to be said for linguistic purism."

Sargent laughed. "Very well," he said, "just this once I'll bow to your zeal for Latin correctitude. We'll skip the third part of question two. It's not much use our starting a hunt for both Benchley and the mummy if we're baffled in the search for either of them separately. Anyhow, we must have covered all the evidence on that point already. Now for question three. It's the crux of the problem. Accident, suicide, or murder? Let's take accident first."

"It's the natural presumption," said Considine. "I don't know that there's any positive evidence for it."

"There isn't a scrap," agreed Sargent. "Let's take the evidence against. What can you think of?"

"The keys found on the body," said Considine, "showing that Benchley hadn't gone to bed and therefore ought not to have been taken by surprise by the fire. The alarm clock with the bell removed, apparently brought in that very day. The essence of clockwork is that it gives a man the chance of bringing about some small action at a fixed time, after he may have left the scene. In other words, it might have been used in some way to start the fire. Percussion caps, you know. Or petrol. Or some electric gadget. I'm not a mechanic, but it ought to be easy enough. Then the key. We know Benchley had the key of the fellows' gate in his pocket when he went to bed."

"Only on Monitor's evidence," put in Sargent quickly. "Remember he's a suspect."

"Only technically," said Considine with some impatience. "I repeat that we know Benchley had the key when he went to bed.

And it wasn't in the ruins when we made our excavations. Accident wouldn't have conjured it away. I think those three points are enough to dispose of the accident theory altogether."

"Taken with the will, I'm sure they do," said Sargent.

"The will?" Considine queried. "How does that come in?"

"You remember it was found in the Bursary. I've spoken to Newton about that, and he says Benchley never kept any personal papers there. The clerks had keys of his desk, so obviously it was most unlikely he would leave anything so private where they would find it. Unless, of course, he particularly wanted it found."

"You mean he foresaw his death and put it there on purpose?"

"I mean that it was put there on purpose, by someone who foresaw Benchley's death or knew that he was already dead. Or rather, someone who knew he would be taken for dead, even if he wasn't really. But I think we've disposed of accident. What about suicide?"

"I'm sure Benchley wasn't in the least suicidal by nature," said Considine with decision. "On the other hand, he had certainly been behaving oddly of late."

"You mean the peculiar manner Devereux spoke of, when he went to see him on Wednesday night," said Sargent. "Remember, we haven't yet tackled the question of Devereux's veracity."

"No," said Considine, "I was thinking more of his giving in to Bonoff."

"You mean he might have committed suicide because he was beaten in an academic argument?"

"If Benchley was capable of suicide at all, the most likely reason was something like that." Considine was speaking now with a quiet certainty derived from intimate knowledge of the man. "To him, it wasn't an academic argument. Egyptology was the whole purpose of his life. He put far more passion into it than most men would into, say, a love-affair. And yet—"

"And yet men have died ere this and worms have eaten them, but not for Egyptology," Sargent misquoted.

"No, Denys, it wasn't even that. It was something more subtle. I was really thinking of the last few letters he wrote to *The Times* against Bonoff."

"They seemed quite as usual to me," said Sargent. "Full of sound and fury."

"And signifying nothing. You know I'm not an Egyptologist, but of course my line of business runs pretty close up against theirs at a good many points, and to some extent I was capable of appreciating the *nuances* of the Benchley-Bonoff controversy."

"Well, what was wrong with Benchley's letters?"

"They were all wrong, really. On the surface, as you say, they were as vigorous as ever; the ordinary cultivated layman would say he was pitching into Bonoff for all he was worth. But from the professional point of view they were not only weak, but deliberately weak. He was harping on all the vulnerable points of his case and slurring over the ones that were really convincing. It was almost as if he wanted to be beaten. And that's extraordinary, because there never was a man more pugnacious than Benchley on a subject that he took to heart. It's so extraordinary that I can't rule right out the notion that his mind might have been giving way."

"And so, that the answer to our question might be 'suicide while of unsound mind'," mused Sargent. "It answers my supplementary number eight, of course. And number nine as well, because then his objection to Devereux as a native of the Isle of Wight would be just a madman's whim. Only insanity seems to me just a little too easy a way out of our difficulties. Have we any positive evidence pointing to suicide?"

"The will," suggested Considine.

"True, but that's consistent with murder as well, if the murderer was going to benefit by it."

"The placing of it in the Bursary would be. But what about the contents?"

"You mean the date of the codicil, just after he'd come back from seeing Bonoff and within four days of his death? That is a remarkable coincidence, of course, but we've no evidence that it was anything more."

"Then there's his not sending his luggage in advance. He was a man of astonishingly fixed habits."

"Yes, so I'd often noticed myself. Witness that horrible old pipe, which he must have had since before we were born. But it's rather a minute point. By the way, do you know where he intended to go?"

"No, I'm afraid not. But then he never did tell anybody. Said he liked to cut himself off from the world of term-time directly vacation began."

"Well, that's that. Still, there might easily have been something about his destination that accounted for his changing his habits about luggage in advance. It's not a point we can build on. Now, what's the evidence against suicide?"

"There's the key in the punt."

"Strong—very strong. I doubt if it can be got round. And even stronger is the absence of the key from the corpse."

"Isn't that the same thing? It couldn't be in two places at once."

"No, but there might have been two keys."

"But it had Benchley's number on it," Considine objected.

"I know," said Sargent. "But I've got an idea. We'll come to it later. In the meantime the key, however you look at it, is strong evidence against suicide. Anything else?"

"I can't think of anything that's really worth much weight in comparison with that."

"Surely his buying the mummy is rather a bad snag in the suicide theory. He spent nearly all his worldly goods on it, presumably knowing he was going to reduce it to ashes within a few days. Practically it was handing over his heiress's livelihood to his pet aversion, Bonoff, and depriving her, into the bargain, of the chance to make up for it by catching a rich husband. He hadn't anything against Miss Carrothers, had he?"

"On the contrary. He was as fond of her as if she'd been his daughter."

"Then the suicide theory makes him out something worse than insane. We can't altogether rule it out on that ground; there's evidence both ways, and we mustn't neglect any of it. But you'll agree that suicide's highly improbable, won't you?"

"So far as you'll allow me to commit myself to any theory, my dear Denys," said Considine blandly. "But that leaves us only murder."

"And I think we're already been over most of the evidence on that point. The sum total of the cases against accident and suicide is the case for murder. And if there's anything to add, we shall come to it under question five, when we're dealing with the various possible murderers. So I suggest that for the moment we only think of the case against murder."

"The case against murder is commonly deemed to be self-evident to right-thinking citizens," said Considine.

"The case against the murder of pedants is very slight," Sargent retorted. "Now what evidence is there against the murder hypothesis?"

"Principally the question of time, I should think," said Considine. "There were people in and out of Benchley's rooms all the evening—Monitor, Devereux, Randolph and Nevern, ourselves, perhaps Bonoff—and even supposing one of them was the murderer, he'd have to be amazingly lucky to dodge all the rest. And as for anyone outside that list, it would be pretty nearly incredible."

"Nevertheless, there's the body," said Sargent. "We've got to credit that."

10
THE CANDIDATES

For some moments silence fell between the two investigators. Each was puzzling over the apparent hopelessness of the problem. Sargent filled a pipe and lit it with lingering preoccupation; Considine rose and walked to the window, where he gazed out absent-mindedly over the sunlit quadrangle. Suddenly he swung round and faced his colleague.

"Denys," he said, "are we making damned fools of ourselves?"

"How d'you mean, Humphrey?" asked Sargent.

"I mean, are we racking our brains over an imaginary problem? Every line we try to follow seems to lead up to nonsense. Isn't it possible we're being too clever, that the verdict at the inquest was right after all?"

"My dear Humphrey, I can't conceive that a college meeting, particularly when it's disguised as a coroner's jury, should ever come to a right decision. In this particular case, I should have thought the alarm clock alone was enough to kill the accident theory."

"There's probably some perfectly obvious explanation staring us in the face all the time," said Considine gloomily.

"Would it also explain the missing key? And the codicil? And Bonoff's visit? Oh, and a dozen other details? Come along, Humphrey, we can't turn back now. Let's get on with question four."

Considine sat down again with a gesture of resignation. "All right," he said. "Carry on. Which is question four?"

"It's the one about the fire. Accidental or done on purpose?"

"Well, that's an easy one, thank Heaven. If Benchley's death wasn't accidental, then it's pretty clear the fire wasn't either. And the evidence is the same in both cases."

"Plus one additional point," Sargent reminded him. "The one we started with. The pipe."

"You mean that Benchley couldn't have been smoking in bed, and therefore that he couldn't have started an accidental fire. But as we've already decided he wasn't in bed at all, it's hardly an additional point."

"No," admitted Sargent, "in strict logic it isn't. I only drag it in because I've still got that idea at the back of my mind that the pipe is going to be the key to the mystery."

"If you're going to work the thing out by spontaneous intuition," said Considine, "I can't help you. I'm just a plain plodding archaeologist."

"No, it isn't intuition," said Sargent. "I suppose I must own up that I've got the beginning of a theory, with the pipe as starting point. But it's pure theory, and rather fantastic. And as it doesn't involve any fresh facts, and the ones we've got certainly don't go anywhere near proving it, I'm not going to burden you with it yet. Let's go on to question five."

"I think you're being indecently secretive," Considine grumbled, "especially after the way you drew me out about my duel of broadswords. However—this is the Who's Who question, isn't it?"

"Yes. We were going to run through the people who were or might have been in Benchley's rooms within twelve hours of the fire, and see what evidence there might be to connect them with the murder. The first is Bloggs."

"Need to take him seriously?" asked Considine with a faint grin.

"Not very," said Sargent, smiling also. "I fancy Jack the Ripper was a different type of man. Still, we've got to be complete. Bloggs had opportunity: he could have gone up at any time without exciting suspicion, though there's no evidence that he actually did later than his ordinary time for folding up Benchley's day clothes while he was at dinner. Afterwards he was on duty for the dance; the Manciple tells me he was in charge of the cloakroom, which was one of the lecture rooms in the big quad, a good long way from the

Bursary. So for practical purposes I think we need only consider him as having had an opportunity to start the clock, not to do the murder, which must have been after dinner—always supposing the body was Benchley's. Inference: Bloggs might just possibly have been an accomplice, but couldn't be the principal. Do you agree?"

"He had no motive. And he was absolutely devoted to Benchley."

"There was that small legacy, but I agree it's not enough to call a motive. He'd have had to be bribed, and I can't quite see a competent assassin trying to buy Bloggs. He talks too much, for one thing. Let's go on to the next, who is Miss Carrothers."

"Really, Denys, you're horrible. I refuse to contemplate the idea of poor Daphne murdering her uncle."

"Nevertheless," said Sargent firmly, "we can't leave her out. We can't afford to be sentimental."

"I leave it to you then," replied Considine.

"All right, I'll go ahead. Interrupt me if I make a mistake. First of all, she had a pretty obvious motive. Benchley was preventing her marrying her boy friend." Considine snorted, but said nothing. "Against that, she was on good terms with her uncle. That's it, isn't it?"

"Couldn't have been better," said Considine shortly.

"We've got to remember that his last-minute manoeuvres deprived her of two-thirds of her expectations, *and* her rich husband," Sargent went on ruthlessly. "It may have been accidental, but there's some evidence he foresaw his death. Still, let that pass. Now what about opportunity. She came into college on Wednesday covered with parcels; one of them might have contained the clock. She was at the dance, and so might have gone up to Benchley's rooms again. On the other hand there's no evidence that she did. She certainly didn't go up when Devereux did, because she was dancing with you, wasn't she?"

"She was," said Considine. "And after that I remember seeing her dancing with an undergraduate—Faraday, I think it was—until supper time."

"Then that, I think, completes the evidence concerning Miss Carrothers. If it's any comfort to you, I don't think this was a woman's crime. She could scarcely have murdered Benchley without firearms, and nothing of the kind was heard by anyone. Nor was any bullet found. So I think we can go on to Van Ditten. You'll be less tender-hearted about him, I expect."

"I'm not tender-hearted about Daphne. I happen to know her, and I know she couldn't be a murderess. It's just as much evidence as your time-table of her movements, and much less capable of being faked. The trouble with you, Denys, is that you've got a policeman's mind; I suppose that's why you won't let a real bobby into the case, because he'd be a rival. But, as you say, let's get on to Van Ditten. What evidence is there about him?"

"My methods seem to be rather blown upon," said Sargent amiably. "You'd better start with a psychological survey."

Considine reflected a moment. "I only met him at dinner that one night," he said at length. "And I shouldn't say he's at all an easy sort of man to estimate. He's got what I believe they call in America a poker face. I gather he made his money on Wall Street, and the stockbroker type, though it has no great reverence for morality, has a habit of keeping within the letter of the law, just because it pays. What I mean is, that they'd be capable of any of the innumerable branches of villainy that your profession so assiduously protects, but not of murder."

Sargent refused to rise to the bait. "Then are we to rule him out, too, on evidence of character?" he inquired.

"Not necessarily," Considine went on. "There's something in him besides stock exchange gambler, which may make all the difference. He's got collector's mania, if ever I saw it in any man; and that's a form of insanity that absolutely destroys the conscience. He'd do you down in a deal with such scrupulous correctitude that all the judges in the House of Lords couldn't find an iota to cavil at; but if it was a question of getting something unique for his collection, he'd go utterly reckless. He might not stop at murder."

"And by 'something unique for his collection' you mean the mummy?"

"It fits the description, doesn't it?"

"It certainly does—rather too well, in fact?"

"How do you mean?"

"I mean that the mummy is so definitely unique that he could never dare to show it to anyone, once it was known that it had been got by murder."

"There, if I may say so," rejoined Considine, "I think you show imperfect knowledge of the collector's mind. They're quite a special sort of lunatic. If he's the genuine article, and I believe he is, he wouldn't *want* to show his collection. He'd prefer to gloat over it by himself. The real joy of it is in having something that nobody else has got. In this case he'd got it into his head that Lewstein was after the mummy as well, and of course that would double its value to him by the mere delight of depriving his rival. By Jove, that gives me an idea!"

"Carry on, Humphrey, let's have it."

"Do you think it's possible that Van Ditten stole the mummy and destroyed it, simply to prevent its getting into Lewstein's hands?"

"Ingenious, Humphrey, ingenious. It gets rid of the difficulty about our finding the coffin empty. But doesn't it water down the motive for murder, which is what we're discussing at the moment, to something impossibly thin? And I should say it would land us in fresh difficulties when we come to the second burglary, the one from the boathouse. I'd been rather taking it for granted that that was done by people who'd already got the mummy and now wanted the coffin; if it wasn't we should have to assume the existence of two separate gangs of mummy thieves. And that offends against the principle of Occam's Razor—*Entia non multiplicanda praeter necessitatem*. I grant you it's a point. But suppose we tackle the Van Ditten direct evidence first."

"There I defer to my learned friend."

"Right. I've collected a few additional facts from Bloggs. We've more or less acquitted him, so we can treat him as a trustworthy witness. He tells me that Van Ditten arrived at three o'clock, just after Miss Carrothers had gone. There he corroborates Collins. He also confirms that Van Ditten was carrying an attaché case, which from his description was big enough to hold the clock. A new point that I got from him was that Benchley had a postcard from Van

Ditten on Wednesday morning to announce his arrival. Bloggs was rather shy about admitting having read it through—one or two words had inadvertently caught his eye as he carried it up—but I cork-screwed out of him the admission that Van Ditten mentioned a previous meeting with Benchley. Did you know anything about that?"

"No, I certainly didn't. But then he was as secret as the grave about everything to do with the mummy. I'm inclined to think that in his heart he was a bit ashamed of his little financial speculation."

"Well, it's a small point," Sargent went on, "but it may fit into place sometime or other. Bloggs doesn't know what time Van Ditten left, but Collins is sure he didn't go by the main gate, so Benchley must have let him out himself through the fellows' garden. He was gone by half-past four, when Bloggs took Benchley's tea up and found him working at his desk. He was back again by half-past seven for dinner. He came in through the garden with the borrowed key, and went up to Benchley's rooms. Bloggs was there when he arrived, and says he only stayed about a minute and then Benchley took him into Hall. After dinner we ourselves saw Monitor and Benchley take him to the gate, and according to Monitor's statement he then returned the key, with which Benchley let him out. Next day we know he left Oxford in a hurry."

"There doesn't seem much evidence against him in all that," said Considine.

"Not much, I agree," responded Sargent. "The significant point is that he had the key of the fellows' gate in his possession for at least three hours; and I'm sure that gate had something to do with the crime."

"But he gave it back long before the crime could have been committed."

"Yes, that's so, provided we assume that Monitor's evidence is above suspicion. But even so, he had it in his possession long enough for an expert locksmith to make a duplicate. You will also note that the key was not found on the body but in the punt. What are we to make of that?"

"Hardly a corroboration of the duplicate key theory," answered Considine. "Its obvious implication is that the murderer got in by the main gate, presumably as a ball guest, took the key from Benchley's dead body and escaped by the fellows' garden. And for that, of course, Van Ditten didn't start with any advantage over anyone else. In fact his having had the key would tell in his favour, but he had only to go out after dinner by the front way and Benchley would probably have forgotten to ask him for the key back. Then he could have come in as well as gone out by the garden way."

"Yes, I agree that seems a simpler explanation," said Sargent. "For all that, I'd like to put on record that Van Ditten had at least the opportunity to make a duplicate. I've a suspicion that more people passed through the fellows' gate on Wednesday night than one key will account for."

"You're thinking of Bonoff," Considine suggested.

"I'm trying to think only of Van Ditten," Sargent replied. "We must do things decently and in order. There is at least the beginning of a case against Van Ditten. We have a motive, though it strikes me as an inadequate one. We have opportunity, both to plant the clock and to do the murder, at different times if he liked. We have suspicious behaviour, in his sudden departure."

"Then oughtn't we to tell the police at once?" suggested Considine. "He's out of our reach, and it'll mean extradition if he's guilty."

"Not so fast, Humphrey," Sargent took him up. "The great charm of a millionaire criminal is that he can't disappear. The American police could lay their hands on Van Ditten at a moment's notice, even if he knew he was suspected, which he doesn't. Meanwhile we've got to note the fatal flaw in the theory."

"And what's that?"

"The same object that theory itself starts from. The key. If Van Ditten had made a duplicate key to get in with, why did he remove Benchley's key from the body? If he hadn't a duplicate what becomes of our evidence of opportunity? The only way I can see out of the dilemma is the absurd supposition that Monitor lied about the key, having first gone out of his way to tell us it had been lent to Van Ditten. And even if Monitor wasn't what Monitor is, can you conceive even of the craziest reason why he should lie to protect Van Ditten against a charge based on his own evidence?"

"Van Ditten might have come in again by the main gate, and out with Benchley's key," Considine hazarded half-heartedly.

"It's not mathematically impossible," Sargent replied, "and that's about all. He'd certainly have been recognized by Collins, and even if he'd come in disguise, or sent an accomplice, we should have to suppose that he'd deliberately thrown suspicion on himself by borrowing a key he wasn't going to use—not for the crime, I mean. No, Humphrey, it won't do. This murder wasn't committed by a fool."

"Then are we going to acquit Van Ditten on that one point about the key?"

"Certainly not. We're going to note an obstacle we've found in the case against him, and we're not going to accept that case unless we find a way over or round the obstacle. No, I fancy we shall have to say more of Master Van Ditten before we write Q.E.D. But let's give him a rest for the moment. Who's next on the list?"

Considine glanced at the paper of questions. "Monitor," he said. "That is, if you're really going to take him seriously as a suspect."

"Yes, Humphrey, I'm going to take him quite seriously. It's the only way. But if it'll comfort you at all, we'll have one of your little psychological testimonials to lead off with. What is the evidence of character?"

"The evidence of character is that he's in every way totally incapable of being mixed up in this or any crime."

"Good. I entirely agree. We'll take that as established fact."

"Then do we pass over him?"

"Certainly not. We're trying to make an exhaustive study of the evidence. Evidence that points to an impossible culprit may be the most important of all. It's something to be explained, and the explanation may contain the solution of the main problem. Now, what have we got against Monitor?"

"Next to nothing, except that he saw Benchley up to bed."

"It's a little more than that," said Sargent. "That in itself is evidence of opportunity. Nobody but Devereux saw Benchley alive afterwards."

"But one witness is as good as a dozen for a point like that," Considine objected.

"Not necessarily," said Sargent. "As we've agreed to acquit Monitor in advance, you won't mind my making the hypothetical case against him as black as it can be painted. Now, supposing Devereux had gone up and found Benchley dead?"

"He'd have given the alarm."

"Are you sure he would? Remember it was known he had a grievance against Benchley, and he'd just been talking big to Miss Carrothers about what he was going to do to him. Isn't it possible he might have got the wind up lest he should be accused of the murder, and that he might have made up the story about his interview—after the fire had made it impossible to check it of course?"

Considine reflected. "Yes," he said at length. "I suppose an unscrupulous prosecuting counsel against Monitor might produce such a theory. Is it part of your idea that Devereux set the fire going?"

"That doesn't come up yet," Sargent replied. "We're making out a case against Monitor, not Devereux. At the moment I'm trying to prove opportunity. Have I done so?"

"After a fashion."

"Right. Then there's motive—Monitor gets a small legacy under Benchley's will. It's a very slight motive, but not quite negligible. Granted he got any legacy at all, it's possible he might have been expecting much more."

"There's a good deal of imagination about all this," Considine put in.

"I know," admitted Sargent. "I'm deliberately stretching the case against Monitor as far as it can conceivably go, just to see where it brings us. Now we've got motive and we've got opportunity. On top of that we've got two little bits of circumstantial evidence. The first is the fact that the mummy coffin, which may or may not be connected with the murder, was found in Monitor's punt."

"Which had been lent for the week."

"Which is alleged to have been lent for the week," Sargent corrected. "So far we have only Monitor's own statement to the effect. While we're acting for the prosecution we're entitled to suppose that it may be incorrect. The second fact against him is the very curious visit paid to his rooms on the night of the crime by Benchley's arch-enemy, Bonoff. Now, what are we to deduce from that?"

"If you want me to deduce that Monitor and Bonoff combined to murder Benchley, in order that Bonoff should get his mummy back and Monitor inherit five hundred pounds, you'd better guess again," said Considine contemptuously. "Since you're so suspicious of interested evidence, you might reflect that we've only got Devereux's unsupported word that Bonoff was in college that night at all."

"My dear Humphrey, you anticipate my every thought. That was precisely the consideration to which I was trying to lead you. Our analysis of the case against Monitor continually brings us up against the name of Devereux. The coffin was found in Monitor's punt, but Devereux had borrowed it. Monitor received a visit from Bonoff, but it's only from Devereux that we hear about it. Incidentally, according to Benchley, Bonoff had ceased to be his enemy, but that's a vital detail that Devereux wouldn't know. On the other hand a thing Devereux might know, being engaged to Benchley's niece, is that Monitor was likely to get a legacy."

"Are you suggesting that Devereux did the murder and tried to plant it on Monitor?" Considine asked.

"I'm not suggesting anything so definite," was the reply. "Obviously the first line of defence of the murderer was the faking of accidental death. If he worked up a case against Monitor as a second line he did it pretty clumsily, because his first lie, about seeing Benchley alive after Monitor had parted from him, tended to cover Monitor."

"No, Denys, I don't think that's sound," said Considine. "You're not quite putting yourself in Devereux's shoes. You forget he didn't know Monitor had been up there. If he was faking a case against

Monitor at all, it would obviously be his cue to suggest that the murder had occurred after his own visit, not before."

"I believe you're right, Humphrey," said Sargent thoughtfully. "We've got more against Devereux than I thought. But then how does the pipe come in?" he added, half to himself. "Oh, damn the pipe, I mustn't let it be an obsession. It looks as if it's high time we turned our attention to the evidence against Devereux. Do we know anything about his character?"

"Not very much, I'm afraid," said Considine. "I'd only met him once before yesterday. It was fairly obvious that Benchley had something against him, but we don't know what. Still, I don't think we ought to pass that over completely; Benchley was a man of pretty sound judgment."

"Then we both saw him at the inquest," Sargent added. "I thought at the time he was keeping something back, and he admitted as much himself yesterday, when he told us his full story—or what purported to be the full story. The difficulty is that it wouldn't pay him to tell the second story, suggesting murder by Bonoff or Monitor, unless he suspected the first one, implying accidental death by fire, was being doubted. Now, do you think he was bright enough to spot that he was being cross-examined?"

"I doubt if we can say more," said Considine, "than that if he had a guilty conscience he'd have realized what was afoot, but if he hadn't he'd probably have taken the interview at its face value. You showed reasonable finesse, for a lawyer."

"Thank you for those few kind words," said Sargent. "I gather we're agreed that there's nothing in Devereux's known character to prove him incapable of the murder, while we've got a definite bad mark in Benchley's unexplained aversion from him. Now what about his movements on the night? He's the last person known to have seen Benchley alive. That was at eleven o'clock. They were having three dances to the hour at the ball; one began at eleven; do you know if he danced the next?"

"Yes, I saw him myself," Considine replied. "I remember the time, because he was dancing with Miss Gatfield, and I spoke to her as they passed to remind her that I was having the last dance before supper with her. That was the dance next to come."

"Then that means he must have left Benchley's rooms by twenty minutes past eleven, when that dance began," said Sargent. "On the other hand he admits he wasn't dancing the next, which would have begun at twenty to twelve; nor was he in the tent; he says he was walking about the quads. So for forty minutes of the hour between eleven and twelve he was without an alibi."

"Unless he produces Bonoff," suggested Considine.

"A rather unlikely event. But I'm not sure that lack of an alibi doesn't rather tend in his favour than otherwise. You see, suppose he'd killed Benchley soon after eleven o'clock. He wouldn't leave his movements unaccounted for later on unless he had something very special to do. And what could that have been?"

"I should have thought that was obvious," said Considine. "He went back to start the fire. If it broke out directly after his known visit to Benchley, it might easily be put down to him. But if it started an hour later, the accidental death theory would be very much strengthened."

"Yes," said Sargent, "I'd seen all that. But then how would the clock come in? If he was going to risk being seen going a second time to Benchley's rooms, he might just as well put a match to something inflammable straight away, and not rig up an elaborate device that mightn't have gone off. Besides, where did the clock come from? If he killed Benchley in the heat of a quarrel it couldn't have been premeditated."

"He might have taken it from some undergraduate's rooms," Considine suggested. "I believe he knows a good many Beaufort men, though he did rather air his unfamiliarity with the college yesterday."

"Well, yes, there's an off chance of that," Sargent conceded rather grudgingly. "In that case we must write down Devereux as having had rather an exceptional opportunity. It goes without saying he had a considerable motive, to remove the obstacle to his marriage. He's told a story that, on the face of it, looks like a fake, though at present we can't disprove a single detail of it. His character, on purely hearsay evidence, is vulnerable. On the other hand, we've got one little fact that seems to me to tell heavily in his favour."

"What's that?" asked Considine.

"The will," Sargent replied. "It looks so obviously planted on purpose to be quickly found. But the one man who most certainly wouldn't have planted it is Devereux, because the codicil is deliberately aimed against him. It's especially improbable because he could easily have destroyed the codicil and left the will itself, which is wholly in his favour."

"Isn't it possible he knew about the contents of the will and hadn't been told about the codicil?" asked Considine. "Then he might have hurriedly dumped it in the Bursary unread, thinking he was securing his fiancée's legacy."

"My dear Humphrey, I leave it to you as a psychologist. Imagine you've just murdered your girlfriend's guardian in order to get her, and are planting out a document in order to get her money as well. If you're remaining on the scene of the crime long enough to do that, don't you think you'd risk a moment just to glance over the thing and make sure it did give you what you wanted? No, Humphrey, once again it won't do. If we're going to convict Devereux, we've got to assume Benchley himself put his will in the Bursary. Possible, of course, but odd. There's the point about the key, too. Why should Devereux take the key from Benchley's body? *He* didn't need to get out of college secretly."

"He might have done that on purpose to suggest an outside murderer," said Considine.

"But he wasn't trying to suggest murder," Sargent objected. "His line was accidental death."

"Sorry," said Considine. "Of course it was. All this is beginning to make my head swim. But the upshot seems to be that we're up against it once again."

"I'm afraid so," said Sargent. "Another good case gone wrong. We may be able to piece it together better when we've got some more information. At present the gaps are too big. So we'll go on to the next suspects. Randolph and Nevern. What do we know about them?"

"Nothing at all. Nothing personal, that is. We don't even know
their real names."

"And therefore there's a presumption they're criminals. But a
sufficient crime to account for their giving false names is the theft
of the mummy. It's almost certain they worked that. But it's surely
incredible that they did the murder as well."

"How do you make that out?" asked Considine. "I can't even
see that they could have worked the theft. We saw them take the
mummy back, we saw it in its place again; and directly afterwards
they were debagged and thrown in the river. I should say they couldn't
have stolen the mummy but might have murdered Benchley."

"Oh, no, no, no, Humphrey," expostulated Sargent. "Don't make
them out raving lunatics. I'll explain to you later how they must
have worked the burglary; but as for the murder, it's wildly impossible. They couldn't have killed Benchley when they took the
mummy back; they were only there a matter of seconds. Therefore
your hypothesis means they must have done it the first time, when
they went to fetch the mummy. And you're not going to tell me
they staged the whole rag just to lead the entire pack of undergraduates straight to the scene of the crime, and to get themselves
captured within twenty feet of the body! No, no, Humphrey, try
again."

"Then are you going to rule Randolph and Nevern out altogether?" asked Considine with an air of disappointment.

"As far as the murder goes, yes," replied Sargent. "We shall
come to them again under the next question. For the moment let's
turn our attention to Bonoff. Psychologist forward again."

"Once more," said Considine, "I don't know the man personally. But his utterances in print are sufficient proof that he's got a
violent temper."

"Are you so sure about that?" asked Sargent in a tone of de-
tached speculation. "Were his letters any more violent than
Benchley's own?"

"No," said Considine. "I shouldn't say they were. They were
extraordinarily similar, in fact; there was really nothing to choose
between them. But you mustn't imagine Benchley was always the

gentle modest soul we used to meet in Common Room. I knew him a good deal better than you, I think, and I can assure you he was capable of losing his temper with the best. I fancy Devereux got a taste of it that night. But as a rule he only let fly on purely academic questions, so everyone who didn't come across him inside his professional sphere thought butter wouldn't melt in his mouth. No, if Bonoff is as much like Benchley in temperament as he is in literary style, I'd be far from putting him down incapable of murder. And if he murdered anybody, Benchley would be the man. He'd been fighting him with words for a dozen years, and I don't think either of us believes much in the alleged reconciliation."

"We've got Benchley's own word for it," Sargent pointed out.

"Oh, I don't doubt Benchley was sincere enough," said Considine quickly. "But this Russian hound is a much lower kind of animal. I don't trust him for an instant."

"Come, come, Humphrey," Sargent protested. "Now you're coming down to sentiment. Bonoff on the face of it had better reason to be sincere than Benchley. He won the argument."

"Yes, I suppose that's so," Considine reluctantly agreed. "All the same, I don't trust him. Call it sentimental if you like, but I don't."

"To tell the truth, neither do I," said Sargent. "Still, we can't write down any definite motive against him. But if we accept Devereux's statement that he was in college at all that night, there's a pretty strong case against him."

"There aren't many facts, surely?"

"Not many, but enough. It all turns on the key—or keys. Bonoff didn't come in by the main gate; I'm disposed to take that as established beyond dispute by Collins's evidence. He didn't come by the river. Therefore he must have come by the fellows' garden. He also went out by that way, if we believe Devereux. Now there may have been either one or two keys, because, as we were saying, Van Ditten might have made a duplicate. But suppose for the moment that there was only one. Then at twelve o'clock, when Devereux saw him getting away, that key must have been in Bonoff's possession. But very soon afterwards, when the mummy was stolen, it must have been in the possession of the thieves. Therefore Bonoff must have been in league with them. But then, how did Bonoff get it? Surely only by taking it off Benchley's dead body. So we seem to convict him of being at least accessory to both the burglary and the murder."

"You're building on rather a narrow basis," Considine objected.

"I am," admitted Sargent. "The whole thing wants a lot of checking. And the first point we might try and check is whether the theory will explain Bonoff's getting *into* college. The only way I can see is that somebody let him in by the fellows' gate; and that somebody, since we're not believing in Monitor as an accomplice, could only have been Benchley himself. But that means a secret assignation between Benchley and Bonoff in the middle of the night; and if he and Benchley had secrets between them, which seems incredible to start with, why in the world should they meet in this college of all places and on the night of a commem ball of all times? I think you'll agree we can't swallow the theory till that's explained."

"Weren't you going to try and work it out on the supposition that there was a duplicate key?" asked Considine.

"I don't think that line makes the case much easier," was the reply. "Its main effect is to get rid of the necessity for a compact between Bonoff and the thieves, because they could have got in and out with one key and he out with the other. But we're still left with the problem of how he got in; because if it was necessary for him to take the key from Benchley's body he must have got in without one. So we still have to imagine a secret assignation with Benchley, with all that that implies."

"Then is that the end of the Bonoff trail?"

"I'd be more inclined to say it was the beginning. We must certainly study Bonoff; and in view of this suggestion that Benchley himself let him into college, I propose we look into the history of their relations with one another. That'll be our next job. Meanwhile, let's go on with the catechism. Question six is about the mummy—how was it stolen? Happily, I think we can solve that one straight away."

"Thank Heaven for that," said Considine wearily. "But I confess I don't see how."

"I really don't think there's much room for doubt," said Sargent. "We saw the coffin back in Benchley's rooms after the rag, and Goddard and Devereux saw it there after the fire had actually started. On the other hand, we also saw a coffin answering the description of the Cher yesterday afternoon. It follows that there must have been two coffins, of which one was a sham. Now you inspected both; which was which?"

Considine knitted his brows in the effort of memory to recall the details of the two coffins. "I'm sure," he said at length, "that the one in the punt was genuine. I was so unprepared for its being Benchley's mummy case that I examined it all over to make quite sure. But the one in his rooms was a different matter. It never occurred to me that it could be anything but the real one, and all I looked for was to see that it wasn't damaged. Besides, the light wasn't anything like equal to the daylight on the river. So I suppose I might have been deceived by a good fake."

"There can't be any question that it was a fake," said Sargent; "and I'll take your word it was a good one. Now I think you'll see how the trick was done."

"Well," said Considine, "I suppose the whole rag was organized to cover the substitution of the sham for the real coffin. But I still don't quite see when it was done."

"There's only one time it could have been done," Sargent pointed out. "The only time Randolph and Nevern were out of sight of their pursuers was when they ran down the little path past the fellows' gate, which is concealed by those laurel bushes. They must have had accomplices there—at least two I should say—who had the gate open with a duplicate key, shoved in the dummy and took out the real coffin. It could be done in two ticks—which is about all the time they had."

"But the sham would never have deceived Benchley," Considine objected.

"It wasn't meant to do so for any length of time," replied Sargent. "By deliberately giving themselves up to the mob as they did, Randolph and Nevern probably expected to distract everybody's attention from the mummy for a few minutes; and even

Benchley himself, if he'd only just been woken up, would most likely have done as you did—looked for marks of damage, but not thought of questioning the mummy's identity. Meanwhile the accomplices had time to get the real one away."

"But they didn't get it away," exclaimed Considine. "They only took it half a mile up the Cher and then abandoned it."

"They abandoned the coffin," Sargent corrected him. "But what about the mummy itself?"

"You mean they wanted the mummy without the coffin?" said Considine incredulously.

"There seem to be three possibilities," Sargent answered. "They may, as you say, have wanted the mummy without the coffin, which seems on the face of it highly improbable. Or the coffin may have been empty all the time, and they may have abandoned it in disgust when they discovered the fact. But you say that's impossible, because Benchley would never have bought it empty. The third possibility is the one we've already discussed, that the coffin was used to carry something out of college; and that must mean the body of Benchley, alive or dead, leaving the mummy behind to be burnt."

"But that makes Randolph and Nevern the murderers."

"It does. However, we've already been stumped by the difficulties of the theory that Benchley was taken out in the coffin, so we won't convict them just at present. For the moment, do you agree that mine's the only possible explanation of how the coffin came to be stolen?"

"Yes," admitted Considine. "There doesn't seem to be any escape from it."

"Then who must be responsible for that crime?"

"The only man who could have made the duplicate key. Van Ditten."

"Exactly. And now I'm going to gratify your sense of British citizenship. I'm going to turn that part of it over to the police—the burglary part that is, without a word about the murder. What's more, I'm going to leave them to answer question seven, about the second theft, concerning which we've got nothing at present to go on."

"Far be it from me," said Considine, "to demur to your unex-pected concession to legalism. But why exactly are you being so modest all of a sudden?"

"Because this crime has got to be investigated in Oxford, and you and I won't be here to do it."

"Indeed. Where shall we be?"

"We shall be hot upon the trail, Humphrey mine. In quest of the elusive Bonoff. We're going to the Isle of Wight."

11
THE PROFESSORS

"OXFORD ON A SUNDAY MORNING in the long vacation," said Sargent, as his two-seater car bustled noisily past Christ Church, "must be the best bit of still life outside Burlington House. And now for the great world beyond the cloister," he added, clanking over Folly Bridge. "Two bright and eager youths, leaving alma mater to seek their fortune: what has fate in store for them round the corner?"

"Mutton!" replied Considine briefly, and if he said more his words were drowned in the screech of rusty brakes as the car turned a sudden bend and swept into the midst of a flock of sheep descending Boar's Hill. Sargent, with muttered profanity, threaded his way carefully through them, and had nearly reached the crest before he spoke again.

"And now let's hear how you got on with the force," he said. "I don't seem to have seen you since lunch yesterday, with all this rush."

"Denys," said his companion solemnly, "I must abandon all hope of a criminal career. The sight of a policeman with his helmet off unnerves me completely. I never saw anything so uncanny."

"My poor Humphrey. Were they unkind to you?"

"Not at all. They played the heavy but indulgent father. They treated me as the poor innocent scholar, not fit to be trusted without the supervision of normal, sane human beings."

"Not quite the most dignified role for a great detective, I'm afraid," Sargent sympathized.

"No, it wasn't," agreed Considine. "But we played up to it all right."

"We?" asked Sargent.

"Oh, I thought I ought to get Miss Foley to come with me. You see, it was from their boathouse the coffin was finally stolen."

"You didn't take Miss O'Connor along too?"

"I thought it was rather unnecessary to bother them both."

"Oh, quite unnecessary. Quite. How you brought yourself to endure even one specimen of—what was it?—boot-faced zeal for learning, is beyond me. All right, Humphrey," he went on as Considine began to splutter indignantly, "I know you made a martyr of yourself in a good cause. Go on with what the copper said to you."

"He talked to us more in sorrow than in anger. Had we but called the nearest constable directly the coffin was found, the thieves would certainly have been under lock and key by nightfall. As it was, it might take some days, and would necessarily put extra work on that much-tried body, the Oxford City Police."

"But he expected to catch 'em all right?"

"Oh, yes. He hadn't any doubt of that. I gathered that the governor of Dartmoor might as well start airing a couple of nice cells at once."

"Did he ask any awkward questions? Anything that might have dragged in the murder, I mean?"

"Dear me, no. He didn't ask any questions to speak of, he was much too busy telling me things for my future guidance. Obviously a poor fool like me couldn't tell him anything worth knowing. But he made us take him round to college, and there he got hold of Newton, and put him through it a bit. He took rather kindly to Newton; all those filing cabinets in the Bursary impressed him. Put on quite a different manner: sort of 'as one practical man to another, and let's leave these visionary pedants to their musty parchments.' I'm afraid if he'd ever seen Newton's book on the Sanscrit affinities of the Greek particles he wouldn't have been so respectful."

"Did he discover anything?"

"Nothing now, so far as I could see. He got a description of Randolph and Nevern from the Manciple, confirmed by Goddard and one or two other undergraduates who are still up. And he measured the fellows' gate all over with a tape measure. Then we took him along to the boathouse, and he did much the same thing there. And finally we took him up to the backwater where the punt was found."

"In the canoe?"

"No; in a police car. There turned out to be a lane leading down from the Marston Ferry Road to within about fifty yards of the backwater. We did come across something there. One of those bolt things that drop off motor cars. Sort of objects that must simply rain out of this thing, judging by the noise it's making. My police-man friend thought it important, because he said he didn't sup-pose a motor car went down that lane once in two years; and the nut didn't look as if it had been there more than a day or two."

"And what inference did he draw?"

"My dear Denys, he wasn't going to trust his inferences with a half-wit like me. But I suppose he concluded that Van Ditten, in a motor car, had a rendezvous with his underlings at the backwater on Wednesday night, and that they then handed over the mummy to be taken away by road."

"Or whatever else the coffin contained?"

"Or whatever else it contained. But you can't convince me it didn't contain the mummy."

"Let's be pragmatists, and say it's convenient for the police to believe the mummy was there. We don't want them looking for more modern corpses. Did that finish your afternoon's work? I looked for you in college about tea time, but you hadn't come back."

Considine looked slightly embarrassed. "As a matter of fact," he said, "Miss Foley asked me to go back to Cherwell Edge for tea."

"Oh, Humphrey, Humphrey," Sargent sighed. "That thou shouldst get thee to a nunnery, after all these stern misogynous years. A detective should have no sex-life. It's lucky I'm removing you from the reach of temptation."

"To be perfectly candid, you're not," replied Considine. "If by temp-tation you mean Miss Foley, she's coming to the Isle of Wight too."

"Not to Bembridge? I can't have you vamped under my very eyes."

"No; she's going to stay with Monitor at Seaview, which is a mile or two away. He's taken a big house there for July and is entertaining a mob of undergraduates of both sexes. But I expect we shall see them occasionally, because Daphne Carrothers is one of the party, and she's sure to be coming over our way to see Devereux."

"The plot thickens," exclaimed Sargent, slowing down to cross the narrow bridge at Abingdon. "We seem to be assembling the whole blinking company in the island. Bonoff and Devereux live there; now Monitor and Miss Carrothers roll up; we only want Van Ditten and his gang and then we shall have all the suspects on our doorstep. All but poor old Bloggs, that is. I'm afraid we shan't get him."

"I shouldn't be so sure that even that's impossible," said Considine with a slight smile. "Bloggs in the long vacation undergoes an annual apotheosis. He blossoms out into the head waiter at some hotel or other. But I don't think it's in the Isle of Wight. I believe it's something incredibly classy on a moor or a links or something in Scotland. Still, as you say, even without Bloggs it's very remarkable how all the suspects seem to be converging on the island. I believe Devereux was meaning to travel to-day, so we may bump into him by Portsmouth. There aren't many boats on Sunday."

"We aren't going by Portsmouth," said Sargent. "We're going to Southampton and Cowes. I did a little research myself yesterday afternoon, but I was dining at Worcester; so I haven't had a chance to tell you about it. I went up to the Bodleian and had out the files of the Southampton local papers of last July."

"What did you expect to find in them?"

"I was trying to get on with my idea of studying the early dealings between Benchley and Bonoff. I didn't get much, but enough to help us along a bit. It appears that Bonoff landed at Southampton on the afternoon of July 6th last year, and Benchley, on behalf of the Egypt Association, met him on the quay. There was a photograph of them shaking hands—one of the usual smudgy newspaper things, but I could recognize Benchley."

"What did Bonoff look like?"

"Oh, a pretty unprepossessing sort of scallywag. More or less tallied with Devereux's description, smoked glasses and so on, though I couldn't make out the scar he mentioned. Then there was about half a column about him—most of it stuff we knew already. But there were one or two points we might do well to remember. To start with, he seems to have brought several mummies with him, and one of them was our old friend Pepi I. He was interviewed by one of the local rags, and swanked a good bit about having discovered it. Said it was the oldest royal mummy ever found."

"That's quite true," said Considine. "I remember how excited Benchley was when it was dug up. He didn't give much credit to Bonoff, though. Said the tomb was really found by some young German whose name I've forgotten, and Bonoff just bluffed him out of his claim."

"That I can well believe, from all I've heard of the old ruffian," said Sargent. "Just cast an eye at this signpost as we pass it; I want to make sure we're on the right road for Newbury. We are? Thanks. Well, about the mummies. Bonoff seems to have made the devil of a fuss about the whole lot of them. Had them in his own cabin on the voyage, taking two extra berths for the purpose, and took them up to his room at the hotel where he stayed at Southampton—the Two Leopards. Benchley went to dinner with him there, and they opened the Pepi coffin and inspected the mummy—showed it to the journalists as well."

"That's interesting," Considine commented. "I'd been under the impression that Benchley saw the mummy for the first time when he went down to the Isle of Wight and bought it last week. Did the paper give any description of it?"

"Only routine journalese—'age-old mystery of the royal dead,' 'mystic glamour of old Nile' and all that sort of thing."

"It didn't mention the split skull?"

"Hullo, hullo, are you beginning to weaken on that after all?"

"Not in the least. I'm as certain of it as if I'd seen it myself. I only hoped the paper would have mentioned it explicitly, so as to convince you. I know your idea of evidence is to attach more weight to the word of an uneducated Fleet Street hack then to the solemn statement of the head of a national religion."

"I can cross-examine the hack, and I've only got the high priest's unchecked affidavit," Sargent retorted. "However, the special correspondent of the *Southern Daily Echo* had a soul above post-mortems. Forty centuries were looking down on him from the tops of the pyramids, and he was well away."

"Oh well," said Considine resignedly, "it was hardly to be expected. There'd have been a gold mask over the face anyway, and Bonoff wouldn't have been likely to take that off just to gratify a reporter's curiosity. Did you find out anything else?"

"I'm afraid not," Sargent answered. "But we're going to Southampton to take up the scent there. As far as the notice in the paper went, Bonoff and Benchley seemed to meet on perfectly friendly terms; but naturally they could scarcely say anything else in print. We may hear something different at the hotel. The squabble over Dionysos was going hammer and tongs at the time, you'll remember."

"I do indeed," said Considine. "I wonder if we ought to have gone over the letters to see if the meeting at Southampton made any difference to it."

"I thought of that," said Sargent, "and went through the whole lot in the files of *The Times*. It was really a liberal education to read it all in one. Do you remember in *King Solomon's Mines* where Captain Good addressed the moon with such a flood of classical bad language as only the imagination of a naval officer could conceive of, keeping it up for an hour and a half without once repeating himself? Well, I'm inclined to think that a Professor of Egyptology, Russian or English, could give points to the navy."

"And you don't think personal contact softened their manners at all?"

"On the contrary. They seem to have got even more ferocious; or at any rate Bonoff did. Some of his letters from Russia seemed at times willing to accept Benchley as a fellow human being; but the ones from the Isle of Wight uniformly regard him as a cheese mite—and one from a very cheap and inferior brand of cheese at that."

"Yes, that was my impression from memory," Considine agreed. "I wonder if there was a personal quarrel at Southampton to put his back up even more?"

"That's one of the things we've got to look into," said Sargent, glancing up at another signpost. "Winchester—eight miles; and Southampton is about thirteen beyond that. We ought to be there in time for lunch. Do you mind if I propose you for Internal Bursar in place of Benchley? Mainwaring and Lake are intriguing to push in Gaunt, who doesn't know Château Lafite from Worcester Sauce."

The conversation swung with alacrity to college shop, and continued on that all-absorbing topic until the car drew up before the Two Leopards Hotel, Southampton, at a quarter to one o'clock.

Seated in a bleak and deserted dining-room, hung with the corpses, behind dirty glass, of large and nondescript fish, Sargent contemplated the menu with an air of cheerless resignation. "But what went ye out into the wilderness for to see?" he announced. "You will be pleased to learn, Humphrey, that your Sabbath day's journey across southern England is to be rewarded with a choice between cold roast beef and cold ham, to be followed either by apple tart or by apricots and custard. Think carefully. This *embarras de richesse* precludes a hasty decision."

"You're too sybaritic, Denys," rejoined Considine. "What could be better than the roast beef of old England?"

"And the canned fruit of new California?" suggested Sargent. "Or shall we postpone that anxious problem? Waiter, we will both partake of your roast beef; and then we should like to speak a word with your exemplar."

"My what, sir?"

"Your model; your pattern; the master of your craft; the controller of your destinies; the snapper-up, I have no doubt, of your less considered trifles. In a word, with the head waiter."

"You don't do that sort of thing very well, Denys," remarked Considine dispassionately, as the waiter went in search of his superior.

"Sorry, Humphrey," Sargent replied. "My heart is far away; that stuffed cod reminds me so poignantly of a dear maiden aunt, long since called to higher service. I am but gambolling to hide my desolation. But perhaps you are right. Let us treat this dignitary with appropriate decorum." He turned to the approaching head waiter.

"Good morning, waiter," he said. "I was going to ask your advice about the wine list. A friend of mine who stayed here a year ago told me you had a particularly excellent red wine. Perhaps you remember his visit and can tell me what he drank. His name was Professor Bonoff."

"Professor Bonoff?" said the head waiter rather stiffly. "That would be the Russian gentleman. It's rather a long time ago, sir, since he was here. But I expect he had the Australian Burgundy— number five on the list, sir. It's what we always recommend to strangers. I'll fetch you a bottle myself, sir." And he was away without waiting for a reply.

Considine broke into a broad grin at the expression of dismay on his companion's face. "This is what I call real poetic justice," he said. "The disingenuous investigator is hoist with his own petard. I'm going to have some beer; I should hate to deprive you of one drop of your chosen beverage. You shall support the British Empire all by yourself."

"No, but really, Humphrey," expostulated Sargent, "this isn't a joking matter. My constitution won't stand it—after two years of the Benchley régime at Beaufort, too. You really must swallow your share. Oh, lord, here comes the potion."

"Now be a little man, Denys," said Considine, as the head waiter hurried up, wielding the flagon rather like a churn, and proceeded to fill two glasses.

"Will you have some yourself, waiter?" said Sargent with a desperate inspiration, noticing the hopeful ruddiness of the head waiter's nose.

"Well, sir," was the reply, "it's very unusual, sir; most unusual, I should say." He looked furtively round the empty dining room. "But as we're so quiet to-day—well, thank you very much, sir." Thirst overcame professional etiquette; he filled a third glass and drank with a gusto in strong contrast with Sargent's wry-mouthed sips.

With one eye on the door through which another customer or, worse still, the manager might appear, but standing in such an attitude as to shield the illicit glass from view, he began to unbend in conversation.

"I'm surprised that Professor Bonoff recommended anything to do with this hotel, sir," he said.

"Indeed," said Sargent. "How was that? Did you have a row with him? He didn't tell me anything about it."

"Well, sir, seeing as he's a friend of yours—" began the waiter diffidently.

"Oh, say what you like about him," said Sargent hastily. "It's really Professor Benchley who was our friend; he came to dine with Professor Bonoff here; but I didn't suppose you'd remember his name."

"Would that be the gentleman with the white beard?" asked the waiter. "Something big at Oxford college, wasn't he, sir?"

"Yes, that's the man," confirmed Considine. "Perhaps you saw in the papers that he was accidentally burnt to death last week."

"Indeed, sir, I'm very sorry to hear it," the waiter replied. "He seemed a very pleasant gentleman, if I may say so. But the foreigner, sir—he was a queer one if you like."

"What do you mean by queer?"

"Well, sir, partly it was the queer things he brought with him. Lot of them Egyptian mummies and whatnot."

"Ah, but that's his trade, you know. He's quite a famous authority on ancient Egypt."

"Still," said the waiter, "it seems an odd thing to carry about with you in your luggage, just as you and I might take a portmanteau. I always thought them things was kept in museums like. But this Professor Bonoff, he had three or four of them, and he wouldn't let 'em out of his sight, not for a moment 'e wouldn't. Couldn't 'ave made more fuss about them, not if they was 'uman."

"So they are, you know," commented Considine. "They've often got real bodies inside them."

"Yes, sir, so I 'ave been informed. Fair gave some of us the creeps it did. We 'ad a lot of trouble with some of the chambermaids about sleeping under the same roof with them. Said they was 'aunted and would bring bad luck. But that foreign professor, 'e fair gloated over them. Took a private sitting-room and 'ad 'em all out and stuck 'em up round the walls."

"You don't mean he had the mummies out of their coffins!" exclaimed Considine.

"Oh, no, sir, not the corpses so to speak. But he 'ad them all out of the packing cases what they came off the boat in, and then he got a lot of young chaps from the papers to come and look at them and take photographs."

"Was Dr. Benchley with him then?"

"Dr. Benchley? Oh, your friend with the white beard, sir. Yes, 'e were there; arrived with the Russian gentleman and stayed to dinner. I took it up to them myself."

"Did they seem to get on well together?"

"Well, sir, I didn't understand anything they were saying, such long words they used an' all. But it didn't seem to me a very friendly sort of party so to speak. They was arguin' something chronic; both talkin' at once, and as soon as one of them said anything the other contradicted it. And the nasty looks they give each other now and then!"

"Did Dr. Benchley stay long after dinner?"

"Well, sir, that's a thing I can't rightly remember, bein' as how it's a year ago an' all. An' then the queer things that happened in the night; I don't suppose anybody noticed what time your friend went home. 'E was gone before the foreign gentleman started to get so excited, that's all I can say."

"What did he get excited about?"

"If you ask me, sir, he got excited about his own imagination. Of course, I was in bed and asleep long before; I only 'eard about all the to-do in the morning. But it seems that this professor, in the middle of the night he suddenly starts ringing his bell like a lunatic and turning out all the night staff and complaining about his bed. Said he'd found a bug in it, if you please. I'm not sure that weren't the queerest thing of all. Of course there ain't any bugs in our beds, though you never know what one of these Bolshies mightn't 'ave brought in in his own clothes. But what I mean to say is, even supposing there was a bug, don't you think it's a most unusual thing for a foreigner to object to?"

"Most unusual," agreed Sargent gravely, while Considine turned away to hide his smile. "But what did he do about it?"

"Do about it? He fair raised hell about it, if you'll pardon the strong language, sir. Made the night porter get the manager out of bed, and talked to him as if he was dirt. Nothing would content my lord but that he should clear out of the hotel then and there, at about three o'clock in the morning it was. He got a taxi and made the driver and the night porter lug all his fancy contraptions, mummies and all, down to it, and he paid his bill and drove off to the Wessex on the spot. If you want bugs in your bed, the Wessex is the place to get 'em; but nobody told 'im that. Too pleased to get rid of 'im, they was. Excuse me, sir. There's another party coming in; I must go and attend to them. Thank you very much, sir."

"Curious story," said Considine when the head waiter had withdrawn. "Bonoff doesn't seem to increase in charm as our acquaintance with him develops. But I'm afraid we haven't gleaned any new facts, have we?"

"Nothing we can get much grip on," Sargent agreed. "We've confirmed, of course, that there was a good deal of personal acerbity even then. I wish we could make sure about the mummy."

"What do you expect to discover here about the mummy?" asked Considine.

"I should like to find someone who actually saw that cloven skull," Sargent replied.

"My dear Denys," said Considine wearily, "you'd much better take that point on trust from my cuneiform tablet. In any case nobody would have seen whether the skull was cloven or not. The embalmers would have pieced it together somehow, and then the whole would have been covered over with a gold mask."

"Nevertheless I should like to find an eyewitness," said Sargent obstinately. "If you don't think you can trace any more fragments of apple among your stewed cloves, I propose we go and seek out the manager."

"I am in your hands," replied Considine. "But I don't recommend you to introduce yourself as a friend of Bonoff's."

The manager of the Two Leopards received the inquiries courteously, but seemed decidedly puzzled at Sargent's explanation of their business. "You say you represent the estate of the late Dr.

Peter Benchley," he said slowly. "I'm sorry if my memory has tricked me, but for the moment I can't recall that I ever met the gentleman."

"No," said Sargent. "I hardly expected the name would be familiar to you. The point that has arisen, and on which we should like to consult you, is rather an unusual one. May I give you a short account of the facts, and will you take it from me that it all leads up to something in which you are not unconcerned?"

"Go ahead," said the manager.

"The position is this," said Sargent. "Dr. Peter Benchley, who died last week in rather unusual circumstances, was the most eminent English authority on ancient Egypt."

"The most eminent in the world," interpolated Considine loyally.

"My colleague was one of his greatest admirers," Sargent explained. "However, his professional eminence is not the point at issue. Just before his death he purchased for a large sum of money a certain Egyptian mummy, which, if genuine, was enormously valuable. The seller was a Russian, a person called Bonoff."

The manager sat up suddenly. "I know that name at any rate," he said; "and I may as well say it's not one I'm particularly fond of."

"Neither are we," Sargent reassured him. "In fact, what I'm now going to say I'd rather not say to any friend of Professor Bonoff's. It might, I fear, be technically actionable."

"You can slander the skunk as much as you like, for all I care," said the manager. "I shan't be taking him into my confidence just yet."

"Very well," Sargent went on. "Strictly between ourselves, then, we have some reason to suppose that this mummy, sold by Bonoff to our late friend, may have been tampered with while in his possession."

The manager looked more and more grim. "I should think it pretty certain to have been tampered with," he said. "I wouldn't buy a bag of acid drops from the swine without a solicitor present. And a policeman," he added as an afterthought.

"We can't go so far as to bring a definite allegation of fraud," said Sargent cautiously. "But Mr. Considine, who is something of an expert in these things himself, thinks that the mummy we have found among Dr. Benchley's effects doesn't quite tally with the one that Bonoff is supposed to have sold him. I may say that the Bonoff mummy is exceedingly well known among connoisseurs. Now I must apologize for taking up so much of your time, Mr.—"

"Manders," supplied the manager.

"Mr. Manders, but I've now got to the point where you and your hotel come in. It seems that this Bonoff, who arrived in England for the first time about a year ago, came straight to you."

"He did," said Manders shortly.

"And that he brought a number of mummies with him, and held a sort of exhibition of them in his room."

Manders nodded in confirmation.

"If we are correctly informed, the press were admitted, and our friend Dr. Benchley was also present. He was the white-bearded, bald man whom you may have noticed."

"I was told that an English professor came to see the Bolshie," Manders agreed. "I didn't see him myself."

"Well, that's not important," Sargent went on. "It's the mummies we're interested in at present. Could you tell us about them?"

"Not very much, I'm afraid," said Manders. "I didn't see them myself—at least, not till they were going away. I was out when this Bonoff arrived, and didn't get back till late at night. But the swine had me out of bed in the small hours of the morning with some perfectly fantastic complaint." With much bitterness he launched out into the story that Sargent and Considine had already heard from the head waiter.

"I see," said Sargent, when Manders had subsided into muttered maledictions. "He does seem to have treated you pretty scurvily. We've seen enough of your hotel to know how absurd such charges must be. But it's a pity you didn't actually see the mummies, so that we could know if there had been a fraud."

"Oh, he was a fraud all right," said Manders with decision. "I know a crook when I see one."

"Well, yes," Sargent agreed patiently. "I expect he's all you say, though neither of us has ever met him in the flesh. But it's really a question of getting evidence to convict him on."

"I'll get the evidence for you," said Manders grimly. He pressed a bell, and to the boy in buttons who answered it gave the order: "Henry, just see if Mr. Dark is in the hotel, and if he is ask him if he can spare me a minute. Dark," he continued as the boy went on his errand, "is the chief reporter of the local paper, and generally comes in here for lunch. He's sure to have been the man that did the story about the mummies; in fact I remember discussing the whole thing with him at the time. He thought—oh, good morning, Dark," he broke off as a small sandy-haired man entered the room. "These are Mr. Considine and Mr. Sargent, of Oxford. They're on the track of that lousy Russian bastard who said there were bugs in my beds."

"Plain-clothes men?" asked Dark, with the pathetic hopefulness of the small provincial journalist, ever compelled, for a lack of better copy, to "splash" the election of a new alderman or the bankruptcy of a local greengrocer.

"Plain enough," replied Sargent, smiling at his eagerness, "at any rate in my case, though perhaps Mr. Considine's socks are worthy of a more appreciative label. But not, I'm afraid, policemen. We're making quite a private inquiry."

"Sorry," said Dark, obviously disappointed. "I'm afraid I've got nothing in the divorce court line. He didn't bring a woman with him. Wouldn't have found it easy to get one to come either. Looked like a cross-eyed monkey."

"We're even less romantic than that, I fear," Sargent warned him. "We're not avenging the domestic sanctities of an outraged Madame Bonoff. Did you happen to meet a certain Dr. Benchley, who came to see Professor Bonoff's mummies when he was here? White-bearded and bald?"

"Yes," replied Dark. "I remember him quite well. One of the real highbrows, he seemed; talked to Monkey-face as if he knew as much about mummies as he did himself. Is he wanted too?"

"I'm sorry to say that Dr. Benchley is dead," Sargent answered. "Mr. Considine is the executor of his will, and I am his legal adviser." He went on to repeat to the reporter the account of the reason for their inquiries that he had just given to the manager. "Now, Mr. Dark, we should be very grateful to you if you could tell us about the mummies, which I understand you were able to examine pretty closely."

The little journalist made a visible effort to concentrate his memory and assumed an expression obviously intended to suggest mature Egyptological wisdom. It is unprofessional to admit complete ignorance of any branch of learning. "Yes," he said, "the Professor showed me the mummies. I can't say I remember every detail; it's such a long time ago. But what exactly did you want to know about them?"

Considine took up the examination. "There were definitely more mummies than one?" he asked.

"Yes," replied Dark. "There were at least three; might have been four; I can't be quite sure which."

"And did you see inside the coffins?"

"Professor Bonoff only opened one of them while the press was there. I saw inside that."

"Was that, do you know, the mummy of King Pepi I, of the Sixth Dynasty?"

"Ah, that I can't be sure of. It was some such name. And it was certainly the prize mummy of the collection. The professor with the beard got frightfully excited about it, and Professor Bonoff told us it was the oldest mummy in the world. Five thousand years old, he said it was."

"I think that must be the one we're interested in," said Considine. "Now, did Professor Bonoff take the lid off that coffin?"

"He did."

"And did you see the inside?"

"Yes."

"Well, what did it contain?"

"It contained the mummy, of course. It looked like a skeleton all wrapped up in musty bandages. Then there were a lot of rings and jewels and things, and some little ornaments that looked like beetles."

"Scarabs," Considine confirmed. "But didn't you notice anything unusual about it?"

"Well—er—I'm not quite sure. Of course, I'm not a specialist in that sort of mummies."

"I don't mean anything unusual about it as a mummy. But was it in any way curious as a corpse?"

"It was terribly shrunken and dried up, if that's what you mean. But it struck me that being so old would account for that."

"Yes, of course, of course." Considine, though still resolved to avoid leading questions, was becoming exasperated with the little man's pompous enunciations of the obvious. "But was there any sign of abnormal formation? Anything about the head for instance?"

Dark shook his own head in negation. "No," he said. "I couldn't see that. The face was all covered up with a sort of mask made of gold. Must have been tremendously valuable if it was real."

"And didn't Professor Bonoff take the mask off?"

"Not while I was there, I'm afraid."

Considine tried another tack. "I wonder," he said, "if you remember what Dr. Benchley thought about it. I expect he went over the mummy pretty carefully. Didn't he look under the mask?"

Dark thought for a moment. "I can't truthfully say I remember a little detail like that," he said at length. "I should think probably he did look there, because he went over every inch of the body with a little magnifying glass, and took a lot of notes. He was still doing it when I went away."

"When was that?" Sargent put in.

"Let me see now. The story would have been going on the home page, which is made up at ten o'clock. So I should think I must have come away somewhere about nine."

Sargent jotted down the time in a small notebook in which he had been following the examination, and Considine resumed his questions.

"Did you get any idea," he asked, "what Dr. Benchley thought about it—I mean, whether the mummy was genuine or not?"

"He was a bit stand-offish about it," replied Dark. "I certainly got the impression he'd have picked a hole in it if he could, and that's why he was so fussy with his little glass and all that. But he admitted it was the real thing in the end. In fact, he was the one who gave me the bit I used in my story, about its being the oldest mummy in the world."

"But you don't think he liked giving Professor Bonoff credit for the discovery?" asked Sargent.

"I don't think he'd have liked giving him anything, except perhaps a dose of poison. I never saw two men who seemed to love each other less than those two professors. Not that they were rude, exactly. But the English one kept making sort of chilly vinegary remarks, and the Russian was just crowing over him all the time about his precious mummy. You know what those ginger-headed men can be like when they get really conceited and showing off. He'd have put an oyster's back up, that Bolshie would."

"You think red hair goes with an irritating manner?" inquired Sargent casually.

"Well, perhaps I'm exaggerating a bit," Dark admitted. "I've just been writing an article on 'Do red-headed men make good husbands?' for Pearl Peri the film star to sign, and perhaps it's got on my brain for the time being. Not that it would matter in any case with this Russian, because it wasn't his own hair. He was wearing a wig."

"A wig!" exclaimed Sargent and Considine together.

"Yes, it was a wig all right. It kept getting crooked and he had to shove it straight again. I thought he was got up to look much younger than he really was. Foreigners are often touchy about their appearance, you know, and I shouldn't be surprised if this one fancied himself as a bit of a gay dog."

"Those smoked glasses he was wearing in your photograph scarcely seem to go with the part," Sargent objected.

"Oh, you've seen the picture in the *Echo*," said Dark with obvious pleasure. "I remember he had them on in that. But he didn't wear them indoors. Might have been better if he had; he'd have looked less like the back of a bus."

"Well, you've seen him and we haven't," said Sargent amiably. "It's been most kind of you, Mr. Dark, to give up your time to telling us all this. We're extremely grateful to you."

"Don't mention it," said the journalist, and then, professional zeal welling up once more, "but you'll let me have the story, won't you, if anything comes of it?"

"You shall be the first to be informed," Sargent replied, and turned to take leave of Manders as Dark withdrew towards the dining-room. "We're no less grateful to you, Mr. Manders," he continued, "and I hope we shall be able to avenge you on Professor Bonoff. And now we must be off. We've got an urgent engagement on the other side of town. By the way, what time does your night porter come on duty?"

"Ten o'clock is his regular time," answered the manager.

"And when Bonoff left he'd have been the only member of the staff awake?"

"Except me," was the reply, with a new grimace of resentment.

"Ah, I think that may be important. Well, good bye, Mr. Manders, and again many thanks."

"What's our urgent engagement?" asked Considine as they took their places in the car.

"You are now, my dear Humphrey, going to show the well-known adaptability—may I say elasticity?—of the archaeological pioneer. You are going to eat a second luncheon at the Wessex Hotel. You are allowed three guesses at the contents of the menu."

Ten minutes later they were interrogating a waiter of the Wessex as to the resources of its cuisine.

"There's cold roast beef, sir," was the reply. "And there's some nice 'am. And after that, will you have rhubarb tart or peaches and custard?"

12
THE LANDLADY

"You see, sir, it's like this," said Mrs. Bunny, clearing two wet bathing dresses and a wireless accumulator from the kitchen table to make room for the tin of steaming rolls that she had just extracted from the oven. "I simply couldn't make ends meet with less than eight children. The more you have the easier the work is in my line of business. Isn't that true, Mr. Considine? Now, Bunny, being a sailor, has probably got dozens of black piccaninnies in the Fiji Islands or somewhere, though he's shy of telling me about them. But what I always says to him is that if he could let me have a few of them to help with the lobsters in the season he's welcome to all his adventures. That's what I say, sir; don't you think I'm right?"

"Well, of course, Mrs. Bunny," said Sargent, "you do shed rather a new light on economics. But then of course not all children, even Fijians, would be quite so resourceful as your little flock."

"No, sir, and that's a fact, they wouldn't; not if they'd been brought up by the sort of black hussies Bunny would pick up with. What's that, Bunny? You picked up with me? Why, so you did, but I'm the exception. I weigh twenty stone, and you can't put it across me like you can your fancy ladies in the bead petticoats. That's why my children are a credit to the Island. No, I don't mean you, Freddie, nor you, Rose; I mean the ones that aren't here. Now look at yesterday, sir. There was seventeen sharras over from Ryde and Sandown, and the whole lot came in here for prawn and lobster teas in the garden. I reckon Effie must have cooked about five hundred gallons of tea; there was a hundred and two lobsters to cut up

154

and Lord knows how many bushels of prawns to boil; the twins did that. We even ran out of tables, and Harry pulled down the old toolshed and knocked the bits into two quite good little tables in half an hour. Now where should I have been if I hadn't had plenty of children, I ask you? Why, I should have had to hire foreigners from London."

Sargent and Considine had now been established nearly a week at Flossington House and Tea Garden. This imposing title covered the rather less imposing home of Edward Bunny, former Petty Officer in the Royal Navy, and now living in very strenuous retirement in the tiny village of Lane End, near Bembridge. Flossington House, the winter residence of the Bunny family, was during the summer months surrendered to a fluctuating number of holiday makers, while the Bunnys bestowed themselves nightly in two corrugated iron sheds at the end of the kitchen garden. No visitor had ever penetrated the secrets of these mysterious structures, either of which would seem to the casual eye more than taxed to accommodate even the gargantuan bulk of Mrs. Bunny alone. The kitchen, on the other hand, was the constant rendezvous not only of the temporary inhabitants of the house itself, but of any visitor to the village who wanted to consult the time-table, use the telephone, get a fishing net mended, borrow a bicycle, ask advice about tides or currents, buy Mrs. Bunny's homemade bread, listen to Bunny's incredible stories of his exploits on a submarine against Chinese pirates, or merely bask in the exhilarating company of the most ramshackle, resourceful, merry and openhearted family in the Isle of Wight. Mrs. Bunny's kitchen would have shocked a Ministry of Health inspector to the point of instant resignation. It measured about ten feet by ten and seldom contained less than five children in addition to Mrs. Bunny herself and such visitors as might have dropped in for half an hour's badinage. The stove would be something more than busy all day long, containing simultaneously a sirloin of beef, three dozen rolls, a large sultana pudding and a bathing dress left by a visitor to dry. The upper surface of the stove would be laden with saucepans containing all manner of comestibles, not to mention a pot of glue required by Freddy for some obscure carpentering operation on which he was engaged in one corner of the room. On the table would be an indescribable confusion of impedimenta relating to every branch of Bunny life. Fishing bait, wireless accessories, a gardener's trowel, a partly dissected clock, a plate of lights for the cat, a lawn-tennis racket waiting to be restrung by Bunny, were all piled into one inextricable heap with the day's fish, meat, vegetables and fruit, and surmounted by two young Bunnys sprawling in an amiable struggle for the possession of a piece of toffee. On a floor littered with the combined debris of a bakehouse, a nursery and a workshop, two dogs and a cat prowled seeking, and finding, what they might devour.

Nobody, however, came to stay at the Warren, as Flossington House was disrespectfully called on the beach, who set much store by the more pedantic standards of regularity and order. Even Considine, with his precise system of archaeological research, had soon discovered that here his principles would not apply. What matter that the butter was for the moment concealed beneath Bradshaw and the blacking. Mrs. Bunny knew exactly where it was, and would lay her hand on it the moment it was needed. Why bother if in the meantime a dish of strawberries and a tin of paraffin were precariously added to the pile? The whole was under the direction of an unruffled and dominant mind, and all would be well.

At the present moment the kitchen was comparatively empty, containing no more than Bunny, his wife, two of their eight children, and their two guests from Oxford. Sargent during his short stay had developed a fascinated interest in his hostess's ebullient fecundity, and had now been drawing her into this discourse on its economic disadvantages. He chuckled happily at the scorn with which she envisaged the employment of London waitresses in the Flossington Tea Gardens—otherwise her twenty-foot square back lawn.

"So you're working up the population of Lane End with the patriotic motive of preventing the importation of foreign labour," he said. "Doesn't it make your island blood boil to have two aliens like Mr. Considine and me about the place?"

"Now get on, sir. You mustn't make fun of me. You know I don't mean the visitors. Besides, I'm not the one to talk; I married a foreigner myself. Bunny's a Portsmouth man, you know; he hasn't lived in the island more than about twenty years."

"Speaking of foreigners," said Sargent, "have you heard any more of Professor Bonoff?"

"No, sir, not a word. He seems to have shut himself up altogether. But then he often does that, you know. One week he'll be down on the beach every day, playing with the children as if he were their uncle, and the next he'll go back into his shell and never show his nose outside the house for ten days on end. I don't know what he does inside, but they tell awful stories about him in the village."

"What sort of stories?" asked Considine. "They don't suggest he's a criminal, do they?"

"Oh dear, no, sir. What an idea!" Mrs. Bunny shook with horror. "Professor Bonoff is a very nice gentleman, queer as he is in some of his ways. Everybody likes him. It's just old wives' tales they tell about him in the village."

"Yes, but what are the old wives saying?" Considine persisted.

"Well, it's all because of those Egyptian monkeys he keeps," said Mrs. Bunny. "No, not monkeys, I know that isn't the right word, but it's something like that. Yes, mummies, that's it, I knew it was one of those learned words. Well, what they say in the village is that those mummies are all full of dead corpses."

"So they are, you know," put in Considine mildly. "That's what a mummy is—it's the embalmed body of an ancient Egyptian."

"Lord, is that so, sir? I thought they were just statues like. But down in the village they say Professor Bonoff does all sorts of magic with them, and that that's what he's doing when he shuts himself up in the house—calling up ghosts and devils and suchlike. Not that I believe in any of it, of course, but that's what they say. And even if it was true I shouldn't care; it would take a pretty hefty ghost to put it across me, now wouldn't it, sir?" and Mrs. Bunny, squaring her massive shoulders in cheerful solidity before the kitchen fire, looked indeed a figure such as an unsubstantial spectre might hesitate to confront.

"But do you think anything unusual goes on in his house?" inquired Sargent.

"Lord bless you, no, sir," replied Mrs. Bunny with decision. "Clever people are always a bit queer, and when a gentleman's a professor and a foreigner at the same time, what are you to expect. I won't say he isn't a bit cracked, but he's as harmless as you could wish. Everybody likes him."

"Well, of course Mr. Considine and I know how cracked dons always are," said Sargent. "But were there any special symptoms in this case? Any unusual kind of straw in the hair, I mean?"

"Now you're laughing at me again, sir," said Mrs. Bunny good-humouredly. "Everybody pulls my leg; it's lucky it's a good solid one or they'd have had it off long ago. But it's funny you should mention his hair, because he hasn't got any. He wears a wig."

"So we heard. Then you spotted it wasn't his own hair too?"

"Spotted it, sir? I should just think we did. We couldn't help it. The first thing the professor did when he got here, he went out for a bathe, and of course his wig got washed away."

"That must have been a nasty jar for him," Sargent laughed. "What did he do then?"

"What does everybody in Lane End do when things go wrong? Come and see Mother Bunny, of course. They make fun of me, but this is where they all turn up sooner or later."

"And were you able to rise to the occasion?"

"Well, what do you think, sir? Can't we generally fix things up? As a matter of fact, it was easy. I just took a pair of scissors and cut off a few yards of Rose's hair, and Bunny made it into as nice a wig as you could ask for. It made the professor look a different man."

"That would certainly be an improvement," said Sargent drily; "at any rate, judging from the photograph I saw. But Bunny seems to be a man of infinite accomplishments. I didn't know wig-making was part of a petty officer's training."

"Everything's part of a naval training, sir." Bunny, looking up from his mending of a shrimp-net, joined in the conversation for the first time. "But I happened to be ship's barber in H.M.S. *Thisbe*."

"Still," objected Considine, "the ship's barber surely doesn't have to make wigs for the crew?"

"Ah," said Bunny, "but you ought to have known Admiral Deephurst, sir. A most particular officer he was about his personal appearance. Always had a looking glass and a brush and comb on the bridge, and went into the battle of Jutland in mess uniform, because we were engaged at dinner time. He refused to sail without a properly trained barber on board to attend to his hair, and so I was sent to a hairdresser's shop ashore to learn the trade. And I learnt wig-making with the rest of it."

"I see," said Sargent. "Then Professor Bonoff is walking round in poor Rose's hair?"

"Oh, no, sir," Mrs. Bunny explained. "That was only a temporary wig. He didn't like the colour of it as a permanency. So directly it was finished he put it on and went off to Ryde to get another one made. In fact he got two, one carrotty and one ginger. He wears them every other day. He says he doesn't much mind what shade his hair is, so long as it's red; but he couldn't wear Rose's yellow all his life. But whenever he meets Rose in the street he always bows and takes his wig off to her."

"Then he's not shy about it? He seems rather a mixture of opposites—so frank about the wig, and yet so retiring about his domestic life. Doesn't anybody ever go inside his house? I suppose he has servants?"

"No, he lives there all by himself—when he is there, that is. Does his own cooking and everything. My twins go down once a week and tidy up the house for him, but that's all he ever has done."

"And do they get attacked by the ghosts?"

"Now sir, don't you go worrying about ghosts. Ghosts just daren't tackle the Bunny family. Elsie and Marjory have been going there every Saturday morning for more than a year, and they've never seen anything worse than the professor himself. Not that he isn't enough to frighten you into fits, till you get to know him."

"Does he let them play about with his mummies?"

"Well, he's rather particular about all those things," Mrs. Bunny answered. "They're all kept in one big room—it used to be an artist's studio before the professor came—and the twins aren't allowed in when he isn't there to keep an eye on them. When he's away that room's always locked up. But they've got a key of the front door and go in and out of the rest of the house as they like."

"Then he isn't always here?" Sargent asked.

"Oh dear, no sir. He's hardly ever here. He stayed for several months when he first came; but since then he's only been now and then for a few weeks at a time. He just comes and goes without telling anyone, and the first we hear of it, as like as not, is when the twins go in on Saturday morning and find he isn't there. Then he may disappear for two or three months and turn up again just when nobody's expecting him."

"Doesn't he ever have any visitors?"

"He's only had one that I know of, all the time he's lived here. That was about a fortnight ago. Another professor it was, a gentleman with a white beard."

"You saw him then?"

"Yes, he came here on his way to Professor Bonoff's house to ask where it was. As a matter of fact Professor Bonoff had the twins down specially that day, to take him some lobsters and lay the table for dinner for him and the other professor. Otherwise we should never have known he was at home even; he'd been away since April and nobody saw him come back."

"And did the twins wait on them at dinner?"

"No; he didn't want them. He just rang up to say that they were to take in two lobsters and some salad and one or two other things, and lay the table and come away again. I asked would he like them to wait at table, but he said no, he had some very private things to talk about to the other professor."

"He's not such a hermit as to dispense with the telephone, then?"

"Why, I never thought of that," exclaimed Mrs. Bunny, obviously taken by surprise. "I always tell people mine's the only telephone in Lane End; it's good for the tea gardens, you know. Elsie!

Marjory!" She went to the window and called to her two fourteen-year-old daughters, who were busy in the garden setting out piles of prawns on the rickety little tea tables. They came running in to the kitchen, their pleasantly bucolic faces split from ear to ear by the grin that was the fixed expression of all the younger generation of the house of Bunny.

"Yes, Mother!" they exclaimed together.

"Has the professor got a telephone down at his house?" asked their parent with some suggestion of anxiety.

"He hadn't up to last Saturday," replied Elsie, to which Marjory added: "Unless it's in the monkey-room, where we're not allowed to go."

"That's all right, then," said Mrs. Bunny with a sigh of relief. "It gave me quite a turn. Not that the professor is ever likely to open up serving crabs to the sharra parties; but somehow it wouldn't be the same thing if we couldn't say ours was the only one in the village. He must have rung up from the station that afternoon when you went down with the lobsters. Did you go in the mummy room that day?"

"Did we, Elsie?" asked Marjory.

"No, don't you remember?" rejoined her sister. "The professor was locked up there himself."

"Oh, yes," Marjory took up the tale; "and he shouted to us that he was very busy and mustn't be disturbed."

"And we were to lay the table, and then go and get two bottles of beer from the Dab and Flounder," Elsie went on.

"Was that after Professor Benchley arrived?" asked Sargent.

"No, I don't think so," Marjory answered. "At least, when we were coming home we met an old gentleman with a white beard who asked if he was going the right way to Pussyholme—that's the name of the professor's house."

"So we thought that must be the friend he was expecting to supper," Elsie chimed in.

"And so it was," confirmed Marjory, "because we saw him coming away in the morning on his way to the station."

"With Professor Bonoff?" inquired Considine.

"No; by himself," Elsie replied. It seemed the twins always spoke alternately, and hence a question addressed to the one was generally answered by the other. "I don't know when the professor went away."

"Oh, he did go away then?" said Sargent.

"Well, he wasn't there when we went down the next Saturday," answered Marjory.

"Besides, we saw him coming back on the sharra from Ryde last week," Elsie pointed out.

"He'd been to London too," added Marjory, "because last Saturday, when we were clearing up, there was an *Evening News* lying about in the hall."

"You can't get it in the Island," Elsie explained.

"There was a lovely serial in it," put in Marjory. "It left off at a most exciting point, where the crook was holding the girl's head down over the rocks, with sharks waiting for her at the bottom."

"And now we shall never know if he dropped her or not," lamented Elsie.

"Quite like a college meeting, isn't it, Humphrey?" Sargent commented with an ironic smile. "I should think the island red-herring fisheries could compete even with Oxford."

"Oh, no, sir," protested Marjory. "You can't get herrings here. But there are plenty of mackerel."

"Well," said Sargent, "the particular fish we're after is still Professor Bonoff. Do you remember what day it was he came back from London?"

"Thursday." "Friday." "Saturday." The twins and their mother all spoke simultaneously and then paused to reflect.

"It couldn't have been Saturday, Mother," Elsie pointed out, "because he was there when we went down to see to the house."

"And it wasn't Thursday," said Marjory, "because that's early closing day at Sandown, and we were too busy serving teas to have been out in the village when the sharra from Ryde got in."

"Then it must have been Friday," concluded all three together.

"Quite a little model of logical demonstration," commented Considine.

"Makes you think twice, sir, before you let yourself get run in by the police," put in Bunny, "now that they have women on the jury. But as a matter of fact it *was* Friday; I remember it myself."

"Now you be quiet, Father," his wife admonished him. "You're the only one that's likely to get run in here, always drinking after hours at the Dab and Flounder."

"Now there's where you're wrong," replied Bunny. "I know the law—island law, that is. I always make a point of not touching a drop after closing time till the policeman's stood the first drink."

"Anyhow, you're all safe for to-night," said Elsie. "The policeman's away."

"He caught a poacher in Mr. Devereux's grounds," explained Marjory.

"And we met him this morning taking him into Sandown."

"And he said he'd have to stay and give evidence."

"And if I know Willie Mursel he'll make an excuse to stay there till Monday," added Elsie.

"Because there's a housemaid in a boarding house there that goes with him to the pictures," Marjory completed the tale.

"And so Lane End is a self-governing community till then," remarked Sargent. "Aren't you afraid of an outbreak of Bolshevism?"

"Now there you go again, sir," exclaimed Mrs. Bunny. "I believe you don't take us seriously."

"Dear Mrs. Bunny," replied Sargent, "we take your whole family with the utmost solemnity. That is why we tremble for your safety when the strong arm of the law is withdrawn. For I foresee that there will be CRIME in Lane End to-night. Hullo, Freddy, what news of the great world?" This was to the twins' younger brother, who bounced into the kitchen entangled with the sprawling legs of the family dog, an animal whose pedigree seemed to combine every known breed in a fantastic welter of canine eclecticism.

"There are two sharras coming down the road, Mum," he announced with the usual family grin. "And the professor's off again. I saw him getting on the boat at Ryde, and he'd got his bag with him. I expect he was going to London."

Mrs. Bunny promptly took charge of the situation. With a hasty glance out of the window to see whether the chars-a-bancs were yet in sight, she unearthed from the chaos of the kitchen table a tray containing a dozen small teapots, stoked up the fire beneath her gigantic kettle, and simultaneously exhorted her daughters to return to their suspended duties. "Now then, Marjory and Elsie," she exclaimed, "don't stand there looking like stuffed bloaters. Get those lobsters out, and fill the milk jugs, and cut some more bread and butter, and see that young Celia doesn't steal any more of the prawns. Freddy, go and see what price George Jones has got up for his lobster teas, and if he's come down to one and nine alter the figure on our blackboard to one and eight. Now then, get a move on, all of you."

The Bunny family launched itself into feverish activity, which to those unfamiliar with their ways might appear as a mere frenzied stirring up of the heterogeneous mass of materials that formed the contents of the kitchen. But in some way known only to genius, Mrs. Bunny contrived to produce daily out of this chaotic helter-skelter a sufficient number of "Prawn, Crab, or Lobster Teas" to maintain the reputation of the Flossington Tea Gardens, and by the time some threescore hungry trippers had sorted themselves out from the two chars-a-bancs and seated themselves at her little wooden tables the miracle had been accomplished once again. But by that time Sargent and Considine had slipped quietly through the bustle and were walking down the lane that led to the beach.

"Curious story that about the wig," remarked Considine.

"Very curious," Sargent agreed. "Can you interpret the cryptogram?"

"I suppose there was some idea of disguise," hazarded Considine very doubtfully. "But it's an extremely queer way to set about it."

"So queer as to be practically incredible," replied Sargent. "He seems to have gone out of his way to let everybody in the village know that the wig was a wig. He seems to have been ostentatiously demonstrating that he wasn't disguised. If he'd wanted to change his appearance, so far as the look of his hair could do it, he had a golden opportunity (in the literal sense of the adjective) by sticking to Rose Bunny's borrowed locks. Instead of which he went back to a slightly different shade of the red that excited so much comment at Southampton. Now what are we to make of that?"

"Need we make anything of it?" asked Considine. "It strikes me you're slipping into the policeman's habit of assuming every action to be guilty until it's proved innocent. After all, this comedy with the wig was played long before the murder—if it was a murder. Surely the natural supposition is that Bonoff just wears a wig and doesn't care who knows it."

"Methinks he doth protest too much," Sargent objected. "My experience is that it's only women who make up in public. A bald man who's sufficiently sensitive to wear a wig is probably vain enough to want to pretend it's his own hair."

"But everybody knew it wasn't," Considine pointed out. "The original wig got washed away in public."

"And you think Bonoff was sufficiently un-self-conscious to forget he was wearing a wig when he went down to bathe? Well, you're the psychologist, of course, but it strikes me as unlikely."

"Can you suggest anything more likely?"

"Nothing that helps us, I'm afraid. All I can see in it is this: if he took all that trouble to prove he wasn't using the wig as a disguise, it looks as if he anticipated that someone would suspect it was. Now that suggests a guilty conscience, for what it's worth."

"Surely it's worth next to nothing. All this is a year before the murder."

"Perfectly true. But remember he'd come straight from his interview with Benchley. There's always the chance that there may be a connexion."

"If there is a connexion," said Considine, "I don't see that we stand the least chance of tracing it."

"Ah," replied Sargent, "that is where the twins' second disclosure comes in."

"Which do you mean by the second disclosure?"

"The absence of the Lane End policeman at Sandown. You heard my remarks to Mrs. Bunny about a probable outbreak of crime during the week-end? The prophecy will be fulfilled."

"How?" asked Considine.

"Alas, Humphrey," replied his colleague, "you are getting into bad company and being led into evil ways. To-night you and I will feloniously, burglariously and of malice aforethought break and enter the messuage known as Pussyholme, being the residence of one Feodor Bonoff. You will remember the statute that commands the Fellows of Beaufort to devote themselves to research."

13
THE COMMONER

THE VILLAGE OF LANE END, which is simply the single street that leads down from the Bembridge-Brading road to the lifeboat house, possesses three centres of social assembly. The first is the Warren. The second is the Dab and Flounder; but that, even under the elastic interpretation of the licensing laws current in the island, is not always open. Besides, it is half a mile away along the cliff, and belongs properly to the hamlet of Forelands. The third is Captain Roger Walters's Studio.

Standing at the point where the macadam debouches on the sand, the Studio seems to represent, in the small compass of a converted army hut, the three great activities of mankind—science, art, and commerce. At a first glance you might suppose that it stood for war as well, for in front of the door is planted a small but dangerous-looking gun. This, however, serves no more lethal purpose than to discharge the rocket that summons the lifeboat crew to their posts. For Captain Walters, having been compelled by advancing years to make his home upon the land, keeps only this slight connexion with the calling in which he spent the days of his youth as commander of a merchantman on the high seas. In one window of the Studio is displayed the collection of meteorological instruments on which rests his claim to be the village scientific expert; with their aid he can interpret the signs of the heavens and tell you when is the time to sail or the time to fish, and when the time to stay at home. One end of the Studio is given up to commerce, in the shape of a counter at which chocolate, bull's-eyes and

167

cigarettes are purveyed to the summer visitor. Here, at most of the hours of daylight, you may meet little girls in gamboge paddlers standing timidly on one leg and opening conversation with such remarks as "Do you like acid drops, Captain Walters? They're my favourite sweets, but I don't get many, because Mummy doesn't let me ask for them." But it is at the farther or seaward end that the Captain's real interests are concentrated; for here is art. Year by year canvases of every conceivable school and period have been accumulating; for the Captain deals in pictures only as an excuse to his own conscience for collecting them; and his friends suspect that he has chosen to set up his emporium in this tiny village mainly because here there are so few purchasers to compel him to part with the treasures he buys with such delight. His is an infinitely catholic taste; and at the Studio you may see and discuss with him works ranging from a chromolithograph of "Dignity and Impudence" to a supposed authentic painting by Tintoretto. One of his most valued possessions is a portrait of Cardinal Beaufort, which he stoutly maintains to be the original from which was copied the famous delineation of the Founder which hangs in Dr. Lacy's library; and Sargent and Considine, after some hours of argument, had failed to make any headway against the wealth of antiquarian learning with which the Captain supported his belief.

As they passed the Studio on their way down to the beach, their attention was caught by the sound of a familiar voice within.

"Most interesting, most interesting," said the voice. "I remember seeing what purports to be the original in a little church on the Adriatic coast; but since you assure me, Captain Walters, with your expert knowledge, that this which you have is the authentic Leonardo, what I saw must have been a forgery. How unscrupulous. But how clever. I quite took it for genuine at the time."

"Hullo, Monitor," said Sargent, walking into the shop followed by Considine, "why aren't you hobnobbing with the Cham of Tartary?"

"I am in more inspiring company, my dear Sargent," replied Monitor. "Do you know my young friends Miss Foley and Miss Carrothers?"

"Mr. Sargent knows me only too well," exclaimed Patricia with a laugh. "I nearly drowned him in the Cher last week. And Mr. Considine too."

"And I expect they're both still more shocked to meet me," added Daphne. "They're my official keepers and guardians, and Humphrey'll have a sticky time explaining to the Lord Chancellor how he let me get into such compromising company as yours, Monko."

"Have you found our mummy again yet, Mr. Considine?" asked Patricia.

"Well, er, no, not exactly," began Considine with some embarrassment. "We're taking a holiday from practical Egyptology at present."

"If you're interested in Egyptian mummies," said Walters, "you ought to go and see Professor Bonoff's collection. He's quite a local celebrity, and he's got some lovely old things at Pussyholme."

"But he hides the light under a bushel rather, doesn't he?" asked Sargent. "From all I hear, nobody except Mrs. Bunny's twin daughters has ever seen the mummies."

"Oh, no, sir, the professor's not quite so secretive as that. He's willing enough to show his mummies to anyone who cares for art, which I'm afraid not everybody in the village does. But he let me see them once; and I know the Vicar's been down and had a look at them. I feel sure he'd be willing to show them to you gentlemen."

"I'm sure they must be most interesting," said Monitor. "Unfortunately we're only over for few hours, and what we were in search of was something so prosaic as tea. We've tried Devereux and he's out. Captain Walters was recommending us a place called the Flossington Tea Gardens. Do you know them?"

"Do we not? We're living there," Sargent replied. "You'd certainly get the noblest tea in the island there, but unhappily the fame of our good hostess has spread too far. At the moment her pearls are being cast before a herd of many swine feeding. Do you think you could hold out for half an hour or so, till they've gone away?"

"We are in your hands," answered Monitor. "May we come and sit on your beach for a little?" The party strolled down on to the sand, Sargent leading the way with Daphne and Monitor, while the other two lingered a few yards behind.

"How did you get here, Monitor?" inquired Sargent. "Have you got your car in the island?"

"Nothing so civilized," replied the doctor. "I was induced to risk my ancient limbs in that." He pointed to where, a few yards offshore, two small sailing boats rode at anchor side by side.

"Which, the yawl?" asked Considine. They were now sitting in a row on the sand, idly throwing pebbles into the water.

"No, ours is the humble dinghy," answered Daphne. "It was a pretty tight squeeze, but she got us over here somehow."

"I didn't know you were a seafaring man, Monitor," said Sargent.

"I'm very far from it," answered Monitor with a grimace. "I'm not sure if I should be more properly described as the passenger or the ballast. Patsy's the skipper; she has suddenly revealed herself as one of the world's great mariners. *Nereis ingreditur consueta cubilia ponto.*"

The two girls exchanged significant glances. "What about it, Daphne?" asked Patricia. "A clear case," Daphne replied. "Not a first offender either. Where do we take him?" They scrambled to their feet and seized each an arm of Monitor, who expostulated with mock indignation.

"What means this outrage on my white hairs?" he asked. "Sargent, Considine, rescue my innocency from these young hooligans!"

"You heard the offence with your own ears, didn't you, Mr. Sargent?" denounced Daphne. "He knows the penalty for quoting more than two words of a learned language in the presence of ladies. He's got to be sconced. I suppose you've got a pub somewhere, Humphrey?"

"There's the Dab and Flounder along the Cliff," Considine was beginning, but Monitor interrupted him with "Don't you pander to their unfeminine vices. If there's going to be any sconcing it shall be in a liquor suited to their sex and their tender years. Tea in fact. Where shall we go?"

"All right," agreed Daphne. "Reprieved for the time being. But you're bound over to come up for sentence when called upon— which is as soon as Patricia and I begin to feel really dry. Now I suggest we go and knock up Mark again for tea. His house is just along the cliff; and perhaps he's back by this time."

To the accompaniment of further badinage, mostly elaborated by Daphne and Patricia at Monitor's expense, the party moved off along the beach to the eastward. It was approaching low water, and the wide seaweed-covered reef beyond the lifeboat house was dotted with little groups of shrimpers tossing backwards and forwards across the shallows the unending argument about the relative merits of the sandy pools and the crevices between the rocks. A small cutter, which had been visible for the last twenty minutes running before the wind from the direction of Portsmouth, was now tacking in an uncertain manner outside the reef, apparently looking for an opening and finding none. Eventually she dropped anchor and her occupants began to furl their sails in an amateurish manner that drew scathing comment from the expert Patricia. Monitor smiled at her vehemence.

"My dear Patsy," he said, "it gladdens my old heart to find that my ineptitude isn't unique. But pardon a humble student of ritual if I ask why exactly it's so much more heinous to fail in rolling up a bale of canvas than in folding the common domestic tablecloth?"

"That's just about the job those three are fitting for," said Patricia scornfully. "But it's no use trying to explain the inner mysteries to a landsman when he's—hullo, hullo. Isn't that—? No, never mind. As I was saying, by the time those three bright lads have finished winding themselves up into a cocoon, they'll be just about ready to foul that buoy." She launched into a flood of nautical technicalities, which did not abate until they reached the point where the lawns of Devereux's old Tudor manor house, White Abbey, spread down to a row of cedars growing almost on the edge of the low cliff. Only Considine had been attending to her discourse with sufficient particularity to observe that its thread was broken at the moment when her eyes, turned for an instant from the sea to the land, fell upon a little wicket gate leading into a garden and bearing the name Pussyholme.

This time they found Mark at home, and soon the six of them were sitting drowsily in deck chairs on the sloping lawn of White Abbey, sipping iced coffee and talking half-heartedly the conventional small talk of Oxford. An antiquated paddle-steamer passed across their range of vision, laboriously churning its way round the island with a load of trippers. Mark, who here on his own territory was very conspicuously the landed magnate, dismissed it superciliously as a "shilling emetic"; but Monitor, to whom even seaside trippers were romantically human, drifted into reminiscence of other ships in remoter seas, and was soon telling a long and complex story of adventures among the headhunters of Borneo in 1874. It was a good story, and he told it well; but before he had finished the sea had changed from azure to violet, the water was lapping over the inner reef, and the distant light of the Nab Tower was winking at regular intervals on the eastward horizon.

"Happily the chief medicine-man turned out to have been at Guy's with me," he wound up; "or I should probably have been the principal entrée. Which word rouses thoughts of dinner; I wonder what time it is. God bless my soul! It's nearly seven o'clock; and Daphne and I are dining with Billy Blount at eight. How long does it take to get back, skipper?"

"About two hours and a half, in the present state of wind and tide," said Patricia uncompromisingly.

"Woe is me; it looks as if that dinner's off, Daffy. And I did so want you to meet Billy Blount. A most attractive man; I'm sure you'd like him."

"Better let me run you over to Seaview in my car," Mark suggested. "Not that I feel so keen as you do on the meeting between Daphne and the fascinating William, whoever he may be."

Monitor smiled. "Billy," he said reassuringly, "is a former policeman whose horse threw him off just as Queen Victoria's jubilee procession was coming along. I had the good luck to catch it and ride it back to Scotland Yard for him, and ever since he's been a very good friend to me. He'd be a more dangerous rival to you, my dear Mark, if I hadn't had the foresight to remove his very dashing left eye after he'd fallen foul of a Boer bullet at Ladysmith. He's not quite the Adonis he was fifty years ago; so I think you may safely persist in your kind offer, which Daphne and I shall most gratefully accept."

"That's all very nice, Monko," Daphne objected; "but what about the dinghy? We can't leave Patricia to bring it back all by herself."

"Oh, that's all right," said Mark. "Of course I'll take Miss Foley back too. I'll get one of the fishermen to sail the boat over for you to-morrow morning."

"Many thanks, but nothing doing," retorted Patricia. "I go down with the ship; an ill-favoured thing, no doubt, but mine own. If I can sail it over with the alleged help of Monko and Daphne, how much more when relieved of that embarrassment. You three get along, or you'll be late. I shall be all right."

"Could I help at all?" began Considine diffidently. "I'm not much use in a boat, but—"

"Sorry, Humphrey," Sargent interrupted. "You forget we're engaged to-night. But I'm sure we could borrow one or more Bunnys for Miss Foley. They're all born mariners, and we could raise any crew she needs from among them."

"Now, my dear good people," expostulated Patricia, "you're all making a ridiculous fuss about nothing. I'm an able-bodied female, more capable of sailing my ship home than the whole lot of you put together. You all seem to think I'm a mid-Victorian clinger, who mustn't be allowed out alone after dark. I'm not Florence Nightingale."

"Speaking as a former medical student who was once firmly trampled under foot by Florence Nightingale," said Monitor mildly, "I should hesitate to describe her as a mid-Victorian clinger. But I'm no match for the neo-Georgian she-pirate. We shall have to leave Sargent and Considine to argue with you. See that she doesn't put to sea on an empty tummy, won't you, Sargent?"

"If Miss Foley will come and share our scratch meal at the Warren I'm sure we shall be delighted," said Considine, as Mark, looking again at his watch, led the way into the garage. In the general bustle of starting up the car Patricia was understood to accept the invitation, and a moment later she was left standing with the two young dons in the drive as the car disappeared in the direction of St. Helen's.

"And now, Mr. Sargent," she said, turning suddenly on her heel as the last sound of the engine died away, "please tell me what is your mysterious engagement."

"Really, Miss Foley," Sargent protested with some embarrassment, "I'm afraid it's rather a private matter."

"Still being as secretive as ever, Mr. Holmes," she mocked. "I shall have to try and pump Dr. Watson. Mr. Considine, can you lay your hand on your heart and swear you're not going sleuthing to-night?"

"I can't let him swear in public," put in Sargent hastily. "Come and make the acquaintance of our excellent Mrs. Bunny"

"Still as mysterious as ever, Mr. Sargent. You seem to have quite forgotten your promise."

"What promise was that?" asked Sargent, as they walked along the beach homewards.

"That you'd let me help unravel the great mummy mystery."

"But that was in Oxford. You surely don't think we could do anything about it here."

"No? Not even at the residence of Professor Bonoff?" Patricia waved a hand towards the wicket gate of Pussyholme which they were at that moment passing.

"Professor Bonoff!" exclaimed Sargent, as if hearing the name for the first time. "I'm afraid I've never met him. But you surely don't suppose a man of his position would stoop to stealing mummies?"

"You're forgetting the rules of the profession, Mr. Sargent. It's the business of the detective to suspect everybody; and you don't seem to have got beyond suspecting me. Well, well; beware of the woman scorned, that's all I can say. I think it's very forebearing of me to come and eat your dinner. Is this the way?"

They turned up the village street in the direction of the Flossington Tea Gardens.

14
THE RESEARCHER

THE BOAT'S SIDE BUMPED CLUMSILY along the stone groin that runs down beside the lifeboat pier, and Sargent clambered out. Considine followed him, and together they hauled the dinghy a few yards up the grating shingle. Then they stood for a moment in silence on the beach, watching the riding lights of the two or three yachts moored outside the reef, as they swung drowsily to the swell of the tide and sent their shimmering reflections along the water towards the watchers' feet.

"Heaven knows what time she'll get to Seaview," said Considine. "There's practically no wind, and what there is is against her."

"My dear Humphrey," replied his companion, "if you'd had a free hand, she'd never have got home at all. If I hadn't ruthlessly hustled her off you'd have been breathing sweet nothings still. From your carryings on anyone would think you'd forgotten you had a felony to commit to-night."

Considine's eyes were still fixed on the sea, and he took no notice of Sargent's persiflage. "She doesn't seem in any hurry to get off," he said. "That's her light, isn't it? It doesn't show any sign of movement."

"I should have said that was the boat that was coming in as we were going to tea," Sargent replied. "The one Miss Foley was so scathing about. Surely that light is hers. Not that it matters; neither of them's moving."

"I wonder if there's anything wrong," said Considine doubtfully. "Do you think we ought to go out again and see if she needs help, Denys?"

175

"Now look here, Humphrey," protested Sargent, "it's time you put that young person out of your head. You've got a serious job before you. And anyhow she won't look at you after to-night, when you're a common burglar. So come along and leave her to look after herself. She knows a lot more about sailing than you do."

With a last look seaward Considine turned away and followed his colleague along the shore towards the wicket gate of Pussyholme. Save for the distant figure of William Walters, pulling his boats above high-water mark and tying them up for the night, the beach was deserted; so they were able to enter the garden and approach the house without taking any precautions to remain unseen. It was a sufficiently commonplace building of stucco, differing only from ten thousand suburban villas by its roof of excellent modern thatch; for this corner of the Isle of Wight is one of the few places in England where the venerable art of thatching still survives and flourishes. The front of the house faced a narrow lane, which joined the main village street two hundred yards to the west; but Sargent and Considine, coming up the path from the sea, approached it from the back, on which side a single-storey extension, about twenty feet square, had been built out into the garden. With its large windows on three sides there could be no mistaking the studio described by the Bunny twins. Sargent walked round it, examining each window in turn and finding all of them latched on the inside.

"If I remember the text-books aright, Humphrey," he murmured, "the next step is for Raffles to insert the blade of his penknife, slip the latch back with a click, and step briskly inside, sighing superciliously over the ineptitude of locksmiths. Have you got a penknife?"

"I have," replied Considine, producing it.

"Well, put it back in your pocket. I wasn't brought up to housebreaking, and I expect I should only slice a finger off. Let us seek for a more excellent way. This flat roof suggests a skylight, and if I know the old man he's sure to have forgotten to lock that. Give me a heave up, Humphrey."

"If you know the old man, Denys," said Considine with some surprise, stooping to allow Sargent to climb on his back, and thence to the roof. "But you don't know him. I thought that day last week when we caught a glimpse of Bonoff at the other end of the village was the first time you'd set eyes on him."

Sargent scrambled on to the leads before replying, and when he did so seemed a little embarrassed. "Yes, yes," he said uneasily; "queer how one's tongue gets out of control. Somehow, I'd built up such a picture of Bonoff in my mind that I'd forgotten it was all imagination. Shows the folly of constructing theories, even unconsciously. And this shows it still better," he went on, stooping over the skylight. "Damned thing's locked. Bonoff isn't quite the absent-minded professor of the comic papers after all."

"What are you going to do about it?" called Considine from below.

"I'm going to put my foot in it and damn the textbooks," Sargent replied, stamping cheerfully on the glass of the skylight. There was a tinkle of falling pieces on the floor of the studio, and in a moment he had it open and had dropped through out of sight. Considine saw the bright point of his electric torch moving in the darkness; then a window was thrown up and he joined his colleague within.

The interior of Professor Bonoff's studio, as revealed piecemeal by the travelling light of the electric torch, was curious in several ways. It was pervaded by a strong smell of mingled chemicals and spices, which seemed to be partially explained when the light fell upon a row of bottles standing on a glass shelf in one corner. Sargent took one down and looked at the label, then handed it with a puzzled frown to Considine.

"Oriental alphabets are your pidgin, Humphrey," he said. "Can you make out what that is?"

Considine took one glance and shook his head. "Sorry, Denys," he replied regretfully. "I'm afraid I'm a bruised reed. This is demotic, which was the sort of undress everyday writing of ancient Egypt. I've got a smattering of hieroglyphic, but this is beyond me. Cuneiform's my script, as I think I've told you before."

"Well, at any rate it's Egyptian, which is something," Sargent replied. "I thought for a moment we'd stumbled into a chemist's laboratory instead of an Egyptologist's study. What's in the bottle, I wonder?" He removed the stopper and sniffed. "Some sort of gum or resin," he decided. Replacing the bottle on the shelf he examined two or three others in the same cursory way. All alike bore the mysterious demotic inscriptions, obviously written by a skilled but modern hand; and their various spicy odours clearly marked them as containing the ingredients that had produced the scent in the air.

"A queer job lot of chemicals, Humphrey," he said at the end of his inspection. "How do we connect them up with Bonoff and Egyptology? Could he have brewed them out of mummies, do you think?"

"Mummy is become merchandise, Mizraim cures wounds, and Pharaoh is sold for balsams," Considine quoted. "They seem the right sort of thing for a mummy to contain; but why on earth should he want to destroy a mummy to produce them? There's nothing new to be discovered that way; it was all done in the middle ages, when powdered mummy was a fashionable drug. I expect Monitor could make you up a prescription based upon it; but it's scarcely worthy of the attention of a man of Bonoff's standing."

"It seems our unconscious host needs further study," Sargent agreed, flashing his torch into another corner of the room. "Here at any rate is an honest-to-God mummy. Cast your learned eye over that. It isn't the one we last saw on the Cher, by the way, is it?"

"Good heavens, no," exclaimed Considine. "That was King Pepi I, Sixth-Dynasty work, anything up to three thousand years older than this thing. This is Roman period, and debased at that. It isn't worth looking at."

"Nevertheless, I think if you don't mind we'll have a look," said Sargent. "Just help me let it down to the floor, Humphrey, so that we can get the lid off."

"I don't suppose there's anything in it," Considine protested. "But I expect you won't be convinced till you've seen with your own eyes that it's empty." He took the foot of the coffin, which stood erect against one of the side-windows, and, Sargent taking the end, they lowered it gently to a horizontal position on the floor. The lifting of the lid showed an inner coffin, painted with the face of a man; this also they uncovered, and then Considine suddenly flung himself down on his knees, with a cry of astonishment, beside the brown swathed figure that lay within.

"Well, I'm damned, Denys," he exclaimed. "There's nothing Roman about this. This is primitive work—more primitive than anything I've ever seen. I'm no Egyptologist, but this mummy certainly doesn't belong to the coffin. Hold the torch nearer; I must look at this."

"What do you make of the head, Humphrey?" asked Sargent, as he threw the beam of light upon the upper extremity of the recumbent form.

Considine bent down and looked closely at the head. "It's a very odd shape," he answered. "Very odd indeed." Very gingerly he ran his hand over the bandages. "There seems to be a fissure—or is it two heads wrapped up separately. No, they're both too small for that; it's two fragments of the skull laid together."

"So that the right ear of Pharaoh fell a cubit's span from the left, so that men took up the head of Pharaoh in two pieces. I the High Priest destroyed him," murmured Sargent softly. "I withdraw all my doubts of your cuneiform tablet, Humphrey."

Considine replaced the inner lid and stood up. "Yes," he admitted gravely, "there can't be any reasonable doubt that this is King Pepi I. And that proves—"

"That the body burnt in Benchley's rooms wasn't the mummy."

"We knew that already from the tablet," maintained Considine stoutly. "No, what it proves is something much more extraordinary. It proves that Benchley paid ten thousand guineas for an empty coffin. It proves that Bonoff was a swindler, which we suspected already. But Benchley? Denys, *can* he have gone off his head after all? It seems the only explanation."

"I think I see the glimmerings of a different one," Sargent reassured him. "But let's collect some more evidence before we theorize. What on earth are these?" He turned the light upon a row of alabaster jars, each about a foot high, inscribed with hieroglyphics, and having a stopper in the form of a head. These heads appeared to be those of a man, two dogs, and a bird.

"Those are Canopic jars," said Considine. "They were made to hold the entrails of the mummy; the heads belong to the gods who protected the various parts. The man is Mestha, who is responsible for the stomach; the dog is Hapi and the jackal Tuamautef; I think those would contain the lungs and heart. And the hawk is Qebhsennuf; I forget what he looks after. Probably the liver. There's nothing out of the way about these. Just a minute, though." He was turning away when some small detail seemed to catch his eye. He snatched the torch from Sargent's hand and bent down again to examine with minute attention a spot on the neck of one of the jars, where the head-shaped cover appeared to have been fixed in place with plaster. "Denys," he exclaimed, "come and look at this seal a minute. It's not a very clear impression, but see if you can make it out."

Sargent knelt down beside him, and together they peered at a small group of marks within an oval border. "What do you make of it, Denys?" Considine asked anxiously.

"You know I can't read hieroglyphics, Humphrey," protested his colleague.

"Never mind reading them, man," rejoined Considine. "Can't you just describe the signs, so as I can see if you agree with my impression?"

Sargent bent again to the jar, impressed against his will by Considine's restrained excitement. "There seemed to be two little squares," he said, "and then a thing like a windmill sail. No, that isn't all; here's something else. It's dreadfully smudged, but I should say it's another of those sail things."

"You're quite sure?" asked Considine. "Very well, now come and look at this scarab." He pulled Sargent down again beside the mummy, and turned over a small beetle-shaped object to show its incised underside.

"Yes," said Sargent, after examining it under the light. "That's exactly the same device as the seal. I shouldn't wonder if the impression was made with it. What do the hieroglyphics mean?"

"They're the name of King Pepi I," replied Considine.

"But my dear Humphrey, why make a fuss about that? If Bonoff has got the mummy, why shouldn't he have the guts as well?"

"Because King Pepi belonged to the Sixth Dynasty, and Canopic jars didn't come into use before the Eighteenth. In the Old Kingdom they used to embalm the entrails and then put them back with the body, under the bandages."

"I see," said Sargent thoughtfully. "That is rather odd. Then you suggest that these jars are faked—and perhaps the mummy too."

"No, the mummy's genuine enough," replied Considine with decision. "If Benchley passed it there can't be the ghost of a doubt. Besides, Bonoff couldn't possibly have known about the cleft head, which we only learnt about from my tablet; it was only dug up last year. But these jars—surely they must be a fake. If not, they'll revolutionize the whole subject. I wish I had Benchley's book here to refer to."

"Never mind for the moment," said Sargent. "I fancy all this is going to fit in rather nicely. Anyhow, let's get on with our search. Here's another mummy, but I think we've got all we want on the mummy tack. Let's leave that to the last. This is a curious object to find in an Egyptologist's working room." He flashed the light on an ordinary metal bath, very long and deep, which stood against the wall on the side adjoining the house.

"Yes," agreed Considine. "It seems a bit eccentric to combine your study with your bathroom. But everything we know about Bonoff shows that he has odd ways. It may be the usual thing in Russia for all I know."

"It can hardly be the usual thing even in Russia to take a bath without any water," Sargent objected. "Look at this. The taps aren't connected up to anything; nor is the waste-pipe. If he wanted to have a bath in this he'd have to carry all the water in in cans. Besides, even the grubbiest Russian would scarcely account for so much discolouration." Flashing the light round the inside of the bath he showed that it was stained a deep brown up to a line about twelve inches from the bottom. "However," he went on, "we must be getting to the next exhibit. We can't be here all night. Possibly this desk may contain some useful evidence. Hold the light, Humphrey, while I run over our friend's private correspondence."

He seated himself at a writing table in the window looking out to sea, and began to pull out drawers. The first he opened contained a heavy pile of typescript, the top page being inscribed: "Religio Pharaonis: A Survey of the Religious Beliefs and Observances of the Ancient Egyptians from the Earliest Times to the fall of the Nineteenth Dynasty, considered in relation to the Anthropology and Comparative Ethnology of the Mediterranean Basin, by Feodor Bonoff, Ph.D., Late Professor of Ancient History in the University of Moscow."

"H'm," grunted Sargent. "Doesn't sound like the opening of a best seller. If the essential clue lies in this, I'm afraid we must let it escape us. Curiously incompetent typist the blighter seems to be. I've never seen so many corrections. He doesn't seem to learn either; it's as messy on the last page as the first." He dropped the mass of papers back into their drawer, and pulled out another, which proved to be full of receipted bills. "Not much in these," he commented after a cursory glance. "The butcher, the baker, the candlestick-maker, and so on. £53 to Bluchers, Wholesale Druggists, but that's only to be expected with all these odd potions about. It doesn't tell us anything new. Ha! this looks more like personal correspondence." He had taken a bundle of letters from a third drawer and was turning them over one by one. "Invitation to lecture at Cambridge, earnest inquirer wants to know if the Great Pyramid confirms her theory that Manchester is inhabited by the tribe of Manasseh, Editor of the *Journal of Egyptology* encloses ten guineas for article on the Attributes of Ptah, begging letter from local parson. Hullo! Hullo! Hullo! look at this, Humphrey. We seem to be hot on the trail at last."

Considine leant over his shoulder, and by the dim light of the torch, whose battery was now almost exhausted, read the following letter:

> "Hotel Hindenburg,
> "Dresden.
> "May 18th, 1931

"Dear Dr. Benchley,
"I am very glad to have convinced you that my fresh-discovered papyrus does your theory concerning

Dionysos disprove. I have now to put before you a proposal.

"I have no wish to destroy your so-distinguished lifework by printing of this irreconcilable evidence. But, owing to the exigencies created by the revolution, I find myself much straitened in pecuniary fortune. Therefore I make you this offer: in return for some suitable assistance on my coming to England I will hand over to you this papyrus, so damaging to your theory; if you then choose to destroy it, you may rely on my entire silence and discretion. I pray you, dear Dr. Benchley, inform me whether this offer commends itself to you, and how much you are prepared to pay for the papyrus.

"I am, dear colleague, very sincerely yours,
"Feoeor Bonoff."

The two investigators raised their eyes together from this strange document, and gazed for a long moment at one another in speechless astonishment. Sargent was the first to find coherent utterance.

"The poisonous septic skunk!" he exploded.

"This knocks me flat, Humphrey. I never dreamt we were up against blackmail."

"I was prepared to believe anything against Bonoff," rejoined Considine; "and though I wasn't expecting blackmail it doesn't surprise me. What puzzles me is why the letter is here; it's in an envelope that's been through the post, addressed to Benchley at Beaufort, postmarked Bonn on the front, and with the Oxford stamp on the back. So apparently it was received by Benchley all right. I can just imagine his reception of it."

"Not a good subject for blackmail, I should think," said Sargent.

"My dear Denys, think what *kind* of blackmail it was. Scholarly rectitude was Benchley's religion. He wouldn't suppress the smallest bit of evidence, however inconvenient to his theories, if you paid him thousands of pounds. I should think he'd have made

Bonoff realize his mistake pretty quickly. But I can't understand this letter. I should have thought Benchley would have taken it straight to the police. And yet here it is, back in Bonoff's possession."

"He may have changed his mind and sent a different letter in the envelope," Sargent pointed out. "I grant you it's a thin explanation, and doesn't account for the envelope being here. But on the face of it—"

"No, no, no, Denys, stop!" exclaimed Considine in sudden excitement. "I've got an idea. I believe we've solved the mystery of the murder after all. Look here, let me think a minute."

"Think on," said Sargent, turning over some more letters and glancing rapidly at their contents. Considine covered his eyes with his hands for thirty seconds or so, and then began to speak slowly and carefully.

"Listen to this, Denys," he said at last, "and tell me what you think of it. Bonoff sent this letter to Benchley just before he came to England. Benchley of course sent him away with a flea in his ear. But they met when he landed, and as soon as they were alone at the hotel Benchley let him have it, straight from the shoulder, as he certainly would have done, for trying to blackmail him in this peculiarly disgusting way. That falls in with what the hotel people said about the chilliness between them. Later on, Bonoff, still after money, managed to patch it up with Benchley sufficiently to sell him the mummy. But at the same time he'd got the wind up about the blackmailing letter, which was still in Benchley's possession; also he didn't really mean to part with King Pepi. He showed Benchley the real mummy, but afterwards sent him a fake, perhaps done with these drugs he's got here, hoping it would arrive after Benchley had gone on holiday. Then he came to Oxford to burgle Benchley's rooms, both of the mummy and of the letter. The mummy was to be got by Randolph and Nevern in the way you worked out; but he himself was going to get into Benchley's rooms to abstract the letter. But he found Benchley in; there was a fight and Benchley was killed. The mummy had already been taken; so

Bonoff took the key from Benchley's body, set fire to the rooms, and escaped. Doesn't that cover all the facts?"

"There's the alarm clock," Sargent reminded him.

"Oh, yes; so there is." Considine considered a moment. "I don't think that's an insuperable obstacle," he resumed. "Bonoff must have brought it with him, and so the murder and the fire must have been premeditated. He must have planned that the body should be mistaken for the mummy—as it would have been but for my tablet. The alarm clock makes it definitely murder, instead of possibly manslaughter. *And* I'm going to see that he hangs for it," he added passionately.

"It's a strong case, Humphrey," admitted his colleague. "It's not all plain sailing, though. You haven't explained how Bonoff got into college, or why he went to Monitor's rooms. Nor why the body was taken out of the coffin, which you see isn't here, though we know that was restolen the night after the murder, another circumstance that wants elucidation. There's the codicil to Benchley's will, too, and the planting of it in the Bursary. Incidentally, there's the pipe. No, Humphrey, it's a good theory, but you've got to dot some i's and cross some t's before you send for the hangman. Meanwhile, however, here's a little more corroboration."

He held out two letters, which he had extracted from the pile on the desk while Considine was speaking. Considine read them through thoughtfully. The first was from the head office of the White Star Line, dated June 30th, acknowledging the receipt of Professor Bonoff's telegram of that day, and consenting to the transfer of the passage he had booked for the beginning of August to one on the R.M.S. *Laconic*, sailing from Southampton on July 2nd. The other, from a firm of carriers in Ryde, announced that the mummy to be left packed in the hall of Pussyholme would be collected at 6 a.m. on July 2nd, delivered to Professor Bonoff's stateroom on the Laconic before noon, and handled throughout with the greatest possible care.

"July the second," exclaimed Considine. "That's to-morrow— or rather to-day; it's long past midnight. I see what you mean,

Denys. He's seen us in the village, suspects we're on his track, and made up his mind to get away at once. We must—"

The sentence was never finished. A new voice broke sharply into the discussion, coming from above. "Hands up, both of you!" it said. "We've got you covered." Sargent and Considine started up, looking in the direction whence the sound came, to see three heads leaning through the dark opening of the skylight, and the barrels of as many pistols levelled at themselves with the steadiness of marksmen well accustomed to their use. Sargent shrugged his shoulders helplessly, and put his hands above his head.

"We don't seem to have much choice, Humphrey," he murmured, and Considine followed his example. Thereupon one of the three on the roof took a second pistol from one of his companions and continued to occupy his menacing position while these two dropped lightly down into the studio. The original speaker walked boldly to the door and switched on the electric light.

"How do you do, Mr. Randolph?" inquired Sargent pleasantly. "And Mr. Nevern, isn't it?"

"Sure, I'm real pleased to find you remember us, Dean," replied Randolph. "I'm only sorry we've got to treat you with what may look a little like discourtesy. But to tell you the truth, we hadn't expected the pleasure of seeing you again so soon. Let's have that rope down, Tom," he called to the man on the roof.

One of the pistols was lowered for a fraction of a second while a large coil of rope was dropped to the two confederates within, who proceeded with methodical efficiency to seize Sargent and bind him hand and foot to the chair on which he had been sitting to examine the letters. As they worked Randolph continued to talk in quiet conversational tones, in which he no longer troubled to conceal the slight hint of an American accent.

"We hope you won't take all this in bad part," he said, "though I'm afraid we shall have to subject you to some slight inconvenience. Now the left leg, please. I hate having to do this, of course, but we're professional men, with our client to consider. That gag quite comfortable? I'm sorry if it isn't, but it's the best we can manage under the circumstances. And now you, sir," he went on, turning to Considine. "I think you'd better take this chair, if you don't mind. As I was saying, we've come to fetch a mummy for a client, and I'm afraid you'll both have to wait here till we've got it away."

"Ah, it's burglary then," said Considine. "I thought so."

"On the contrary," protested Nevern. "It's a simple commercial transaction. If you'll allow me to say so, the burglarious entry seems to have been made before we arrived, judging by the state of that skylight. We're only acting as agents for the purchase of the mummy. I understand that our client is sending Professor Bonoff a cheque for seventy thousand dollars as soon as we deliver it. A very fair price, don't you think?"

"This conversation must now cease," Randolph interrupted before Considine could reply, and bent over him to force a gag into his mouth. Then, standing back, he surveyed the two trussed and helpless dons with simple childlike pride.

"Nothing like doing it by kindness, is there, Cal?" he inquired complacently of Nevern. "There's many a gang back in the States that would have thought it necessary to take these two guys for a ride. But one of the things I learnt at Cambridge was the advantage of keeping within the law. It's a little more trouble, but it lends distinction to the firm."

"I've a kinda notion we're not strictly within the law even now," replied Nevern. "It's a bit fussy in these parts. But we've treated them as lawfully as they did us. Which reminds me, they owe us two pairs of pants. Shall we have theirs?"

"Not on your life," answered Randolph with decision. "Dons haven't got any taste in dress. We'd better get down to serious business. Ready for a job of work, Tom?" he called to the man on the roof.

Tom dropped down into the studio and all three bent over the mummy coffin, still lying open on the floor. Randolph, who seemed to be the leader of the gang, tools a small notebook from his pocket, and carefully compared something drawn on one of its pages with the scarab on the breast of the mummy. He clearly knew well what he was doing, and was quickly satisfied.

"This is his majesty all right, boys," he announced. "Got the mortician's outfit, Tom?"

"All waiting outside," replied Tom. He went to the seaward window and threw it up; Nevern followed him and stepped out with him over the low sill. A moment later, to the surprise of the two prisoners, there was propelled gently into the room a familiar object—the painted outer coffin of King Pepi I, which they had last seen lying in Monitor's punt on the Cherwell a week before.

Obviously the three gangsters had planned their moves in advance. Considine writhed in his bonds as Randolph and Nevern started to lift the body of King Pepi; but to his relief they handled it with punctilious care, taking it up bodily with its inner coffin and depositing it without a jolt or ajar in the outer case that they had brought with them. Randolph seemed to divine the archaeologist's anxiety, for he turned to reassure him.

"Your friend's going to a good home," he said comfortingly. "Our client's a real cultured man. And we're taking it over in a sailing boat so it shan't get shaken up. All ready to move, Cal?"

"All ready," replied Nevern. "Sure it's safe to leave these two guys alone?"

"We shouldn't be so inconsiderate," rejoined Randolph. "Tom's going to stay and keep them company till the ship's out of sight. Just give us a hand, Tom, to get the deceased on the trolley, and then you can take post."

The three lifted the coffin with care and thrust it feet first through the window on the seaward side of the studio, themselves climbing out after it. In the first dim light of dawn they were just visible, apparently fixing the mummy upon a small vehicle, which appeared to Considine to be an ordinary garden wheelbarrow. As he watched, however, he was surprised to feel the impact of a drop of water on his forehead, and with a cramped wriggle succeeded in turning his eyes upwards sufficiently to bring the edge of the skylight, immediately overhead, into his range of vision. In the square opening was framed a head and a crop of sodden black hair, together with the upper part of a female body, clothed in a damp green bathing dress.

THE MUMMY CASE MYSTERY

"Sorry I can't rescue you," said Miss Patricia Foley in a hoarse whisper. "I should only find myself compelled to join you; and you've told me already my company isn't wanted. But we'll see if you can't be avenged, dear Sherlock. Au revoir."

The head vanished into the darkness again, just as Tom re-entered through the window and seated himself on the only unoccupied chair in the studio. A few minutes later a not very rhythmic plashing of oars was heard from the direction of the sea.

15
THE TRAVELLING FELLOWS

To Sargent and Considine, with aching backs and tormented limbs, it seemed that the rotation of the earth had been arrested, and the world left in a condition of perpetual and depressing twilight. Tom was not a conversationalist; having smoked one pipe in complete silence, he closed and latched the broken skylight, climbed out by the windows, shut it behind him, and disappeared. The prisoners were left gazing out towards the sea, more perceptible to their ears than to their eyes as the faint breeze of early morning began to ruffle up a ripple clearly audible in a sleeping world. Sargent could see no more than the suggestion of a line between a dark and a lighter grey, which must be the horizon; but he noted that where the riding lights of the two yachts, the unknown cutter and Patricia's dinghy, had shone as they entered the studio, no light now appeared. He had not seen—neither of them had seen—the cutter lurching from her moorings as the stars began to pale, and the dinghy following lightless at a discreet distance, the contrasting grace of its movement betraying, if there had been any to see, the guidance of skilled hands, fully competent to maintain an indefinite pursuit in spite of the larger boat's apparent advantages.

As the slow light grew, the incoherent clues to the mystery of Benchley's death chased one another like riotous hares through Considine's brain. The inability to communicate with Sargent, who seemed to be dozing, was a worse hardship than the biting constriction of the ropes, for he felt sure that Sargent by now had some central idea in his head, which would make sense of all this mass of seemingly inconsistent facts. True, there didn't seem to be much doubt left of Bonoff's guilt. The evidence of the studio was damning. Or was it? Slewing his eyes round through the narrow angle that his bonds allowed him to survey, Considine ran over the objects of their night's investigation. The Roman-Egyptian coffin, now relieved of its incongruous Sixth-Dynasty occupant. That showed that Bonoff had deliberately defrauded Benchley of £10,000. The writing-desk, with the letters still lying on it. Here was evidence that the Russian was a blackmailer; and surely a blackmailer would stick at no crime. (Would he though? Wasn't there something in that peculiarly base and cowardly character that would shrink more abjectly from the distant thought of the gallows than criminals of less ignoble motives? Considine strove to recall a passage of the old fifteenth-century Chief Justice, Sir John Fortescue, who vaunted the virile qualities of his countrymen, of whom so many more were hanged every year for crimes of violence than was the case in France. There was something in it, after all. Was not the writer of that letter too creeping an animal to plan and carry through a murder?) His gaze travelled on to the bath, and he made out just a glimpse of the four Canopic jars beyond it. More evidence of fraud; not content with selling Benchley an empty coffin, here was the brute manufacturing faked antiques. It seemed a clumsy fabrication; but of course the ignorant public would swallow anything—even a Canopic jar with a Sixth-Dynasty seal. Considine reluctantly admitted to himself that Bonoff's reputation was sufficient to "get away with" even that with all but a small circle of expert archaeologists. But what did all this prove, he asked himself again. That Bonoff was several sorts of rogue: yes. But murder? The case on that charge seemed still to be just the same as ever. Bonoff had been seen in college on the night of Benchley's death, but not near Benchley's rooms. That really was all. Seen too by only one witness, who might have been mistaken—probably was mistaken, for though Bonoff might have got out with his victim's key after the murder, how could he possibly have got in? Unless Benchley himself let him in. But why should Benchley be admitting his own assassin in the dead of night? Curious as had been their relations during the year of Bonoff's residence in England, Considine could not imagine that the two men were intimate friends. Bonoff had tried to blackmail Benchley; and though that had apparently been smoothed over, he had added injury to insult by selling him a counterfeit mummy. Could Bonoff have counted on Benchley's not having yet opened the coffin, and decided to murder him, under cover of a friendly visit, before the fraud was detected? Surely an incredibly wild gamble. Indeed, as Considine reflected, the fraud must have been detected already, for had not young Devereux actually found Benchley examining the mummy? The merest glance must have exposed the imposture to his expert eye. But the bath? Had Bonoff some chemical process for converting a late mummy into the semblance of an early one? Considine pondered the idea for a moment and then dismissed it as too absurdly fantastic. He knew Egyptologists who might conceivably be deceived in that way; but not Benchley. No, that was quite incredible.

But what *had* Benchley been doing in these last days? Wearily Considine racked his brains to remember and fit together the curious details they had collected about their colleague's behaviour. His curiously submissive acceptance of the victory of Bonoff in their archaeological controversy—the unexpected codicil to his will, and its apparently deliberate "planting" in the Bursary—the breach of the habit of years in not sending his luggage in advance: all these were small things in themselves, but they needed explaining. What other explanations was there than that Benchley had been anticipating his death? But then, surely that made havoc of the idea that he had himself let the murderer into college. Yet how else could Bonoff have got in? Considine had not always been a don; as an undergraduate he had discovered by personal trial the truth of the reputation enjoyed by Beaufort, with its barred windows and spiked walls, as the most difficult college in Oxford to enter by unauthorized ways. Where the ingenuity and agility of able-bodied young men, familiar with all the ground, had been so repeatedly baffled, was it likely that an elderly foreign scholar, new to Oxford, would be more successful? But it followed (didn't it?) that Bonoff had been let in by somebody other than Benchley. He could not have

come by the main gate, nor yet by the river; there remained only
the private gate in the garden. And of that only the fellows had
keys. Therefore, Bonoff must have been let in by one of the fellows. Who could it be? Monitor? Absurd; and yet Monitor was the
only fellow who had been remotely connected with the case. There
were four links between him and the death of Benchley: the legacy,
Bonoff's visit to his rooms, the punt, and the pipe. Sargent seemed
to attach a lot of weight to the pipe; what significance could it have?
It did bring in Monitor—oh, but this was nonsense. You're getting
delirious, Considine told himself, if you're going to start seriously
thinking of Monitor as an accomplice with the murderer of his best
friend. But who else was there? Oh, of course, Van Ditten! How fool-
ish not to have thought of that before. He had the key in his possession for several hours, and must have made a duplicate for Randolph
and Nevern, who surely must be in his pay. But that wouldn't do.
Randolph and Nevern had deliberately gone back with the sham
mummy (the second sham mummy?) to let themselves be seized within
a few feet of where Benchley's body lay. If they were privy to the murder, such conduct would be beyond the wildest aberrations of lunacy.

At this point Considine's exasperated reflections were interrupted by the trampling of feet the other side of the locked door,
and by the shrill voices of the Bunny twins. The carriers had arrived from Ryde to remove the mummy that was to accompany
Bonoff to America, and Elsie and Marjory were taking joint charge
of the operations.

Considine looked across at Sargent, who had awaked from his
uneasy sleep and was straining at his ropes in a desperate effort to
throw his chair over sideways or at any rate make sufficient noise
to attract attention. But the gangsters had taken every precaution;
both chairs were firmly secured to legs of the heavy oak table, and
the utmost efforts of the two prisoners could produce nothing more
than a slight creaking of timber. This was drowned by the ponder-
ous noises without, or lost in the brisk chatter of the twins; and
within ten minutes of the workmen's arrival the front door
slammed, a motor started up, and the crunching of the wheels of a
heavy van died away in the distance.

Profound silence descended once more, for visitors to Lane End in June do not rise early. Fishermen and proprietors of lobster pots, indeed, keep more matutinal hours, but they must have gone out to their work long before. For what seemed endless time the monotony of waiting dragged on. Considine's cricked neck, it seemed, must snap at any moment; the tickling in the small of Sargent's back, which ought to have been scratched hours ago, grew to the enormity of one of the major tortures. A brilliant patch of sunlight, falling through the skylight, afforded by its motion the only clue to the passage of time; but that motion was so slow that it seemed that a new Joshua must be laying his spells upon the world.

At last, when it seemed to them both that their confinement must have lasted for weeks, a firm step was heard striding up the path from the road, round the house and into the garden. A moment later, to his unspeakable relief, Considine saw the face of Mark Devereux peering in at the window.

Mark's expression showed amusement rather than surprise. He scaled the studio wall with the practised ease of the noctambulant undergraduate. Leaping down through the skylight, he drew a large clasp-knife from his pocket, and had slashed to pieces the ropes binding both Sargent and Considine within half a minute of first coming into view.

Considine was so stiff and sore from the long constriction that he was unable to stand upright, and could at first only roll in agonized convulsions on the floor, rubbing his arms and legs in a frenzied effort to restore the circulation. Sargent, in equal physical distress, was mentally too heavily preoccupied to notice it, but sat still in his chair, and directly the gag was out of his mouth began to speak.

"Thank you very much, Devereux," he said. "What time is it?"

"Five minutes to ten," replied Mark. "I've ordered breakfast for you at White Abbey. We'll get along as soon as you feel ready to move."

"No time for breakfast," answered Sargent curtly. "We've got to catch the *Laconic* from Southampton. I suppose you don't know what time she sails?"

"Must be somewhere about high water," said Mark; "and that's just before one o'clock. You're certainly running it pretty fine. Have you got your passage booked? I had no idea you were going away so soon."

"We only made up our minds to go about one o'clock this morning. But—"

"We!" interrupted Considine in protesting tones. "I like that, Denys. *I* haven't made up my mind to do anything so silly; not till I've had some breakfast, anyhow."

"Sorry, Humphrey," said his colleague. "This is an emergency. What's the earliest we can get to Southampton, Devereux?"

Mark, who seemed bewildered by the curious reception of his errand of rescue, was impressed by the urgency of Sargent's manner. "If you really must catch the *Laconic*," he said, "there's a boat from Cowes to Southampton at eleven, which'll just do it in time. D'you think you can manage to walk to the Warren while I get the car out? You can? Good. I'll ring up Southampton while you pack. I've got a brother-in-law there who's a director of the White Star Line, and I think I can manage to squeeze you into the ship somewhere through him. Luckily they're all sailing half-empty now, owing to the slump."

"Come on, Humphrey, my lad," exclaimed Sargent, seizing Considine by the arm and marching him towards the door. "Damn! I forgot this door was still locked. We must go as we came, like thieves in the night. See you at the Warren in about a quarter of an hour, Devereux." He climbed out of the window, catching his breath in a sudden spasm of pain as he did so, but not abating his haste. Considine had to be helped over the sill by Devereux, and then collapsed groaning on the grass and protesting that he could stir no further. But Sargent would give him no mercy: clutching him firmly by the arm, he hustled him ruthlessly off towards the Flossington Tea Gardens.

"That's what I call a profitable night, Humphrey," he said, as they emerged on the road and turned to the right, while Devereux went to the left towards White Abbey.

"I'm glad you think so," replied Considine. "Personally, I'm crippled for life."

"Physically I'm a bit of a wreck myself. But what a golden opportunity you've had for some undisturbed reflection on our little
mystery."

"I've been racking my brains for about eight hours, and it seems
to me rather more entangled than ever. Do you see any light?"

"I've solved it."

"My dear Denys! You don't mean you know who did the murder?"

"I hope to have the pleasure of introducing you to the murderer in person on board R.M.S. *Laconic* this very evening."

"Oh, Bonoff!" Considine sounded disappointed. "Of course, if
that's all, I've solved the problem myself long ago. But *how* did he
do it? That's really what baffles me."

"That mystery also is solved, Humphrey mine," replied Sargent.
"But I'm not going to do your thinking for you. The exercise is left
to the student, as the textbooks say. Here we are at the Warren.
You've got just ten and a half minutes to equip yourself for the
New World. But meditate on our little problem on the way to
Southampton. If you concentrate your thoughts on Benchley's old
pipe you oughtn't to find it too difficult."

At twenty-five minutes past ten the two were seated at the gate
of the Warren in Devereux's car, which was submerged in a great
cloud of Bunnys. Rose and Freddy were strapping suitcases on the
luggage carrier, while the twins, who had undertaken the packing,
ran backwards and forwards between the house and the car with
objects forgotten and having to be stuffed in at the last moment.
Harry was cracking the claws of a lobster on the radiator, while
Susan tied up a bulging parcel of rolls hot from the oven. Three
more young Bunnys, with broad and helpful grins illuminating their
faces, scrambled busily about the car, though in what precise way
they were speeding their guests' departure it was difficult to say.
Just as the engine started Mrs. Bunny herself emerged, flushed
and out of breath, from the front door, and thrust into Considine's
hand a tattered copy of *Baedeker's Guide to Western Canada*.
"Here you are, sir," she exclaimed. "It was left behind by a visitor
ten years ago; I expect you'll find it useful in America. Good bye,
sir, good bye; and don't forget to come to Lane End next year."

The car moved off, shedding Bunnys right and left, and two minutes later was skimming along the road that encircles Bembridge Harbour in the direction of St. Helen's.

"And now," said Devereux to Sargent, who sat beside him in the front seat, "am I allowed to ask why you're off to America in such a tearing hurry?"

"It's rather complex," Sargent hedged. "And time's very short. Hadn't you better tell me first how you managed to find us? I'm afraid we've been too rushed to thank you properly; but we owe you more than you know." With a roll in one hand and a lobster's claw in the other he began his belated breakfast.

"It's really Miss Foley you have to thank," Devereux answered. "I got a telephone message from her to go and release you."

"Miss Foley!" exclaimed Sargent. "Where did she telephone from?"

"From the porter's lodge at Beaufort."

"The devil she did! How did she get there? We last saw her in a bathing dress on the roof of that infernal studio."

"So I gathered. As far as I could make out on the telephone, she recognized two of those toughs in the cutter last night as Randolph and Nevern, the two blighters who tried to rag your commem ball. We debagged them, you know, after you and Mr. Considine had gone."

"I fancy I did hear rumours of some such outrage. There are occasions when decanal authority need not be too vigilant."

"Well, when Randolph and Nevern went ashore in their dinghy last night Miss Foley smelt a rat and swam after them. I think, by the way, she deliberately hung about here instead of letting me take her back with Daphne and Dr. Monitor, so as to do a bit of detective work on her own."

"I expect she did. But go on."

"When she got up to the studio and looked in the window they'd already started tying you up, and she saw it wouldn't be any good interfering, or they'd capture her too."

"Couldn't she have knocked up somebody and got help?"

"I suppose she could," Devereux admitted. "To tell the truth, I rather think she wanted to score off you a bit. Gave me the impression you'd been doing some sleuthing of sorts, and wouldn't let her in on it. So she thought she'd steal a march on you and show what she could do by herself."

"She scores her point all right," said Sargent grimly. "I only hope she hasn't done us in altogether. Are we going to catch this boat?"

"Easily," Devereux reassured him. "We'll be in Cowes in ten minutes now. Well, as I was saying, Miss Foley watched those three steal the mummy, and when they went back to their cutter with it she slipped down to the beach after them in the dark and swam out to her own boat. She'd put out the riding light before she started; so they probably thought she'd sailed off while they were ashore. Anyway, she got her sail up and followed them over to the mainland without being noticed, dressing on the way; and when she saw where they were bound for she got ahead and landed half an hour before them. She was a bit contemptuous of their seamanship."

"Where did they land?"

"I'm not sure. Somewhere in Chichester Harbour—Emsworth, I should think. Anyhow, there was a fourth tough in the offing waiting for them with a lorry, and when he went down to the water to meet Randolph and Co., Miss Foley got into the lorry and hid under a big packing case. They loaded the mummy into the lorry and went off towards London; but at Petersfield they knocked up a pub to get some breakfast, and all three went inside, leaving Miss Foley with the swag. So she just started up the motor and drove off to Oxford. She's handed over the mummy to Mr. Newton, and wants to know if there's any reward."

"She'd better apply to Mr. Considine for that," said Sargent with a smile. "As Dr. Benchley's executor, of course, I mean. Is this Cowes?"

"It is. You've got about three minutes to spare. Won't you enlighten my curiosity?"

"I'm afraid it's too long a story to tell in three minutes," said Sargent, as the car drew up at the foot of the pier. "But you can probably guess what we expect to find on board the *Laconic*."

"I suppose you're after Randolph and Nevern," suggested Devereux, as all three scrambled out and hastily unstrapped the suitcases.

"Put it that we're after whoever committed the crime," said Sargent, running for the boat. "We've no reason to suppose that pair gave us their real names."

They caught the boat with thirty seconds to spare.

16
THE BURSAR

"WE RAN THAT PRETTY FINE, DENYS," said Considine, leaning over the rail of the *Laconic* to wave a farewell to Charles Goring, Devereux's brother-in-law, who had personally met them on their arrival at Southampton and driven them over to the ship, putting them aboard within five minutes of her departure for New York.

"Yes," rejoined Sargent. "There's a good deal in having a friend at Court."

"We seem to have caused a small sensation by our dramatic arrival," Considine went on. "It looks as if every passenger on the ship had turned out to watch us board."

"All but one," said his companion. "Did you notice him?"

"Who do you mean?"

"As we came down on to the quay there was a man standing at the rail just by that lifeboat. He had flaming red fuzzy hair and big blue goggles—not a pretty sight by any means. But just as all the rest came flocking over to stare at us, he slipped into the background. And I've had a good look along the deck and he certainly isn't in sight now. I'm afraid he isn't glad to see us."

"I think you're imagining that, Denys," Considine objected. "After all, he's only seen us once in the distance at Lane End, and would hardly suspect we were after him. He can't know us from Adam."

"My dear Humphrey, you underestimate your fame. You'll be surprised to find, when we call on him, how well he does know you."

200

"When we call on him? Are you going to tackle him in his cabin?"

"It's the only way we're likely to meet him. Now that he's seen us, I'm prepared to bet he'll be confined to his bed with acute sea-sickness for the entire voyage—for the first time in his life, by the way. He's been an excellent sailor hitherto."

"You seem to know a lot about him."

"I do. I've been studying him longer than you think. Let's go and look for some lunch."

By the time they came on deck again after lunch (having ascertained that an empty chair at the next table was intended for Professor Bonoff, "who was not feeling very well"), the ship had emerged from Southampton Water and was creeping slowly towards the Nab Tower. To port, the spire of Chichester Cathedral caught the sun beyond the harbour mouth; to starboard they were able to make out Lane End lifeboat house and the row of white dots which were William Walter's bathing huts. Sargent leant on the rail and watched with obvious regret as their home of the last week slipped astern.

"Don't you wish we were back on that beach, Humphrey?" he asked. "With nothing heavier on our minds than an undigested Bunny lobster? I'm sorry now we ever mixed ourselves up in this business."

"I'm not," replied Considine stoutly. "I'd go through a good deal of unpleasantness to bring to book the brute who murdered poor Benchley."

"Alas for your simple mind," Sargent sighed. "I'm afraid you're in for a shock, Humphrey, but you'd better face up to it now. We'll go and call on the invalid. Number 17, I gather, is his cabin. That'll be on the other side, and a bit forward."

He led the way along the boat deck, and, having threaded the intricate passages of the great ship's interior, arrived with some difficulty outside a white-painted door bearing the number 17. Murmuring "I think in the circumstances we won't knock," he grasped the handle determinedly and threw it suddenly wide open.

DERMOT MORRAH

The cabin contained two beds. One, which had been prepared for the night, was empty. The other was occupied by a large packing case, whose sliding lid had been removed to show the solemn staring features of a mummy that lay within. A man was bending over it, examining the surface with minute and loving care. He had blazing red hair, and wore large steel-rimmed smoked glasses. A white scar, about two inches long, showed low down on his left cheek.

"Good afternoon, Benchley," said Sargent. "May we come in?"

The man with red hair swung round with a start, at first of astonishment and then of terror. With one hand he leant for support on the edge of the packing case, while he tried to speak; but only incoherent sounds came from his lips. Then suddenly he shot out a trembling arm towards the small table at one end of the cabin. But Sargent, anticipating the gesture, sprang in front of him and seized the little pillbox for which he was reaching.

"Come, come, Benchley," he said, as the red-haired man sank despairingly on the bed. "It's not as bad as all that. We're not the police, you know, nor are we likely to give you away to them. I'm sure you had a perfectly good reason for disposing of Bonoff. Here, try some of this. It's from my private supply of '48, and you can take the hint next time you're buying for the college cellar." He held a flask of brandy to the lips of the half-fainting old man, who sipped and appeared to revive a little. "Here, Humphrey," Sargent went on, "you must take some too; you look as bad as Benchley."

Considine did indeed show how great had been the shock he had suffered. He gazed with speechless consternation at Benchley—for the wig and glasses, the shaven chin and the scar, could not for a moment disguise his identity from his old colleagues—and passively accepted the stimulant Sargent proffered. Then he sat down mutely on the bed at Benchley's side. For several minutes there was complete silence in the cabin. Benchley was the first to speak.

"It wasn't murder," he burst out at last. "Please believe that. At least it might be technically; I'm not a lawyer. But it wasn't murder in the ordinary cold-blooded sense."

"I'm glad to hear you say it," replied Sargent. "But won't you tell us how it happened? We're both old friends."

"Personally," interposed Considine, "I don't want to hear any more. If Benchley says he didn't murder Bonoff, his word is good enough for me."

Benchley was evidently cheered by his former pupil's loyalty. "Thank you, Considine," he said. "But I think I'd rather tell you everything. Only I suppose Sargent knows a good deal of it already. I can't think how you found me out."

"This was the principal clue," said Sargent with a smile, taking a bulky object from his pocket and handing it to Benchley. "I abstracted it from Monitor's rooms just before we left Oxford."

"My pipe!" exclaimed Benchley, springing to his feet to take it, with greater animation than he had yet shown. In a moment he was down on his hands and knees beside his suitcase on the floor, and was rummaging among pyjamas and socks. He rose to his feet with a cry of triumph, holding a briar pipe and a tin of tobacco. The former he cast contemptuously through the open porthole into the sea; from the latter he began hastily filling the meerschaum, and a moment later was filling the cabin with thick and pungent smoke.

"I haven't the least idea how this could have put you on the trail," he said between puffs; "but I'd cheerfully have committed a real murder to get it back."

"I'll tell you how the pipe helped us when you come to that part of the story," replied Sargent. "You were going to tell us about Bonoff. He was blackmailing you, wasn't he?"

"He certainly was," exclaimed Benchley. "He did a thing I couldn't have believed possible for any man who'd ever even begun to be a professional scholar. He actually stooped to suggest that I should pay him to suppress an historical document that happened to conflict with my theory. He wrote to me about it before he came to England—the most nauseating letter I've ever received. You wouldn't believe me if I told you what he said in it, but you can take it from me—"

"As a matter of fact we've seen the letter," Sargent broke in, to cut short what looked likely to be a prolonged piece of denunciation. "Why didn't you take it to the police?"

"Because I wasn't going to foul my own nest. After all, the brute was known to the world as an Egyptologist, and I couldn't bear to think that a member of my own profession should be branded as such a blackguard. Why, I was implicated myself in a way. I was one of those who invited him to come to England when he was turned out of Russia, and I subscribed to the fund for providing him with a home—though that wasn't publicly known of course."

"That would be why you were chosen to go and meet him at Southampton?"

"That was one reason. But I happened to be going there in any case. I was just starting on my holiday; I'd meant to catch a boat for Finland that evening. Nobody knew that; you know of course that it's my foible never to tell anyone where I'm going—except Ernest Monitor sometimes. But even he didn't know last year."

"Anyhow, I gather you didn't go to Finland?"

"I did not. It was a great disappointment. It's one of the few countries Ernest has never been to, and I wanted to take him by surprise. But *Dis aliter visum*. The evening's events upset all my plans." Benchley, with his pipe belching fumes, seemed to have completely lost consciousness of his position, and had relapsed into his common-room manner of academic detachment.

"We were hoping you'd tell us exactly what the evening's events were," said Sargent.

"I thought you knew that already."

"We know the principal event."

"Which was?"

"The death of Bonoff. And your departure to Bembridge as his substitute. But we don't know any details."

"I see. In fact, you really want to know how I killed him?"

"It is rather important, isn't it?"

"Well, yes, I suppose it is, from your legal point of view. I'm afraid you as a lawyer may disapprove. To be perfectly frank, I killed Bonoff in a duel."

"A duel!" exclaimed his two juniors together, and Sargent added: "I never thought of that."

"Yes, a duel," Benchley repeated. "I know you young fellows are all iconoclasts; but personally I think it's one of the duties of people like ourselves, holding academic position, to try and keep alive historic customs. I like to show, too, that it's possible, in a humble way, for a man of letters to be something of a man of action as well. I've always been rather proud of the Fellows of Beaufort who went out to fight the Prince of Orange in 1688. And so I thought it was more in the tradition of the college to tackle a creature like Bonoff myself than to go whimpering to the police. Not that I really meant to kill the fellow. What I had in mind was just a little duel in the academic manner."

"Is duelling an academic habit?" asked Sargent.

"Well, perhaps not in Oxford nowadays. Old traditions decay, you know, they decay—'lest one good custom should corrupt the world', I suppose. It's one of the reasons why I deplore all this growth of athleticism. But Oxford isn't the only university in the world. You may not know that I was a graduate of Bonn as well, and I learnt there to stand up for myself. That's where I got this scar, in a students' duel. You've never seen it before, of course, because I grew a beard to cover it. But I always kept a pair of German university duelling swords, thinking they might come in useful one day. And so they did. So they did."

"You don't mean to say you fought a German students' duel in Bonoff's room at the Two Leopards," exclaimed Considine.

"Yes, I did," replied Benchley placidly. "Why not? It wasn't quite formally correct, of course—no seconds and so on, but I did the best I could in the present rather degenerate state of the law. And I'm afraid the terrain wasn't all it might have been. It was desperately cramped, which was what led to the unfortunate result. I'd really intended just to chip a bit out of his ugly face—give him a mark something like this one, which for a man of his vanity would have been quite adequate punishment. I could have done it too, in the open, without the least risk. I was a bit of a swordsman once. But scuffling about among all that furniture—why are provincial hotels so cluttered up with whatnots, by the way?—Bonoff was squirming about to get out of my reach when he tripped over a bit of carpet and came down with a bump on the edge of the fender. He was a heavy man, and it must have been a smashing blow on the skull."

"And is that what killed him?" asked Sargent.

"It was. I suppose it was concussion—or perhaps heart failure— I'm no doctor. But it was perfectly clear he was dead."

"Then what did you do?"

"I sat down and got out my pipe and spent half an hour thinking it all over. I remember my first thought was that after all I was rather sorry Bonoff was gone. I don't mean on any personal grounds—he was a nasty specimen of humanity, and I don't pretend I felt any remorse whatever. But after all he was one of the great scholars of our generation, and there was his book, promising to be an epoch-making work, and no one living competent to finish it. All that research wasted because a man of genius was also a blackguard. And then—I hope I'm not boring you with all this reminiscence of my personal reactions?"

"Not at all," replied Sargent. "They're really the essential bits to fill up the gaps of the story. We know most of the mere external facts."

"Well—as long as I'm not getting too prolix. I'm getting on in years, as I expect you two boys are only too conscious, and one gets garrulous, you know. Well, I was thinking how lost I should be, after all, without Bonoff to argue against, when suddenly two ideas came over me both at once. The first was that I was, in all modesty, the only man alive capable of completing his work; and the second was that I was in rather an awkward situation over his death."

"And that's really the order in which the thoughts came to you?" asked Sargent.

"Why, yes. It's the way one's been trained of course. I've been an Egyptologist most of my life, and so naturally I thought first of the Egyptological problem. You're a lawyer, and equally naturally you'd have thought first of the legal difficulty. It's all a matter of habit."

"Well," said Considine with a smile, "it may be because I've only been an Assyriologist a few years, but such detachment is frankly beyond me."

"I don't insist on it," Benchley went on. "But anyhow, that's how these ideas drifted across my mind. And then I settled down to try and think out something that would solve both difficulties at once. As it turned out, it was fairly obvious I had a good many points in my favour. First of all, nobody in the hotel seemed to have heard the noise; if they did, I expect they put it down to our shifting heavy mummies about. Secondly, it was the beginning of the long vacation, I had no more engagements till October, and nobody knew where I intended to be until then. So I had the best part of four months in which to work out my little problem. Now the first difficulty of any murderer—by the way, Sargent, am I a murderer?"

The lawyer reflected a moment. "Really, Benchley," he said, "it's rather an embarrassing point to have to answer offhand. But I'm afraid I'm bound to say that the law is likely to take that view. If in seeking to cause a person grievous bodily harm you cause his death, that is murder in law; and I don't see how you can challenge a man to a duel without intending to do him grievous bodily harm."

"Yes, well, I expect you're right. It's a point that had puzzled me a bit, as a layman, and I'm glad to have a professional view. I might plead that obliterating a bit of Bonoff's rather forbidding face would do him the reverse of harm; but I suppose a jury wouldn't see that as I do. However, as I was saying, the first difficulty of a murderer is to conceal the body, and the second is to prevent the discovery that the murderee is missing. Now the solutions of both those difficulties happened in this case to be particularly simple. I gather you spotted them yourself."

"I did," replied Sargent, "though I shouldn't have if I hadn't been put on the track already by a detail we picked up in Oxford. But I was rather struck at the Two Leopards by the ingenious way it was contrived that nobody who saw Bonoff arrive also saw him depart."

"That was the weak point," Benchley agreed; "though of course it was unavoidable. I'd better explain the details, perhaps. First I bundled the body of Bonoff into one of the empty mummy cases, and swabbed up what little blood there was; luckily it had all gone on the marble of the fireplace, so I could get rid of it without leaving any pronounced stains. Then I went through his luggage and found a razor, with which I shaved my beard off; rather clumsily, I'm afraid; it was the first time in forty years that I'd handled such a thing, and the so-called safety razor didn't exist in my day. In fact, I think there was more blood shed in that operation than in— well, the murder, if that's the right word. Then I put on Bonoff's wig— another stroke of luck for me—and undressed and went to bed."

"But I gather you didn't sleep very well," put in Sargent.

"On the contrary, I slept like a log. You'd hardly believe how exhausting it had all been. But I can generally manage to wake up when I want to, and in this case I was awake again about three. Then I'm afraid I had to do something of an injustice to the staff of the Two Leopards hotel."

Sargent and Considine exchanged a glance and a smile. "I don't think you need go into details about that," the former said. "We've had it all *agitato* and *con espressione* from the horse's mouth."

"Well," said Benchley, "I'm glad to be able to skip that part; I really regretted having to do it more than finishing off Bonoff. But you see how it worked out. The day staff of the Two Leopards saw Bonoff in and the night staff saw me out; we were both unknown in Southampton and neither there nor at the Wessex did anyone who'd seen Bonoff see me impersonating him. I left by the first boat in the morning for Cowes, and went straight to the house that had been taken for Bonoff at Lane End. There again nobody knew either me or him, and it was quite easy to step into his shoes. It was more difficult to step into his hat, because his wig didn't fit at all, and it looked pretty suspicious to turn up in what might be taken for a disguise. So I made the first opportunity of getting rid of it, by going out to bathe and getting it washed away. Then I had another made, which did fit, but I rather ostentatiously let everyone know it was a wig, just to make it seem that I wasn't really trying to conceal my natural appearance. As indeed I wasn't; I was relying entirely on not meeting anyone who knew me in my real character.

"Now I come to what really made the whole thing worth while, though it arose so to speak accidentally. You know I read chemistry in the Schools, and all my life I've been deeply interested in the technique of mummification. But it's impossible in this country to get a fresh corpse to experiment on; even for medical purposes they only seem to be supplied pickled; and anyhow, not being a doctor, I hadn't the facilities for getting one. But this affair with Bonoff gave me the opportunity of a lifetime. I spent the long vacation making him into a mummy. I did it in the full style of the Eighteenth Dynasty, with the seventy days' soaking in a bath of natron—sesquicarbonate of soda they call it nowadays—and all the rest of it. It was really the most fascinating occupation, and in the course of it I solved quite a number of perplexities that have puzzled Egyptologists for generations. There's nothing like the empiric method in archaeology. I even found a set of Canopic jars among Bonoff's belongings, which had been sent after him from Russia, so I could dispose of his internal organs in the correct way."

"You made a mistake there, didn't you?" asked Considine.

"Ah, you spotted that, did you?" said Benchley with an approving smile. "Well, I'm glad it was my old pupil who detected the anachronism. As a matter of fact, I foresaw even then that Bonoff might ultimately have to masquerade as King Pepi, so I deliberately sealed the jars with Pepi's cartouche. Strictly speaking, as you say, it was all wrong to associate Canopic jars with the Sixth Dynasty, but I never thought they'd have to meet your expert scrutiny.

"I won't go into all the technicalities of the mummification now, interesting as they are. I've written a full account of it, which I shall hand over to you, Considine, and I hope you'll publish it after I'm—that is to say, when the time is ripe. But I must get on with the story. At the end of the vacation I went away to a little village in Dorset, called Studland, where I spent a fortnight growing my beard I again, and was in my place at Beaufort, as you'll remember, at the beginning of Michaelmas term. Meanwhile I'd

been writing letters to *The Times* in Bonoff's name against the
theory of my own 'Dionysos at Memphis', and directly I was supposed to be back in England myself I started replying to them in
my own name. For the next academic year I thoroughly enjoyed
myself keeping both sides of the controversy going at once. The
Bonoff letters were all typewritten and posted in London, where I
used to go pretty frequently; and I don't think anyone at Printing
House Square had the least suspicion that Bonoff and Benchley
were now the same man.

"Still, I obviously couldn't keep both my characters going in-
definitely; one of them had to be dropped, and after consideration
I decided it would have to be Benchley. You see, the facts of the
controversy made it clear that Bonoff was right on the main point
at issue—that indeed was the trump card in his blackmailing
game—and to keep Benchley alive and kill Bonoff would involve
me probably in perpetuating my own false theory. And that, I think
you'll agree, would have been betrayal of historic truth. So I decided Benchley must go.

"One of my difficulties was that Bonoff was very hard up. I
managed to finance him a bit by writing for the learned periodicals; but unless I let him take to blackmail again it rather looked
as if he would starve. Then it struck me that I could kill two birds
with one stone. I put the mummy of Bonoff into the coffin of King
Pepi I and sold it to myself as Benchley at a fancy price. In that
way I transferred most of my private fortune into Bonoff's name
and at the same time transferred Bonoff's body to my rooms at
Oxford. My idea was to get it destroyed by an apparently accidental fire, allow it to be taken for my own corpse, and retire to live
the rest of my life under Bonoff's name.

"So far everything had worked out with surprising smoothness.
But at the last minute things began to go wrong. One complication
was introduced by my niece, Daphne Carrothers. I'd always hoped
she'd marry you, Considine; but when I heard she'd got herself
engaged to young Devereux of New College, who I knew was pretty
well endowed, I thought it a stroke of good luck, seeing that my
plan looked like depriving her of her legitimate expectation of being my heiress. And then I got a shock when I discovered that

Devereux had a house at Lane End, and that I was threatened with
having my own niece coming to live on my doorstep. Of course I
couldn't allow that; my disguise wouldn't deceive Daphne for ten
minutes; but it was too late to turn back, so I had to do the best I
could by making the will that I expect you've seen. I thought that
by making Daphne a ward in Chancery I could delay the marriage
long enough to give me time to find another home before she came
to live in the island, without depriving her of the chance of marrying a rich husband as soon as she was twenty-one. But it involved
working up an entirely artificial quarrel with young Devereux,
who's really a charming boy and will make as good a husband as
Daphne could desire. It also forced me to hurry on the climax of
my little plot, lest they should make a runaway match of it before
the court of Chancery could acquire jurisdiction to stop them.

"The second unforeseen obstacle was that the news of the transfer to Benchley of the mummy of Pepi I came to the ears of an
American collector called Van Ditten. I think you met him; he dined
with me ten days ago. He descended on me at Oxford and tried to
buy the mummy—offering, I may say, double what I'd paid myself
for it. Of course I couldn't part with it; but he was the persistent
type that will take no refusal, and I knew that unless I acted quickly
I should be so pestered by him that I should never get the chance
to carry out my plan in quiet. So, although I'd originally meant to
work it when the college was empty, somewhere about the beginning of July, I decided to take the risk of staging my fire in the
middle of the night of the Commemoration Ball."

"As things turned out, it was rather a happy choice," remarked
Sargent. "If you'd left it a day later Van Ditten would have got away
with the mummy of Bonoff and the fat would have been in the fire.
Perhaps you don't know that your rooms were burgled that night."

"No!" exclaimed Benchley. "I certainly didn't. I don't see how
that can have happened."

"I'll explain afterwards," replied Sargent. "Won't you go on with
your story?"

"Well, I think you must know the rest," Benchley continued. "I
was forced to ask Van Ditten to dinner that night, but I got rid of
him as soon as possible and went up to my rooms, where I took the

mummy out of the coffin and put it in my bed, with some unin-flammable objects of mine attached to it to support the identifica-tion. There was one untoward incident, for just as I'd got the lid off the coffin Devereux came in and we had a bit of an argument. He saw the mummy uncovered, as Van Ditten had done during the afternoon; and I'm proud to say that neither of them detected its modernity. But they weren't experts, of course. However, Devereux departed after about twenty minutes, and I then shaved and dis-guised myself as Bonoff. I rigged up a contraption with an alarm clock and a candle to go off at 1.15, soused the mummy in paraffin, and slipped out into the fellows' garden, and so away by the gate in Grammar Lane. I walked up Headington Hill to a place where I could see down to the college, and waited there till I saw the fire break out. If my alarm clock affair had broken down, of course I should have had to try again some other night. But I soon saw a satisfactory conflagration started, so I caught the early morning train to London and so on to the Isle of Wight. There I thought I was all right, until you two turned up and gave me another shock; but I dodged you in the village for a day or two and then made a bolt for America, intending to take up my duties at Yale a month before my time, and make some arrangement to get the contents of my Lane End house sent over later. That's all, I think."

"You've left out one important detail of your movements," Sargent reminded him. "After leaving your rooms for the last time, you didn't go straight to the gate in the fellows' garden, did you? No," he added, as Benchley was about to answer; "let me explain how the thing looked to us. Devereux told us that he'd seen Bonoff coming out of Monitor's rooms. That single statement led Humphrey and me to explore all sorts of false trails, and we couldn't make head or tail of it. I lay awake all night puzzling over it, and at last I got a sort of flash of inspiration and saw the point. It was the pipe, wasn't it?"

"It was," Benchley admitted. "But I don't see how you could have deduced that."

"I didn't deduce it; it was sheer inspiration, as I said. The only way Monitor seemed to be connected with the case was through the pipe; and suddenly I realized that that pipe was a bait to draw you across the world, let alone the quad, even in a moment of the utmost emergency. Wasn't I right?"

"You were," agreed Benchley. "But it seems absurdly far-fetched, considering you had no reason to suppose the fire was anything but an accident or that I was still alive."

"Ah, I didn't detect that," rejoined Sargent. "That was Humphrey. You must get him to show you his cuneiform tablet afterwards. But take it from me for the moment that we knew something extraordinary had happened in connexion with you, Bonoff and the mummy. I got the idea sent straight from Heaven that whoever went to Monitor's room that night must have been after the pipe, and that meant you were impersonating Bonoff. After that I was always on the lookout for evidence to confirm my suspicion, and bits gradually accumulated. First there were the accounts we got at the Two Leopards; I noticed there how nobody had been allowed to see both you and Bonoff after you'd been left together that night. Then in the island, when the Bunny twins described the visit of the strange professor, I noticed that though they saw the Oxford professor with the beard, they only heard the voice of the Russian professor with the clean-shaven face and the scar. In the end we broke into your house and found the blackmailing letter from Bonoff to Benchley, and that finally gave the show away. A blackmailer is the sort of knave who's very seldom a fool, and if he gets back his letters he's most unlikely to preserve them for the police to find. That was what clinched the case; but without the pipe we should never have made a start."

Benchley took the pipe from his lips and gazed at it reflectively. When he spoke it was in tones of quiet resignation. "I see," he said. "Strange that my oldest friend should be the cause of my downfall. But I won't reproach it. Tell me about this burgling of my rooms at Oxford."

Sargent proceeded to tell the story of the rag at the Commemoration ball, and of his deduction that under cover of it Van Ditten's agents, by the use of the hastily forged duplicate key, had succeeded in stealing the mummy, or rather the empty coffin while the mummy itself lay behind the locked door of Benchley's bedroom. Benchley was shocked at the suggestion that the false mummy substituted could have deceived him even for a moment, but confirmed Sargent's inference by revealing the fact, which had puzzled him for ten days, that the key returned to him in the dark that Wednesday night by Van Ditten, though otherwise resembling his own, bore no number on its haft.

"I can't be quite sure," Sargent went on, "what happened after the mummy was pushed through the gate to the confederate of Randolph and Nevern who was waiting in Grammar Lane. But I should imagine it must have been something of this sort: he put it into Devereux's punt, which they'd stolen deliberately with the idea of putting suspicion of the theft on the man who was known to have a grievance against you. That implies that they were pretty well up in the situation; but I've ascertained that Van Ditten had been some time in Oxford, no doubt investigating. Then, after Randolph and Nevern had been debagged and thrown into the river, their colleague picked them up and they all went off to the backwater to keep their assignation with their employer. By the time he turned up he'd heard all about the fire at Beaufort, attributed it to his gangsters, and naturally had the wind up lest he should be made an accessory to murder. When he also discovered that the coffin was empty, he'd have been furious as well as terrified, refused to take delivery of the goods, and driven off in his car, leaving the gang with the baby. They, I take it, abandoned the mummy and went home. But after we'd brought in our verdict of accidental death, no doubt they took heart again and got into touch with Van D. with a proposal to complete the contract by getting the body as well. Meanwhile Miss Foley had found the mummy and removed it to the Cherwell Edge boathouse; but Randolph and Nevern were probably watching the river, saw where she put it, and stole it again that night."

The other two agreed that this was a plausible explanation, and Considine followed Sargent with an account of the inquest on the burnt body and of the cuneiform tablet with which he had disproved the theory that the remains were those of King Pepi I. Finally, the two young men between them pieced together the story told them hastily by Devereux of the recovery of the mummy by Patricia Foley and its return, coffin and body together, to the custody of the Bursar of Beaufort.

When they had finished, Benchley knocked out the ashes from his pipe and leant back in his chair with an expression of serene content. "*Nunc dimittis*," he said. "I couldn't believe it would all turn out so well. The only thing I regretted in the whole business was the apparent necessity of destroying that unique and wonderful mummy."

"You mean the mummy of Bonoff?" asked Considine.

"No, no," Benchley replied, "I wasn't thinking of that. Of course, I can't pretend it wasn't a disappointment to have to burn my own work—work of art, I think I may in all humility call it. But I'd put the essential results in writing, and after all, the mummy itself, proud as I might be of it, was my own personal loss. In some ways the pipe was more of a wrench. And I had the consolation that by letting my own mummy go I was preserving something infinitely more precious—the mummy of King Pepi himself. No, what worried me was the need to destroy the coffin—not unique of course in the sense that the actual mummy of Pepi was unique, but still a dreadful loss to the world. Believe me, I racked my brains for weeks to think of any conceivable way out of my dilemma without sacrificing it; and even now, if my plan had worked out as I originally intended, I don't think I could ever have forgiven myself. But now you tell me that even the coffin has been saved. In the last year I've finished Bonoff's book for him, and in it I have completed both his life's work and mine. In anticipation of this discovery of yours I've made another will, which will set all little Daphne's affairs straight again for her. I've learnt by practical experience more than any man in modern times has known about the process of mummification; and I've been enabled to bequeath it to posterity. I've even removed that dreadful Victorian excrescence from the top of the Bursary. In fact everything I'd ever hoped to do in the world is done, and I'm quite content to leave it. So now, my dear Sargent, perhaps you'll give me back my box of pills, since I'm sure, for the honour of the college, you'd rather it was ended that way than by the gallows."

"Gallows be damned!" exclaimed Sargent vehemently. "And pills be damned too," he went on, tossing the little box out of the open porthole. "Thank Heaven law's a more human study than Egyptology. You don't imagine two fellows of your own college are going to hand you over to the police?"

"Why else should you have taken all this trouble over detecting me?" asked Benchley in a toneless voice.

"Why should you have devoted so many years to finding out how the Egyptians made mummies?" asked Sargent. "Pure academic curiosity. But since we've now solved our intellectual problem, it's time to tackle the practical one. How are we to get you back to Beaufort?"

"I'm afraid that's quite impossible," said Benchley. "If I reappear Bonoff disappears, and there will be inquiries that must bring the whole thing to light. No, if you're really not going to do your legal duty with the detected felon, I've got to live out the rest of my days as Bonoff."

"Nonsense, my dear Benchley," Sargent retorted. "If you can kill Bonoff once you can kill him again. I've got a plan. What's in that coffin?"

"Just a mummy I'm proposing to lecture on in America."

"Is it a very valuable one?"

"Not particularly."

"Right. I expect a suit of your clothes would look very nice on it. Now, supposing we bored a few holes in the coffin, do you think you could support life inside it for, say, a couple of hours?"

"I suppose it's not impossible. But what exactly—"

"Now listen to me, Benchley. You've done enough. Please let me take charge." Sargent dropped his voice to a lower tone and began to speak long and earnestly. His two colleagues listened with grave interest and a growing excitement.

THE PASSENGERS on the R.M.S. *Laconic* noticed with some amusement the sudden intimacy that sprang up during the voyage between the two young Oxford dons who had come aboard so dramatically at the last moment and the distinguished but eccentric-looking

Russian professor with the scarred face and the fiery red wig. The
three, who soon acquired the nickname of "the conspirators," were
continually in one another's company, always engaged in vehement
conversation, and yet no word that passed between them was ever
overheard by the most deliberate and assiduous eavesdropper. Few,
however, of those who speculated about the mysterious subject of
their discussion were prepared for the unexpected incident that
saddened the end of the journey. It was thus recorded in a London
newspaper:

"Professor's Tragic End

Dr. Bonoff Drowned

In The Atlantic

From our own Correspondent

"Newly appointed Professor of Egyptology at Yale
University, Dr. Feodor Bonoff, the world-famous
Russian Egyptologist, recently resident in England,
fell overboard from the R.M.S. *Laconic* last night,
and was drowned. The body has not been recovered.

"I am informed that a letter addressed to the
Captain was found in Dr. Bonoff's stateroom, in
which he is alleged to have said that he had determined
to end his life, having lately discovered that he was
suffering from an incurable complaint. ("Incurable" is
good,' muttered Sargent when he read this passage, 'for
fatal concussion of the brain, *plus* mummification, *plus*
total destruction by fire.') With the letter was found a
will, drawn up the night before, leaving his valuable
collection of Egyptian antiquities to the Ashmolean
Museum at Oxford and his other property to go to
the augmentation of the salary of the Khedivial Professor of Egyptology in that university. (This chair
is at present vacant, owing to the tragic death last
month of the late Professor Benchley.)

"The will concludes with the request that his belongings on board the liner, including a valuable

Egyptian mummy needing very careful and skilled handling, may be put for the time being in the charge of Mr. Humphrey Considine, whose acquaintance the testator had made during the journey to New York. Mr. Considine is a Fellow of Beaufort College, and Reader in Assyriology in Oxford University.

"Interviewed on the landing stage at New York, Mr. Considine said that he and his friend Mr. Sargent had become very friendly with the late professor during the voyage, and were with him to a late hour on the last night of his life. They had said good night to him, and were on their way to bed, leaving the professor alone on the deserted deck, leaning over the rail and smoking a last cigar. Suddenly they were horrified to hear a splash, and turned round to find that their friend had disappeared. Though the alarm of 'Man overboard!' was given at once, the ship circled, and the boats were lowered, no trace could be found of the unfortunate *savant*.

"Mr. Considine, who seemed deeply moved by the tragedy, was unable to give me any more particulars, since he had to hurry off to his hotel, not being able to rest, he told me, until he had fulfilled his friend's last wish by putting his treasured mummy in a place of safety."

EPILOGUE
THE PROVOST

THE FELLOWS OF BEAUFORT sat round their common-room table at dessert on the first night of Michaelmas term. The candle lights were reflected from silver and mahogany and the dull red glow of port in cut glass, and the peace of Oxford's centuries lapped them round. Mr. Provost Lacy fingered his snowy bands and beamed at Benchley, who sat beside him, with the childlike benevolence of the very old.

"My dear boy," he said, "I can't tell you how glad we all are to see you back. Only this afternoon I was telling my granddaughter how your loss saddened the opening of the new term. And then to find you appearing in the hall with the dramatic suddenness you young men love. I believe we're the very same party that dined together on Commemoration night—except that I think there was a guest present then. We're threatened with a little change, I'm afraid; perhaps you're aware that our young friend Considine is about to be married—to a Miss Foley, a most admirable young lady, I believe, but I cannot but deplore these drastic new departures of the junior fellows. In my younger days such a step would of course vacate a fellowship. And that reminds me, my dear Benchley, that the curious circumstances of your return have raised a most difficult problem. Most difficult. Most difficult. I doubt if there be a precedent." He twirled his glass absently between his fingers and relapsed into silence.

"What is your problem, Mr. Provost?" asked Benchley politely. "I am sorry if my resurrection has caused the college embarrassment;

219

but you see, till two hours ago I didn't know I was dead. I've been a little out of touch with civilization."

"Ah, yes, ah, yes," murmured the Provost. "You've been in the Saharas, you say, with—with—"

"With the Sheikh Mahmoud bin Said," supplied Benchley. "A most interesting man, though unknown outside his own country. But he has a great future."

"Yes, yes, yes. You shall tell me about him some day. But my problem is really very perplexing. You see, we have announced that your fellowship has been vacated by death. Now that raises the most difficult question, whether we ought to go through the form of re-electing you. On the other hand, it may be said that the fellowship, once announced to be vacant in due statutory form, can only be filled by a fresh election. On the other hand, it might be held that the announcement, referring as it does to a death that has not taken place—and which I trust, my dear Benchley, will not take place for many, many years—is itself null and void. And I have to determine this extraordinary dilemma by to-morrow morning, when it will fall to me to give a ruling whether you shall attend as a fellow the college meeting whose business may include a motion to re-elect you to your fellowship. My dear Benchley, you in your quiet retreat in the desert cannot imagine the complexity of the problems of thought and conduct that beset the mind of the Head of a House. Believe me, I have often thought of retirement, at any rate when I reach the age of ninety-five. But the decanter is empty; let us pass it down to Sargent."

Benchley gravely took the decanter and handed it, carefully keeping it a few inches off the table, which empty decanters must not touch, to Monitor, who sat on his other side. As it passed on down the line Monitor murmured to his old friend: "I wonder if after all, Peter, you may not have had problems of your own, not so much less perplexing than the Provost's."

"What have you got up your sleeve, Ernest?" asked Benchley in the same low tone.

"Oh, nothing, nothing, Peter," replied Monitor. "I was just wondering about your death and resurrection. You don't seem the only

one to have returned from the grave. But perhaps I'd better keep
to myself the melancholy honour I had at the beginning of August
of prescribing for the Sheikh Mahmoud bin Said on his deathbed.
I wish Sargent would be quicker with that corkscrew. I want to
drink your health."

The hum of after-dinner talk subsided for a moment as the
Provost and Fellows of Beaufort College, Oxford, suspended their
several conversations to take an informed and critical interest in
the opening of another bottle of port.

COACHWHIP PUBLICATIONS

COACHWHIPBOOKS.COM

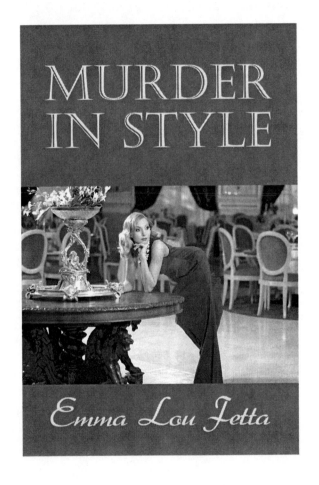

ISBN 978-1-61646-232-1

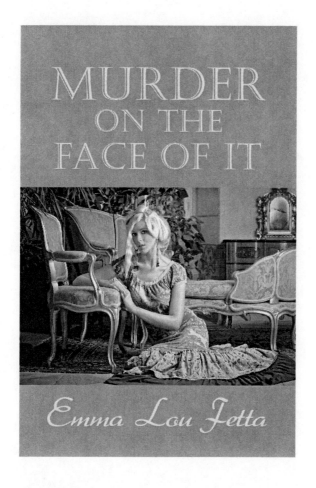

MURDER ON THE FACE OF IT

Emma Lou Fetta

ISBN 978-1-61646-233-8

COACHWHIP PUBLICATIONS

COACHWHIPBOOKS.COM

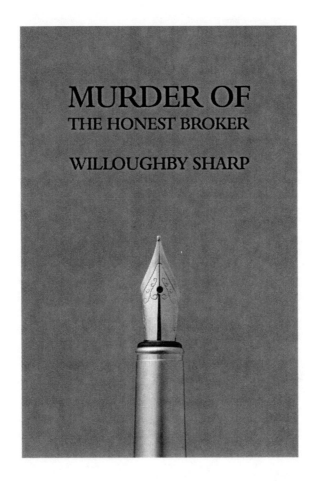

MURDER OF
THE HONEST BROKER

WILLOUGHBY SHARP

ISBN 978-1-61646-211-6

COACHWHIP PUBLICATIONS

ALSO AVAILABLE

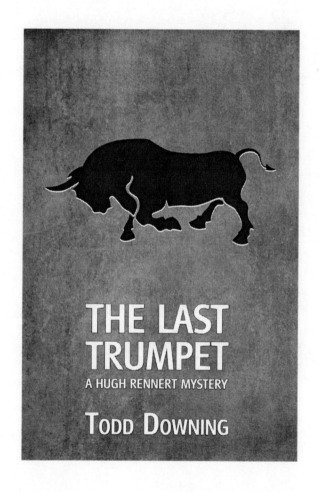

THE LAST
TRUMPET
A HUGH RENNERT MYSTERY

TODD DOWNING

ISBN 978-1-61646-152-2

COACHWHIP PUBLICATIONS

COACHWHIPBOOKS.COM

MURDER
À LA RICHELIEU
THE ADELAIDE ADAMS MYSTERIES
ANITA BLACKMON

ISBN 978-1-61646-222-2

COACHWHIP PUBLICATIONS

ALSO AVAILABLE

THERE IS
NO RETURN
THE ADELAIDE ADAMS MYSTERIES
ANITA BLACKMON

ISBN 978-1-61646-223-9

COACHWHIP PUBLICATIONS

COACHWHIPBOOKS.COM

CLUES AND CORPSES

The Detective Fiction and
Mystery Criticism of Todd Downing

CURTIS EVANS

ISBN 978-1-61646-145-4

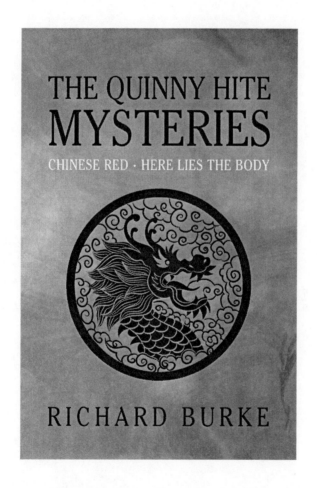

CPSIA information can be obtained
at www.ICGtesting.com
Printed in the USA
FSOW02n0133201215
14453FS